Mallets Aforethought

Mallets Aforethought

A
Home Repair Is Homicide
Mystery

Sarah Graves

LARGE PRINT

This large print edition published in 2004 by
RB Large Print
A division of Recorded Books
A Haights Cross Communications Company
270 Skipjack Road
Prince Frederick, MD 20678

Published by arrangement with Bantam Dell Publishing Group,
a division of Random House, Inc.

Publisher's Cataloging In Publication Data
(Prepared by Donohue Group, Inc.)

Graves, Sarah.
Mallets aforethought : a home repair is homicide mystery / Sarah Graves.

p. (large print) ; cm.

ISBN: 1-4025-7943-8

1. Tiptree, Jacobia (Fictitious character)—Fiction. 2. Historic buildings—Conservation
and restoration—Fiction. 3. Women detectives—Maine—Eastport—Fiction. 4. White,
Ellie (Fictitious character)—Fiction. 5. Inheritance and succession—Fiction. 6. Female
friendship—Fiction. 7. Large type books. 8. Eastport (Me.)—Fiction. 9. Mystery
fiction. I. Title. II. Series: Graves, Sarah. Home repair is homicide mystery.

PS3557.R2897 M35 2004b
813/.6

Printed in the United States of America

**This Large Print Book carries the
Seal of Approval of N.A.V.H.**

Mallets Aforethought

CHAPTER 1

The body was all withered sinews and leathery skin, seated on a low wooden chair in the tiny room whose door my friend Ellie White and I had just forced open. Slumped over a table, one arm outstretched, the body wore a sequined chemise whose silver hem-fringe crossed its mummified thigh.

Masses of bangles circled the knobby wrists and rings hung loosely on the long bony fingers. From beneath black bobbed hair the hollow eye sockets peeked coyly at us, the mouth a toothy rictus of mischief.

Or malice. A candle burnt down to a puddled stub stood in an ornate holder by the body's arm. A tiaralike headpiece with a glass jewel in its bezel had fallen to the floor.

Ellie and I stood frozen for a moment, neither of us able to speak for the horridness of the surprise. Then:

"Oh," breathed Ellie, sinking heavily into the window seat of the dilapidated parlor we'd been working on. It was Saturday morning and around us the aging timbers of Eastport's most decrepit

1

old mansion, Harlequin House, creaked uneasily.

Only the wind, I told myself. Outside it was blowing a gale. But the fact brought little comfort, since after a century or so without maintenance, the old mansion's skeleton was probably less sturdy than the body we were staring at. Being sealed in the room had apparently preserved it like some denizen of King Tut's tomb.

"A woman," Ellie added, her voice still faint with shock.

"Yes," I responded, sniffing the air curiously. Thinking . . . something. I just didn't know exactly what, yet.

The parlor was lit by a couple of lamps we'd brought from home, the power in the house having been turned on only the day before. This morning was meant to be a work party but it seemed the storm had discouraged all but the two of us. Around us lay damp swathes of stripped wallpaper and the scrapers and putty knives we'd been using to pull down chunks of cracked plaster.

It was behind one of those cracks we'd first found the faint outlines of a hidden aperture, and of course a secret door had been irresistible. Who wouldn't want to learn what lay behind it, where it might lead?

But now I reentered the chamber cautiously. Its air smelled of the dust to which its occupant had partially returned, and of something else, the faint whiff I'd caught earlier: *not* dusty.

Not in the slightest. The lamplight barely reached

the back of the little room. As my eyes adjusted to the gloom there, I made out the shape in the corner.

And identified it, wishing I hadn't.

"Let's get out of here," I said, exiting hurriedly.

"Don't worry, I'm fine," said Ellie, misunderstanding me. "I just felt strange for a minute."

Her speedy recovery was little more than I expected. Ellie wasn't usually much daunted by dead bodies, antique or otherwise. Her shaky reaction to this one I put down to the fact that at the moment she was as pregnant as a person could be without actually wheeling into the delivery room.

"Help me . . . oof! . . . up." Gripping my hand, she struggled to her feet. "I swear this isn't a kid, it's a Volkswagen."

"Only a little longer," I comforted her distractedly, still staring into the hidden room.

"It'd better be," she retorted. "If this baby doesn't come soon I'm going to start charging it rent."

There were two bodies in there.

"Lots," she emphasized, "of rent."

One old body. And a new one. "Ellie, have you ever heard any stories about another door into this room?"

She could have, if one existed. An ancestor on Ellie's mother's side, Chester Harlequin, had owned the house in its heyday.

"No." She peered puzzledly at me. With her red hair softly framing a heart-shaped face, green eyes

3

above freckles the color of gold dust, and a long slim body blooming out at the middle like some enchanted flower, Ellie resembled a storybook princess and was as tough as Maine granite.

But she was in trouble now and she didn't even know it.

Yet.

"I'd never even heard of *this* one," she added. "I have seen photographs of this parlor, though, back when—"

Her gesture took in the ramshackle interior wall where the door had been concealed, its trim removed and panels smoothed over by a coat of plaster topped with the same fusty vines-and-grape-leaves pattern as the rest of the ornate old chamber.

"—the wallpaper was new," she said. "Last time this room was redone was sometime back in the twenties."

Although when it was hung, that paper had probably looked ultramodern. In its time Harlequin House had been a showplace, with parquet floors, marble mantels, and chandeliers so grand and numerous that the house for a while was dubbed "the crystal palace."

Why someone had also walled a body up in it was a question I supposed might never be answered—not after more than eighty years. Which I guessed was truly how long the woman had been dead; the state of the plaster, the wallpaper, and the body's own costume all testified to it pretty convincingly.

Yet there were no additional obvious entrances to the room, and the inner walls were all of unplastered boards. Any break in them, however well repaired, would have been clearly visible. In short it appeared that the room had been sealed since the first body was entombed. So how'd the second one gotten in there?

"I know her," Ellie said suddenly. "I've seen old pictures of her wearing the dress and the tiara. It's Eva Thane, the woman my Uncle Chester was . . . So *that's* what happened to her."

"Ellie, wait." She'd gotten her wind back and was about to reenter the room, her shock giving way to the curiosity that was among her most prominent character traits.

"Why?" she demanded impatiently. "I want a closer look at . . ."

Then she understood, or thought she did. "But you're right of course, a flashlight will help." She drew one from her smock pocket.

The windowless room was enclosed on all sides with a center hall at its rear, kitchen to its left, the parlor plus a vestibule and coatroom to its front and right. The house was so huge that a square of missing space wouldn't be missed, especially tucked as it was to one side of an enormous black marble fireplace.

Ellie aimed the flash past me and sucked in a surprised breath. "Him," she exhaled, recognizing the dead face instantly just as I had, despite the unpleasantness of its disfigurement.

But having been unnerved once, Ellie was not about to show faintheartedness a second time. "Well," she continued briskly, "*this* certainly isn't going the way we planned."

Which was an understatement. Begun just today, the Harlequin House fix-up was supposed to be a labor of love. Assisted by a small army of local volunteers, we were to ready the old dwelling for a gala put on by the Eastport Historical Society, and in doing so perhaps up the chances that someone—anyone!—might actually take the place off the Society's impoverished hands afterwards.

And the first corpse, I thought, might even have helped. A long-dead flapper from the Roaring Twenties could have been just the hook this old money-pit needed to snag the attention of a buyer with cash vastly exceeding common sense.

But the newer body was of more than historical interest.

Way more. "We have a problem, don't we?" Ellie said.

She was starting to catch on. Eva Thane's antique corpse dropped off her mental radar as a new and more unpleasant light dawned.

" 'Fraid so," I agreed unhappily. The dead man was Hector Gosling, Eastport's most irascible real-estate mogul as well as the current president of the historical society. His face was smudged with grime, as were his clothes, a condition that would have been unthinkable while Hector was alive. But even filthy and hideously exaggerated as it was now, that furious teeth-baring grimace was an all-too-familiar expression.

Combined with his position, however—feet and head on the floor, midsection arched tautly, agonizingly up like a drawn bow—Hector's look didn't say *fury* or anything like it.

What it said, unfortunately, was strychnine.

I am the type who goes more for structural guts than shelter-magazine glory, so if Harlequin House had been mine I'd have started renovation with the underpinnings, the wooden sills and the foundation. At the same time I'd be tearing off the roof, all the trim, and the chimneys and siding. All the windows would come out, too, as would the wiring, plumbing, and heating. Inside, I'd pull down every last bit of the cracked, ancient plaster, and fix all the lath.

Only when the house sat four-square on its footings with its mechanicals updated, its windows made weathertight, insulation layered onto it, and its new trim and clapboards coated with oil-based primer and paint would I even give a thought to wallpaper.

Whereupon I would reject it. These old houses have been smothering in garish floral patterns and gloomy scenic designs for long enough, in my opinion. They need paint in a nice light color scheme, off-white woodwork, and freshly sanded floors.

But as I say, the house didn't belong to me. So for a little while Ellie and I went on puttering and pondering, deciding what we would say when we summoned the authorities.

And what might need doing afterwards.

"I mean, George and I have a problem. But mostly George does," Ellie said. "Or he might have."

At last we gathered our tools and arranged them on some newspapers at the center of the room. I'd acquired the "clean up as you go along" habit soon after I bought my own old house and began repairing it.

"Not," she added, "that anyone will *believe* he could've . . ."

"Of course they won't," I agreed hastily.

But privately I wasn't so sure. Ellie's husband George was your go-to guy for nearly everything in Eastport. In our little town on Moose Island, seven miles off the Maine coast, George was the man you called if you had bats in the attic, a bad drain, or a pet parrot scared by Fourth of July fireworks into a copper beech tree.

But George was also Hector Gosling's worst enemy. Or next-to-worst, after whoever'd murdered the old schemer in this awful manner. Strychnine— the very idea made me shudder.

"Anyway, I guess we'd better call Bob Arnold," Ellie said. It was sinking in now, what this discovery could develop into.

Although, in the call-the-authorities department

at least, we were in luck. If anyone knew George's good character better than Ellie, it was Eastport's police chief Bob Arnold. So George might still catch the break I already thought he might be needing.

"I mean we can't very well just wall Hector up again. Can we?" Ellie asked, briefly hopeful.

Actually we could have. Powdered lime for Hector, quick-set plaster for that door, fresh wallpaper, and in a few hours we could be sitting pretty in the corpse-concealment department.

And nobody would ever deliberately go looking for Hector the Objector, so called because no matter what anyone ever wanted to do, he could be counted upon to come up with a dozen reasons why they couldn't or shouldn't.

That is unless they wanted to unload parcels of real estate at fire-sale prices. But . . .

"No," I replied grudgingly. "We can't take the chance. If we hadn't wrecked the door getting it open, we could say we'd never *gotten* it open and never seen him. But people will know we've been working in here. So now if anyone else ever *does* find him, we'll have an awfully hard time explaining ourselves."

Oh, it would have been lovely just to walk away and forget him. Poison was too good for Hector, and as for a decent burial, any hallowed soil you tried putting him in would only spit him right back out again the way you would a bad clam.

"We had better just let Bob get the process in

motion," I told Ellie. State police, medical examiner, crime lab van from Augusta: the whole, as Chief Arnold tended to call it, dog-and-pony show.

"All right." Ellie sighed. "We should find George, too, let him know what's going on."

Give him a heads-up, she meant, before some state cop began surprising him with pointed questions. Not that he wouldn't have all the answers sooner or later, but George always mulled things over a while before supplying any and hesitation would make him into an even better suspect.

Of course he would be cleared eventually; maybe even soon. But until then I thought he could be in for an uncertain time.

"He's at the marine tech center this morning," Ellie added, "helping drop in new pilings for the dock, and the granite slabs for the boat ramp . . . mmph!"

An odd look came over her face. "A Volkswagen," she gasped wincingly, putting her hand on the fireplace mantel and leaning against it, "that kicks like a *mule*."

As we stepped from under its portico, the windows of Harlequin House peered dourly down at us through a mess of fallen gutters and sagging trim, its mansard roof rotten and the breaks in its wooden gutters home to generations of pigeons. Hunched arm-in-arm we dashed together under wind-whipped maples, unkindly shoved along by gusts bearing rain in overflowing buckets.

Power lines swung wildly overhead as we rushed through the storm-lashed streets. "I guess," Ellie gasped, "they won't be putting that dock in today after all."

"If this keeps up they won't even have to demolish the old one. Yeeks," I finished, nearly blown off my feet. "You okay?"

"Fine," she replied grimly.

For a woman who was carrying the equivalent of a compact car she was moving right along; when I was waiting for my own son, I was lucky if I could move from a chair to the couch. But she just kept putting one foot in front of the other, and much as I dislike the damage they cause I adore these storms. They're the closest I'll ever get to being on the ocean in heavy weather.

So I risked a glance back toward the bay where rows of white shingled cottages faced bravely into the gale, shutters rattling and weather vanes aimed stiffly northeast. The sign over the Happy Landings Café swung on its chains as the wind rose to a banshee howl. Gouts of heavy spray burst massively upward, racing waves battered the breakwater, and the stinging rain tasted of sea salt, as trudging forward again we at last caught sight of home.

My home: the big white 1823 Federal house loomed suddenly out of the storm at us, its many-paned windows gleaming a golden welcome from between green shutters. Water gushed from its downspouts, streamed down its brick chimneys, and sheeted along its clapboard sides as if someone had opened a spillway above it. But thus far it didn't look as if the sump pump had gone on. No water, I saw with relief, poured from the pipe leading from the cellar window.

So one thing was going right, anyway. In the driveway a heap of old truck parts hunkered atop mismatched tires.

"He's here," Ellie managed breathlessly, seeing the vehicle.

George, she meant. We staggered up the porch steps and into the back hall, shedding our wet jackets and sodden hats as my black Labrador, Monday, danced and wagged her tail in joyful greeting.

"Hi, girl." I patted her silky head, then reached to bestow equal attention on our red Doberman, Prill, who demanded nothing, adored everything, and received her petting with solemn gravity.

George was at the kitchen table drinking a cup of coffee and listening to the radio's report of the storm's unexpected power. Wearing a green flannel shirt, faded overalls, and battered work boots, he got up quickly when he saw Ellie.

"Hey, hey," he said, frowning a sharp question at me as he took charge, guiding her toward a chair. "You look all in."

He was the one who appeared exhausted, his chin stubbled and his eyes deeply shadowed with fatigue. He'd been working harder than usual lately

12

to buy things the baby needed and to pay doctor bills, and the strain was beginning to show.

With him at the table was another local guy, Will Bonnet; he and George had grown up together. Will took in Ellie's drenched condition silently, then went back to the newspaper he was reading.

"I'm fine." She leaned affectionately against George but didn't sit. "I just need to get these wet clothes changed, that's all."

Wisely, George backed off. Ellie was the oxygen in his air, the stars in his sky, his own personal moon over Miami. But he knew better than to try making her do what she didn't want to.

"Hop in a warm bath, though, why don't you?" I said, putting the kettle on. "Seriously. You're giving the kid a chill."

Which was the secret: most of the time you couldn't get her to do anything strictly for herself. For the baby, though . . .

"Dry clothes of yours are in my dresser," I called after her as she went up the stairs. Over the years I'd known her, our two houses had intermingled until they had become virtual annexes of one another. "Clean towels in the linen closet."

Then I turned to George, who was still eyeing me narrowly. He was a small man with dark hair, grease-stained knuckles, and the milky-pale skin that runs in some downeast Maine families. But his size was made up for by an alert, banty-rooster bearing and thrust-out chin; most folks didn't give him any backchat.

"George, she wouldn't let me get the car," I began before he could reproach me. "It was either stand in the cold rain arguing with her or make a dash for it. It wasn't raining when we started out earlier."

He relented. "She is hard-headed, isn't she?" *Hahd*—the downeast Maine pronunciation. The radio started in on a fiddle-and-banjo version of "Beaumont Rag," a tune that always makes me feel like dancing.

But not now. I glanced around the big old barnlike kitchen with its tall bare windows, pine wainscoting, and bright braided rugs on the hardwood floor. It seemed a haven against any storm.

Still, I had a feeling the sensation of safety wouldn't last much longer. There was a window sash standing in the corner by the washing machine; I'd removed it earlier and now just to keep my hands busy I began tinkering with it.

"George. We found two bodies in that house." A length of metal weatherstripping lay atop the washing machine, along with a sharp chisel, a hammer, and some small nails. "And one of the bodies is Hector Gosling's."

He'd returned to his chair to wait for Ellie so he could take her home. Now he peered blankly at me, his look unreadable.

Will looked up too. By contrast he appeared delighted. "Ain't that," he pronounced succinctly, "a goddamned shame."

"We haven't told anyone," I went on. "We need to inform Bob Arnold."

I'd already nailed weatherstripping into the sash channels. Now I turned the window sash so the bottom edge faced up. "And George, the police will want to speak with you."

But George shook his head. "Bob's mom took ill last night in Kennebunk. State boys'll be covering us till he gets back."

Which was not welcome news. Something Bob Arnold might've given instantly—such as for instance an ironclad character reference for George—wouldn't be available at all from a cop whose usual task was patrolling the interstate, 200 miles away.

"Anyway, why would they want to talk to me? And who's the other one?" he inquired mildly. George had a way of not getting too exercised over anything not relevant to him.

A dead body, for example. If it wasn't his or Ellie's, and it wasn't someone from my household—my son Sam, my husband Wade Sorenson, my ex-husband Victor, who lived down the street, or any of our animals—then to George it was an item to be read in the newspaper and that was the end of it.

But Will, a big, handsome fellow with jet-black hair, blue eyes, and a deeply cleft chin—in red plaid shirt, narrow jeans, and polished boots, he was the Hollywood version of Paul Bunyan—had begun looking even more interested. "Yeah? Whose was it?"

"The other one's too old to make any difference to us," I said. Let Ellie tell the rest of that story, I decided, sometime when we didn't need George awakened to his own personal peril.

A bomb might do it. Or an air-raid siren. George's feisty nature was controlled by a routine of daily habits; in his youth he'd been a terror, racketing around with Will Bonnet and getting into all kinds of mischief. But with time—and after an incident that he didn't like talking about, nowadays—he'd learned to behave.

"They'll want to speak with you," I told George, "because you are the one who hated his guts the most."

If your window locks with a top clasp that holds the bottom sash down tightly, you can make it draft-free by installing some weatherstripping on the bottom edge of the window.

"And," I added to George, "everyone knows it."

There was another more specific reason, too, but I didn't want to mention it yet. Maybe I wouldn't have to at all. I positioned the length of weather-stripping in the window well, cut it to fit by tapping the chisel on it with the hammer, and lay the cut-to-fit strip on the bottom edge of the sash.

"Join the club," George said, perusing a section of the newspaper he'd picked up. "Can't think of many who didn't hate him. Can you?"

"No." I began nailing the weatherstripping to the sash with little taps of the hammer. "But they weren't talking it around that if they could find a good way to do something to Hector, they'd do something to him."

He looked unimpressed. "So you think I should get my ducks in a row? Trump myself up a good old-fashioned alibi?"

Tap, tap. "That's just what I think you should do, but a real one, not trumped up." I didn't think he was taking this seriously enough.

"And the more wide-ranging and comprehensive the better," I went on, "because . . ."

Because we didn't know yet just when Gosling had died. But a week earlier while Ellie was at a baby shower, Will and George had gone out on the town together. They'd ended up in Duddy's Tap, drinking beer and regaling the crowd with hilarious schemes.

And what all those schemes had in common, I'd been told the next day by one of Duddy's regulars who'd been there too, was the sudden, violent, and unsolvable murder of Hector Gosling.

"I just think you ought to," I finished, lifting the sash and placing it back into the window opening. The sash trim went up in a twinkling; I hadn't even bothered taking the nails out. Now I slid the sash experimentally up and down, then locked it.

It worked, the weatherstripping pressed tight by the locked window. "Nice," Will Bonnet observed.

"Thanks." A little burst of pleasure flooded my heart. "And it will be even nicer this winter."

"Hey, there." George's face brightened as Ellie

returned, a towel around her head and the rest of her swathed in an enormous hot-pink sweater. With it she wore fuchsia leggings with crimson flowers printed on them, and a lime-green crocheted vest. Purple legwarmers, plaid socks, and sandals completed her costume.

"Oh, I feel *so* much better," she beamed.

Will Bonnet grinned at her and I suppose I must have, also. You couldn't help it; combined with the outfit, her smile made her look like an explosion at the happiness factory.

"George, did Jake tell you what we found?"

"Ayuh. She seems to think folks'll b'lieve I did it."

"Well." The smile dimmed a few watts. "Bob Arnold *is* going to want to talk to you. So you'd better be ready."

But she didn't sound nearly as concerned as before. I hadn't mentioned the Duddy's Tap stuff to her, feeling it was not a part of my duty as a friend to tattle on George. Now I guessed she must have thought things over again and decided that we were just worrying too much, earlier.

Which left me for the role of Chicken Little. "Bob isn't around," I started to tell her as I began clearing up tools and scraps of weatherstripping. But she'd begun rubbing the towel over her hair and wasn't listening. On the other hand, the sky wasn't falling, either . . . so far.

"Hector was a crook," George declared. "Whoever's done for 'im should've done it sooner.

Before"—he emphasized this with a shake of the sports pages—"Gosling and his quack pal Jan Jesperson got near my Aunt Paula. Rest," he added sadly, "her poor addled soul."

This was the crux of the matter and the reason for George's dislike of—black hatred for, actually—Hector the Objector.

That Hector *didn't* object to swindling town ladies out of their money. Or anyway, that was the rumor: that over the years he and his partner in crime Jan Jesperson had conspired to identify women who were alone in the world, and befriend them.

Next, people said, Jan wielded a pill-bottle and Gosling worked the social angle. Hector wooed the ladies with old-fashioned courtliness while Jan turned them into doped zombies from whom it was child's play to extract shaky power-of-attorney signatures.

And after *that*, it was Katie-bar-the-door: estates looted in the name of investment opportunities, ladies dumped into distant "assisted living" facilities that later turned out to be little more than grim boarding-houses and sometimes much less.

"She's not a quack, though," Will corrected George. "Not a doctor at all. She's what they used to call a detail man. Or," he added, "in her case, detail woman."

I turned curiously to him. "How do you know?" Jan Jesperson was in her late sixties or so, I estimated: single, retired, and tight as a tick about her private life.

"Did a little research," he replied wisely. "Used to be, the drug companies all had salesmen. They would go around to doctors' offices with a satchelful of samples."

Ellie's ears had pricked up, too. "And that was Jan's job? She sold pharmaceuticals?"

"Yup." He preened, happy to be listened to. "See, doctors now don't make all the decisions the way they once did. Somebody needs medicine, they could be stuck with what the insurance company or HMO will pay for. Used to be different. A good detail man kept his customers happy and satisfied, just like any other salesperson, kept them using *his* company's line of goods."

"And you learned all this how?" I persisted.

He hesitated. "Well, you know those services on the Internet where you can get background checks on people? I thought maybe if I could find out something on her, I could get her to go away."

My face must have showed how likely I thought this was.

"Hey, it could happen," he protested. "Matter of fact you're right, it didn't turn up any juicy stuff. I didn't want to pay what a serious search costs. Lot of dough."

And anyway, talk about bait and switch. Some of the online services promise the moon and deliver green cheese.

"But she'd won herself a business award once so there'd been an article about her," Will added. "Little more reading on the drug business, I could figure out what she did. And it was like I said, sales."

"Very enterprising of you," I commented, then turned to George. "And how about you? Any online investigating you want to tell me about? Or any other kind?"

George on a computer was as easy to envision as me on a high wire. He had enough to do in the real world, never mind the virtual kind. Still, if the browser on Ellie's computer was going to reveal a suggestive history—a search on Hector's name, for instance, or on Jan's—I wanted to know about it.

But he just made a face. "Nope. Sales is right," he told Will. "Sold my Aunt Paula a load of bull."

"So you think Jan might have been squirreling drug samples away over the years?" Ellie asked Will. "And maybe used them when she and Hector were softening up their victims?"

"Don't know," he replied. "Don't even know if it's possible. Fake her records or something. But it'd make sense. Even went and asked her once. I said, what's the deal with you and Gosling? How come bein' friends with you two's so bad for the health? And she told me, watch what I was saying or she'd slap a lawsuit on me."

He bridled, remembering. "That's a hot one, *her* suing *me*. I told her so, too. Those poor women shut away far from home . . ."

"If a person goes into care in Eastport," George agreed, "it is different. Nursing home, or the poor farm here in town."

It wasn't a poor farm. It was a place to live if you weren't quite sick enough for constant nursing and you weren't quite well. But everyone called it that and it had the best water view on the island.

"There people can check on you, even if it's only when they are visiting their own folks," he said. "People *know*."

"George," I began, trying to think of some way to change the subject. But too late: he was on his horse again.

"Poor old Aunt Paula," he mourned. "Witch that she was, I had a soft spot for her. Wouldn't have let those two Evel Knievels go to town on her if I had known."

"Not your fault," Will reminded him. "She wouldn't talk to you. How were you to know those vultures had their claws in her?"

It was the reason Will himself had come home to Eastport: his own last living relative, his elderly aunt Agnes Bonnet, was a natural next target for the predatory Hector and Jan.

"If you hadn't told me what'd happened to Paula," he added to George, "*I'd* never have known."

"How is she, Will?" Ellie inquired kindly. For it seemed Jan and Hector had gotten a start on Agnes, too.

Will shrugged sadly. "Not good. I don't know what that woman might've given her, and *she* says she never gave her nothing."

Anything, I corrected him silently. Will was a

charming guy, but he was a little rough around the edges.

"Doctors can't find a thing. She's so fragile, though, it could have messed her mind up even after she stopped taking it."

It occurred to me that the doctors might not be doing drug tests. So his Aunt Agnes *still* could be taking it. Whatever it might be.

"You know, you might want to look around in the house."

He was living with her now, caring for her as best he could despite her increasing dementia. "In case there is anything, she might be confused and think she should swallow it," I added.

Which was a nicer way of saying *in case she's as sneaky as any other addict.* My own son Sam used to hide pills in ballpoint pens or rolled up in his toothpaste tube. Once he glued capsules behind his ears; when he pulled them off some cartilage came too, and he'd needed plastic surgery.

"Yeah, huh?" Will replied thoughtfully. Before coming home to Eastport he'd been in Boston for a dozen years, and city life had made him quick to pick up on the behaviors people might be getting into. "Yeah, maybe I should," he agreed.

"That Jan Jesperson," George said, understanding also what I was suggesting, "is one tricky piece of work."

With this I had to agree, if only because nothing alleged against Gosling or Jesperson had ever been proven. On the face of it, George's aunt had simply died of old age. By the time George heard about it she'd been cremated, on instructions that Gosling and Jesperson had helped her issue shortly before she expired.

"You know anything yet about the estate?" Will asked.

George shook his head. "Don't guess I'm going to, either, at this late date. You aren't in it, they don't tell you about it."

Which we assumed must be the situation: that George's aunt had left her estate to that pair of shameless carrion-eaters.

"But it's not about the money. It's that I could've tried harder," George insisted stubbornly. "She could've had us, 'stead o' bein' alone in that big house of hers, rattlin' around amongst a lot of tarnished silver and dusty old furniture."

He looked at Will. "It was her own choice the way she shut herself off from everyone but I don't b'lieve she'd've ever been suckered by 'em if she wasn't so lonely. Aunt Paula was always smart. You, though, you're lucky. You got back before things got too bad."

Will shrugged sympathetically. "Maybe. I hope you're right, but we'll see. Agnes was in pretty sad shape when I arrived."

George got to his feet. "Anyway, I better go double-check the stuff I was using this morning. I need to make sure the rain didn't seep in and wash it anywhere I don't want it to go."

Will followed him to the door. "I should get

moving too. Almost time for Agnes's lunch." He'd been a restaurant manager in Boston and hoped to start one of his own, a seafood joint, here in Eastport.

Which was another story; I had my doubts about it.

"At least she's eating well," Ellie told him approvingly.

But then George's remark struck me. "Stuff? I thought you were working out at the marine center, putting in the new dock."

"Weather's too bad." He took his slicker from its hook in the hall and draped it over Ellie's shoulders.

"So I got started on those red ants over to Cory Williams's. Christ in a handcart, but he's got a case. Never saw so many."

Decades ago some big schooner must've come in here with stowaways: European fire ants. Furiously aggressive and equipped with a fierce formic acid bite, the ants had multiplied.

"And you know," George went on, tucking Ellie's hair under the earflaps of his sou'wester, "Cory's trying to raise little pigs. Pot-bellied pigs, sell 'em as pets. Says people keep 'em in their houses like dogs. Smart as dogs, too, he says."

At this Prill and Monday got up from the dog bed where they were lying together and left the room, which was probably only a coincidence. Meanwhile, with that day-glo yellow slicker and black rain hat laid on over the rest of her outfit,

25

Ellie appeared to be wearing an entire storewide clearance sale.

"I'll make the cop call," I told her quietly. "And you call me if anything happens." The baby, I meant, and she promised to.

"So Cory," George went on, "has to eliminate the ants."

Unlike the rest of us, who doused ourselves with bug dope in summer and with cortisone ointment on the many occasions when bug dope didn't work. Boric acid sometimes got rid of them, though, and was unlikely to have been the stuff that eliminated Hector.

For that my money was still on strychnine. The awful grin on his face was a giveaway. So I felt better.

Temporarily. "Turned out, Cory's got another problem, too, with all the feed and the straw and the refuse," George added.

"Yup," Will agreed, pulling on a windbreaker. "Although he keeps those pigs so clean you could lie down next to 'em and sleep. He's set up such nice pens for 'em, you might not mind it."

I would mind. But it was what George had said that had my attention now. "Other problem?" I asked.

George checked his pocket for his key ring, pulled out a massive one loaded with the fifty or so labeled keys he used on a regular basis, working around the island for people. It also held a truck key as backup for the one in the vehicle's visor.

"Seems no matter how clean you are with 'em, if you keep 'em outdoors," George said, "the feed spills, coupla grains here and a coupla grains there, pretty soon you've also got—"

Ellie looked at me and I looked at her, and I could feel our hearts sinking together like anchors. Because she'd seen Gosling too, and I knew she'd have come to the same conclusion as I had.

Strychnine is controlled, now. For all practical purposes the ordinary person can't even buy it. But once upon a time many households had a tin of the stuff. People used it to kill . . .

"Rats," said George, stepping out into the storm.

My sentiments exactly.

My name is Jacobia Tiptree and when I first came to Maine, my old house needed more rehab than your average heroin addict. The roof leaked, the floors sagged, and the cast-iron radiators were antique, charmingly ornate containers clogged with mineral deposits and rust.

And speaking of addicts, back then my son Sam needed rehab too. It was why I'd brought him to an island in remote downeast Maine, as a last resort before the horrors of locked hospitals and teenage boot camps.

In the city he'd been a young teen going on twenty or so, running in a wolf pack of friends with eyes as blank and shiny as dimes. Too old for spankings and too young for jail, scornful of school and contemptuous of kids who actually went there, the boys roamed Manhattan with money in their pockets and mayhem in their hearts.

When I polled the others' parents, hoping for help, I found attitudes ranging from "boys will be boys" to the extremities of tough love; those parents at any rate who could be located and who were sober enough to express an opinion. One youngster, whose dad was a well-known rock star (see sober enough, above) lived in a penthouse with views more extensive than the kid's own faraway stare. With him lived a maid who spoke no English, his mother's boyfriend (she was climbing Mount Everest and writing an article about it for *Vanity Fair*), and a down-on-his-luck former dot-com honcho to whom the kid had, for no particular reason that I could discover, given a key.

Not that my own situation was any less ridiculous or desperate. Sam wasn't yet hooked on heroin but only because he liked other substances so much better. And some of them changed my son into someone neither of us recognized. One night as he was leaving our apartment I caught at his sleeve; in response he swung around, put his hands on my throat, and began squeezing. And when I looked into his eyes to try snapping him out of it, croaking his name through the diminishing space in my airway, no one was there.

No one at all. Why he stopped choking me and slammed out, I have no idea; the next day he didn't remember any of it.

And then there was Sam's dad; when I mentioned a divorce he'd pledged a civil, even cordial arrangement, then hired a pack of lawyers who were about as civil as wolverines. Victor was amazed that I'd thought when we were married he would be faithful. To him this was as foolish as believing that once people landed on other planets there would be air there.

Just because people needed it. Just because, actually, they were dying without it. When, after he showed absolutely no sign of leaving—he did get his own phone line which his girlfriends began using; the hots-line, Sam started calling it—I threw him out, Victor had a hissy fit that deteriorated into a meltdown.

And even when it was over—all I wanted was custody, which he didn't want but fought savagely for anyway just on principle—he kept pestering me bizarrely. For example he stole my wedding dress, wrapped a dead fish in it, and sent it to me in a box.

And Sam, of course, opened it. "It doesn't mean anything," I remember telling our son. "He's angry and his feelings are hurt."

Sam looked at me, and despite the hots-line I could see him thinking that if his mother weren't such a bitch maybe his dad wouldn't be driven to such extremes, and he wouldn't be opening a package in hopes of finding a Game Boy and coming instead upon a lace-wrapped carp.

So maybe it was that: Victor, and not Sam's

addiction or the increasingly dismal task of being a hot-shot financial advisor in Manhattan. Which I was, and I was a whiz at it, too; big clients and bigger commissions. Let the rest have their fifteen minutes of fame on the financial networks, touting stocks they owned and barking at competitors like a company of trained seals. I was the real deal and publicity was the last thing I wanted or needed.

But the money business had changed and so had the city, and probably so had I. Looking back on it now it seems so impossible that I could have stayed, it's hard to come up with one reason, a single motivating factor for my departure.

Bottom line, I just needed a planet with air on it.

CHAPTER 2

Out in my driveway, George's truck sat stubbornly refusing to start. No surprise; the old vehicle was so unreliable that none of the rest of us would drive it at all if we didn't have to. This time I poured a thin stream of gasoline from a Big Gulp cup straight into the carburetor while he turned the key—kids, don't try this at home—and he got it going.

"Meet me?" he called to Will Bonnet through a cloud of blue exhaust and a rumble of rotting muffler.

At the Mobil station, he meant. The truck spent more time on their repair lot lately than it did on the road. But he couldn't afford to replace it so he kept it going with rebuilt parts.

Will waved agreement and headed for his aunt's house to get her car, itself only recently returned to running condition. In a muddled try at maintenance (and a sad one; not long ago she'd been the sort of person who rotated her own tires), Agnes had put melted bacon grease into the crankcase instead of motor oil.

Once they'd departed I got on the phone. Soon

I was telling a Maine State Trooper what Ellie and I had found, and where.

"People aren't in there gawking at it, poking at it with a stick or anything, are they?" he wanted to know.

From which I deduced Trooper Hollis Colgate's opinion of the general public. But I held my tongue, merely saying that I didn't think anyone else would be visiting Harlequin House today; the other volunteers in the fix-up project were too sensible to brave the weather. Then I let the other shoe drop.

"Listen, there are actually two bodies in there. Gosling's, and another one from a long time ago."

A silence. Then, "How long?"

I told him, adding what I knew about the deceased's probable identity but not mentioning anything else about it.

Such as the fact that it had a small hole in its head, above its right eyebrow. Ellie hadn't noticed.

"So maybe this Gosling guy might've found it first and the shock got to him?" Colgate said. "You happen to know if he had a condition, might account for his passing away so suddenly?"

No, I felt like retorting, and I especially didn't know of any that would've enabled him to walk through a wall, then end up stiff as a board and wearing a grin out of your darkest nightmares.

"You would," I told the policeman mildly, "have to check into Hector's medical history for that."

"Yeah." Still hoping he didn't really have to rush up here, sixty miles on winding two-lane Route 1 in a storm. I could hear it in his voice so I described Hector's body in further detail.

His tone turning crisp, he asked only a few more questions before promising to arrive within the hour; by the time I hung up I was convinced at least that Trooper Hollis Colgate was nobody's fool.

But whether that turned out to be good news or bad news only time would tell. Sitting in the phone alcove I watched the panes of the big old double-hung windows in the dining room get battered by the rain. The caulk beads I'd run atop the storm windows were holding, so the window wells weren't filling with water.

Not yet, anyway. Next summer, I mused, I would remove all the aluminum storm-window frames and grind the trim down to bright unweathered wood. After that maybe it would hold paint, which it hadn't the last time, peeling away in thick strips almost before I finished applying it. But back then I hadn't yet discovered the Johnnie Cochran rule of preparing old houses for painting: "If the wood is grey, the paint won't stay."

Finally, I intended to caulk *under* the frames, squeezing the seal tight to form something more durable than the current temporary fix. For a while I'd considered also packing the screw holes with plastic wood, since removing the screws would strip the holes smooth, rendering them useless. But the best plan was to drill them a little bigger and tap in dowel pins; that way there would be at least some good wood in those old windows.

And you never know, I thought as I sat there watching the torrential rain. That little bit of good wood might end up being what held the house up, if push came to shove.

There was plenty I could do while I waited for Colgate but the more I thought about it, the more it seemed like a bad idea to leave those bodies alone until he'd seen them. So finally when he didn't show up I left a note on my back door and went over.

No one was there, but the rain had slowed down to a drizzle. I went in and grabbed some tools. The front steps were broken and if teams of investigators were going to be tramping in and out of here, it seemed only charitable to make it safe for them.

Fortunately I'd been eyeing those steps for a while, with special attention to the old black cast-iron railing. I'd soaked the bolts holding it on with WD-40 every day for a week. So now when I dropped a hex wrench on them they unscrewed cooperatively.

Next I pulled the railing off and went to work on the wooden treads, which despite their rot didn't come off as cooperatively at all. Eventually I bashed them up enough so that I could get at the nail shafts holding them on with a coping saw: *zip, zop*.

Last came the hard part. Usually when you replace stair treads you've prepared yourself by measuring and cutting the new ones. I by contrast had prepared by noticing some old boards and figuring I could jury-rig something.

This plan, it turned out, might have been too optimistic, especially since I only had the coping saw, no tape measure or pencil, and nowhere to prop the boards while I cut them.

On the plus side, the boards did turn out to be wide enough. So I just laid them on the risers, nailed them down, and cut the ends off. The coping saw was most emphatically not the proper tool for the job. Fortunately, however, I am naturally equipped with the one tool that is most essential for old-house fix-up.

That is, bonehead stubbornness. I even had a strategy for getting the railing back on without a drill, using a nail to make the pilot holes for the wood screws.

The trouble was, I couldn't keep the railing straight and turn the screws back in at the same time. If I held the railing up I couldn't reach the screw holes, and when I could reach the screw holes the railing overbalanced itself and fell over, pulling the screws out.

So after several attempts I abandoned this portion of the step-repair program. Still I considered it reasonably successful, since even without a railing no eager-beaver homicide detective was going to hustle up those steps on his way to a nice juicy murder case, and end up instead in the hospital with a broken ankle.

And in a bad mood. The last thing we needed around here was a cop of any kind in a bad mood.

We didn't get one, either.

At first.

"State or federal?" my father asked two hours later. I was still waiting for Trooper Colgate and after hanging around at Harlequin House for a while longer I'd decided to come back home.

"State." The crime, I meant, that George had been in trouble over, back when he wasn't very much older than Sam was now.

It was the event George didn't like talking about. "Trial or plea?" He was a lawbreaker from way back himself, my old man, and he knew the ropes.

"Pled," I replied. "Took it for someone else. Drugs belonged to his friend, who had a sheet already, would've gone to prison. So George stepped up. But that won't be in the record, of course. And it'll take two minutes for it to come up on their computers, that old conviction."

My father was a lean, clean man with pale blue eyes, strong hands with knobby knuckles, and thinning white hair pulled back in a straggly ponytail that he fastened with a leather string.

"Well. There are convictions," he said consideringly. "And then there are convictions."

We were in my cellar inspecting the leaking part of the foundation. These days he was a magician at tricking stones and mortar into stable configurations. But years earlier, before he changed his name and became a famous fugitive, he'd been what passed in those quasi-innocent days as an urban terrorist.

He gestured at the part of the cellar wall he hadn't already replaced. "All this here has got to go," he decreed. "Leaks now, and the water between the stones'll freeze later. Every year, worse."

He kicked pebbles into the gutter at the foot of the wall. Called a french drain, it was meant to carry water back outside.

It didn't. "Nonviolent crime," he said. "Took his medicine, been a good boy since. I doubt one old pop'll hurt him much. An actual threat, though. Malice aforethought. That'll hurt him."

"Maybe the police won't hear about that." But I was grasping at straws. My father looked up at me from where he was examining the sump pump, the old trace of a feral twinkle still in his eye.

"How long did it take you to hear about it?"

I let a breath out, defeated. "Twelve hours." People liked Ellie too much to have gone to her with the Duddy's Tap story, or she'd know, too.

"Okay," I conceded, "I get your point. They're going to look hard at George. He had a motive and odds are he also had access to the method."

On that big ring of his, George had a key to nearly every garage, barn, storage hut, and garden shed on the island, as well as to many houses. And he'd been rat-killing for Cory Williams.

With I didn't know what, yet, but the way things

were going I could hazard a guess. "As for opportunity, we don't know when Gosling died. But George doesn't punch a clock. Nobody keeps tabs on him. He sets his own schedule and mostly he works alone."

I thought a moment. "Still, it would've been pretty stupid. Saying you'd like to get rid of a person and then going out and doing it."

But my father was already shaking his head. "Cops think all criminals *are* stupid," he pointed out.

He reached over and tested the float mechanism on the sump pump. "They never seem to get the reason, though. Which is that the stupid ones are the only ones *they* ever meet."

When water leaked into the cellar it flowed into a barrel I had set into the floor, its upper rim an inch or so below floor level. As water in the barrel rose, it lifted a float attached to a long rod, which in turn was hooked to the pump switch.

And—voilà. Or viola, as my son insisted on pronouncing it. Sam has dyslexia, tries to be good-humored about it.

Mostly. "All you can do now is see how things play out. Nice gadget," my father added approvingly.

Then out of the blue: "Not so easy to go on the run with a wife and baby," he said, still examining my flood-control arrangement.

You could buy sump pumps but I'd built mine out of toilet tank innards and an old bilge pump, for the economical fun of it and because George had bet me a dollar that I couldn't. My father now fiddled with the float and set it so the pump switched on sooner.

"Don't want to let the barrel get full," he counseled. "Get a big run in, barrel's full, pump might not be able to keep up."

It hadn't been easy for my dad when he ran, his own wife blown to smithereens, his toddler daughter ending up under a heap of rubble in the tiny yard of a Greenwich Village town house.

The daughter being me. He tinkered with the float angle, his knobby fingers working meticulously. "How's that other situation of yours coming?"

George's public hatred of a guy who'd turned up with a bad case of the deads wasn't the only situation complicating my life just at the moment. "I don't know. I'm waiting for a call."

He got up from his crouched position by the sump pump under the hanging bare lightbulb and turned to the old foundation. The stones were granite chunks that had been quarried on the mainland and barged here, two centuries earlier.

He probed the old mortar with a finger. It sifted out like sand. Through some of the gaps you could see daylight, yet other parts were as solid as if the stuff had been laid in yesterday.

"You can't tell by looking," he said, "what's salvageable. You can hit it with a mallet, even, some'll fall out, some not. Put real stress on 'er, though, you find out what she's made of."

Uh-huh. "So when can you start fixing it?"

He stroked his chin. "After the frost is out of the ground."

Which in Maine could mean anytime from April to the middle of August. Now it was October, after which came winter, and after that would be what we get here instead of spring: mud time.

And *that*, as Sam would've put it, would be the wrench in the monkey-works. "You know," my father said gently, "you might want to put another pump down here. To take the excess."

"Yeah." I frowned at the earthen floor; maybe the dogs could help me dig the new hole. He started upstairs.

"As for George, what he tells them is this," he said. "He tells them the name of his attorney, period. Nothing more without counsel."

My heart thumped. "You think it could be as bad as that? I mean, *everybody* likes George. He couldn't possibly have . . ."

He turned and looked down at me. "Jacobia, it doesn't matter that he's a good guy, even if he didn't do it."

If, he'd said. I noticed it right away.

Not a slip. After his years on the run, you didn't slide too many fast ones past him, and he never paid anyone the false compliment of thinking they were too good to be capable of something.

Thinking *that* was what had put him on the run in the first place. Because he hadn't triggered the blast that killed my mom and as good as orphaned me, years ago.

His best friend had. In the kitchen he picked up his leather satchel. "Better make myself scarce before the *gendarmes* arrive," he warned me. "I need to get back to Jody Jones's place, anyway."

He was building a new chimney for Jody, whose record in the bill-paying department was not exactly stellar.

"Okay," I said. My father went along so normally most of the time, you'd never guess how many years in prison were waiting for him if he were ever captured. "How are you going to get Jody to pay? Hold a gun to his head?"

That had been tried but Jody had a habit of bursting into tears when he was threatened, to the point where he'd earned the nickname, "Old Blubber-Puss."

"Nope. I've got a secret method. He'll weep, all right, and he won't quit till it's cash on the barrel-head. Wade back soon?"

"Uh-huh," I said, not quite able to hide the annoyance in my voice. "Later tonight."

After such a long time of not being able to care for me, my dad liked the idea of Wade being my protector. In fact, he liked it more than I did.

"Good," he said. I looked up to find him gazing at me. Folks used to tell me how much I resembled

41

my mother; her folks, who'd raised me until I lit out for the big city.

"Dad." I stopped him at the door. "I'm sorry. Lots of things on my mind, is all. I'm glad you're here."

He replied with a small smile. Not enough, but we had that. It killed me that even with all he'd done for me lately, he still thought it was all he deserved.

And that sometimes it was what I thought too. "It was a long time, though, wasn't it?" he asked quietly.

Like I said, not much got past him. He wasn't the only one still trying to make sense of what we were to one another: what could be salvaged.

And what, perhaps, was too damaged to save.

"Tell George what I said," he added, and went out.

Trooper Hollis Colgate pulled his squad car into my driveway and hustled for the house through what remained of the nor'easter now barreling away from us into New Brunswick.

"Had to wait at the causeway in Machias," he said of the delay. "Tide was high, took an hour for the storm surge to clear off the road. Plenty of trees down, too. Lots of fender benders, other general nonsense."

I caught the drift. This had better not be a false

alarm. Colgate glanced around, noticed that our electricity was still on.

"There's a generator on our island," I explained. "When the power lines from the mainland go down, men from town go over and fire it up."

Colgate nodded. "Handy," he said, looking around some more.

Suddenly I felt glad we weren't displaying any obvious signs of careless living. To help George—assuming he needed it and it was possible—I needed good credibility with Colgate. And while waiting for him I'd been too preoccupied to play Holly Homemaker.

Sam was at the kitchen counter making some sandwiches. "How do you do, sir," he said when I introduced him to the officer.

With dark curly hair and hazel eyes, Sam was ridiculously handsome, not to mention much older than any child of mine had a right to be. I watched with pleasure as his manners registered with Colgate.

"D'yado," echoed Sam's friend Tommy Pockets, a red-haired, freckled boy whose round cheeks and big ears gave him a striking resemblance to Howdy Doody.

The boys went back to fixing their late lunch. "Are you all right, ma'am?" Colgate asked.

My eyes were red from weeping, a fact I'd tried to disguise with cold washcloths, unsuccessfully. Between my dad's departure and Colgate's arrival I'd had the call I'd been waiting for. It was from an associate of mine in the city who had law enforcement connections, and it hadn't conveyed welcome information.

"I'm fine," I told Colgate. "After I spoke with you I had some bad news on another matter, that's all. Nothing to do with why I called you."

Sam glanced at me. *Later,* I telegraphed at him. "Would you like some coffee?" I asked Colgate, "or—"

"No, thanks," he replied with a practiced smile. He had good teeth, a ruddy complexion, sandy hair, and caramel-colored, pale-lashed eyes. His husky build might go to fat later, but for now it was easy to imagine him engaged in outdoor activities: fishing in summer, hunting in fall, and snowmobiling in winter.

"Maybe we could take a ride to the scene," he suggested. "I can get a feel for just what the situation is."

All business, but pleasantly enough. We weren't chums but we weren't adversaries either.

"Sure. Sam, if you could please feed the animals before you go out . . ." The dogs and our Siamese attack cat, Cat Dancing, were milling around the kitchen, agitating for snacks.

"Sure. Good to meet you," Sam said to Trooper Colgate. "Mom, I could stick around if you want," he added.

Once upon a time, the only reason Sam would stick around was in case there might be a chance to steal money from my purse. I was thanking my stars that our situation had changed and getting ready to turn down his offer when it hit me.

"Sam. The CPR course your father is teaching at the clinic? Listen, I hate to tell you this, but I signed us both up for it at the last minute and forgot to tell you."

I looked helplessly at the clock. "And *then* I forgot . . ."

The class had begun an hour ago. "I'm sorry, Sam, I knew you needed it for the semester, and—"

Tommy listened in silence. Just Sam's age and working at the Mobil station, he was tutoring Sam in algebra and geometry so Sam could take a challenge exam and get three college credits.

But to start the new semester as a sophomore, Sam needed four. "Damn," I said. Even dead, Hector the Objector could really mess you up. But Sam only grinned.

"Don't worry, Mom, it's a great idea. Dad'll catch me up on what I missed today. But *you'd* better watch out for him."

At this Tommy did smile. He was such a good kid, I had to hide the way my heart ached for him; working at the gas station was fine as far as it went, but even the older men employed there thought what I did: Tommy should try for more.

Now, while he had the chance. "Yeah," he teased me, "I heard if you miss one of Dr. Tiptree's classes or you even come late, he lets the other students practice on you."

Which sounded like something my ex-husband would do. As a man who delved into other people's craniums for a living—back in the city, Victor was the guy you went to when your case was so hopeless that the other brain surgeons switched to doing nose jobs just to avoid you—he'd left squeamishness in the dust.

Unless he could use it against you. Meanwhile Tommy chose this moment to change the subject. "Uh, listen, if I could get hold of a pair of alpacas, could I raise them in your backyard?"

The kid was always looking for ways to make money. "There's this guy here in Eastport," he explained, apparently taking my stunned silence as an invitation to continue, "raising pot-bellied pigs. Like, for pets. But alpacas are way more valuable."

Cory Williams; the guy with the red ants. The reminder sent a pang through me as Tommy went on. "Their hair, even, is worth a fortune. But the yard at my house is too small."

"How will you get alpacas?" I asked, momentarily diverted.

As it happened an old client of mine had just written to me on this very subject. Alpacas were the hot new back-to-the-land investment for urban rat-race escapees.

"Dunno," Tommy said. "I figured I better have a place to put 'em, first."

Besides a big yard, alpacas needed a fence, water troughs, a warm barn, feeding arrangements, grooming tools, and an area for a communal dung pile, which somehow I didn't think my neighbors would appreciate.

Also, a breeding-age male alpaca went for upward of twenty thousand dollars. "In this case I think you'd better find out how to get them first," I told Tommy.

Next I supposed he'd want to raise mushrooms in my cellar, which was at least a suitable environment. And if I didn't get it fixed soon, he would be able to raise trout down there, too.

"Come on," I told Trooper Colgate. "We'd better go do this before my ex shows up and starts demonstrating the kiss of life."

We went out into a thin rain. "Have a fair amount of trouble with your ex-husband, do you?" Colgate asked mildly.

Delicate. But fishing, definitely. I decided to level with Trooper Colgate. "He's a real pain in the ass. But he's Sam's father."

I didn't even try explaining it all; for one thing I didn't understand the accommodation we'd come to, myself. But Victor had moved here and given up everything to be near Sam, and I had begun getting over my own bitterness enough to give him credit for that.

"Yeah." Colgate nodded when I'd finished my summary, as he drove carefully through the rain-washed streets. "I've got two teenagers myself. They live with my ex-wife in Auburn. What we do for our kids, huh?" He turned on Water Street, past the nineteenth-century brick storefronts facing the bay. I scanned the pier and the tugboats tied there, the *Pleon* and the *Ahoskie,* looking for my husband Wade. But I didn't see him.

"Your boy seems like a good kid." Colgate turned left again, spotted the mansard-roofed mansion set back from the street.

"He is," I confirmed. "He's doing a work-study this semester out at the boat school. Back to U. Maine after the break."

Colgate pulled over. "This it?" He got out his notepad and a utility flashlight. "Let's have a look."

The yard was an overgrown thicket of sumac, barberry bushes, and wild raspberry. A small forest of whippy, resilient softwood saplings grew around the rear of the structure.

"Nice new step," he remarked, glancing down at my handiwork as we went in.

"Thanks." I couldn't resist bouncing on it a little. Solid, definitely solid. But it was the only thing so far about the whole morning that felt that way. And although I had my hopes because Colgate seemed like a serious and solid Maine State Trooper, I still suspected matters would get worse.

Inside, the smell was a mixture of old varnish and dry rot. A wide stairway curved up to the second floor, a carved mahogany banister turning with old-fashioned gracefulness at the landing.

"Quite a place," Colgate commented, peering around.

I led him into the parlor. "There," I said.

He aimed the flash, went in where the bodies were. I stayed out. Somehow in my mind the skeletal tree branches outside had gotten mixed up with Eva Thane's withered arms; I didn't want to see her again. Or Hector either, his body still taut with the agony of his last moments.

"Uh-huh," Colgate said emotionlessly from inside the little room. Then: "You're Wade Sorenson's wife, aren't you?"

"Yes." When there was freighter traffic, Wade guided the big vessels in and out of the local waters; the rest of the time he sold and repaired guns, both collectibles and utility weapons. So between boats and firearms, almost everyone around here knew him.

"Quite the shooter."

Wade, he meant. It was how I'd gotten to know Wade, too; on the target range. "You poke around in here?" Colgate asked.

The question snapped me out of a pleasant memory. "Enough to see them. That's all. My friend knows who the old one is, though, or thinks she does."

"Really." He came back out again. "How's that?"

"Her uncle owned the place, back in the early 1920s."

Chester Harlequin, *bon vivant* and disgraced local physician, had given the house and himself a bad name that lasted to this day. "Ellie has photographs of him and the other people who lived here,

49

and she recognized that headpiece. The tiara."

"Right. And the other one is Hector Gosling?"

He glanced casually around some more as he asked, taking in the broken plaster, cracked windowpanes, a patch of the ceiling fallen to the floor and shattered. But his tone wasn't casual.

"Yes. Everyone knew Hector," I said. "No one liked him."

Might as well get that right out there; plenty of suspects. Just because George hated Hector for a reason, that didn't mean someone else couldn't have killed him for some *other* reason.

"Anybody around here dislike him particularly?"

Drat. I hesitated a beat too long and felt him hear it. Being a cop would've given him ears like a bat, especially for a lie. "My friend's husband had a beef with him," I replied.

I explained it briefly. "But," I finished, "George couldn't have done it. You really need to look for somebody else."

"Okay," Colgate said. He'd stopped smiling but he hadn't locked up behind a thousand-mile stare. And maybe it was better he heard it right away, not wonder later why I hadn't told him.

"Just a sec," he said. "I want to check one more thing."

He went back into the little room and emerged a few moments later with a clear plastic bag in his latex-gloved hand. Inside the bag was a scrap of paper with some writing on it.

"Well?" I couldn't read what it said.

He was frowning, thoughtful. "Well, what?"

And obviously he wasn't going to tell me. "Can you at least reveal whether or not you happened to find the gun?"

"You spotted that, did you? Single gunshot to the head on the female deceased." He looked shrewdly at me and stripped the glove off. "No, I didn't find it. But here's some good news. Just one door." He waved at it. "But it's not a locked-room mystery anymore."

The mystery, he meant, of how someone got Hector through an eighty-year-old wall. It had been my big question, too.

Or one of them. He looked at me some more. "So what was the news *you* got, that you were crying about not long before I got here?"

Wham, out of left field. But not entirely; the news could've been George confessing to me that he'd done the deed.

So I leveled with Colgate again. "A friend of mine in New York was a fugitive from the Federal authorities for a long time. He got picked up a few days ago, they've got him over a barrel."

Friend was putting it mildly. If not for Jemmy Wechsler I might have ended up with a bullet in my own head, all those years ago when I was little more than a child and alone in the city.

"And you knew where he was? This friend of yours?" Colgate asked.

In other words, did I need an attorney, too?

"No. But he was . . . probably I shouldn't say this, but he was a hero of mine. And now he's either going to prison or into the witness protection program."

Witless protection, Jemmy always called it, because you had to be witless to get in a position where you needed it. And even more so to believe in it; I mean, that it could protect you.

Or that anything really could. "He was a mob guy," I said. "Handled their money. Few years ago, he stole a big bunch of it and disappeared."

Colgate whistled. "Nervy move. And you were a pal?"

"Yeah." It was Jemmy who'd taught me to survive and thrive in Manhattan. Now he was in trouble and I didn't know whether to be sad, scared, or furious with him for letting it happen.

All of the above, I figured. "Anyway, that was the news," I said to Colgate. "Nothing to do with this."

We headed for the door. "What did you mean about no locked-room mystery?" I asked. "And what's in that plastic bag?"

He held the big old ornately paneled door for me, scraped it shut behind us over the uneven wooden floor as we left the house.

"Body goes in, there's got to be a way in," he said. "That, like the man says, is elementary."

I put the key in the lock and jiggled it, waiting for the tumblers to fall. A good hard kick would have pushed the old door right over, or someone could've broken a sidelight window and reached through to turn the dead-bolt knob.

But no windows were broken and the door hadn't been kicked. I handed Colgate the key when I was finished with it; everyone on the historical society's volunteer team had one.

As did George. "Same with a gun," Colgate added. "Gotta be a way out for it, too."

I wondered if someone took the gun eighty years ago when Eva Thane was shot in the head, or later when Hector was put here.

"And I don't know if you noticed," Colgate continued, "but there was an old carpet on that floor."

Right, an ancient red rectangle, its vaguely Oriental design mostly obscured by dust. I'd barely paid any attention to it. Now Colgate strode to the squad car ahead of me through sodden autumn leaves torn down by the storm.

I stood still, working it out. He was already on the radio, reciting his unit number, location, and situation.

"A trapdoor? Is there a trapdoor under that rug?"

He glanced over, nodded to confirm. Which encouraged me; if he thought I was screwing around with him he wouldn't have told me anything.

Waiting for him to finish, I leaned against the squad car. As the storm pulled off, the wind had swung around out of the south, bringing with it a burst of warmth and a false smell of spring mingled with a hint of wood smoke. Crows cawed, blue sky peeped between the departing clouds, and shafts of sunlight beamed down onto the puddles shimmering in the streets.

Maybe everything would be all right, I thought.

Colgate hung up his radio, came around to me. "Found this in Gosling's pocket."

He held up the plastic bag. The paper inside had been torn from a lined notebook, the kind you could buy anywhere, marked with a heavy hand. Close up it was easy to read the single word block-printed on it: GUILTY.

The smoke smell got stronger. "You or your friend happen to put it there?" Colgate asked.

I stared at him. "No, of course not. Why would we?"

"Don't know. That's why I'm inquiring. Maybe for the same reason a nice woman like you turns out to know so much about an ugly thing like strychnine poisoning?"

"Don't be silly. Anyway," I went on, flustered, "aren't you supposed to leave the evidence where it is? For the crime scene people?"

His gaze didn't waver. "Not if it might not survive intact."

"Oh, for heaven's sake, why wouldn't it?" But as I asked this I heard a faint crackling sound and glanced back puzzledly at the derelict old building's sagging clapboards.

Smoke seeped from between them. "If things

don't go right, I might end up hauling those two bodies out, too," Colgate went on.

Harlequin House was on fire.

In the old days, many of my clients believed the Big Three Myths: that they could run a hotel, operate a good restaurant, or manage a major league baseball team, given the opportunity.

Thinking this, I blew out the candles on the dining room table and switched on the lamps, their glow reflecting softly in the old gold-medallion wallpaper. It was six in the evening and through the front windows I could see the blue-white blaze of the floodlights set up around Harlequin House, blocks away.

"So what'd you tell him?" Wade asked. "When he asked how you knew so much about strychnine, I mean."

Dark figures moved in the lights, cars leaving and others arriving. An occasional brief siren-whoop pierced the night.

"The truth," I replied. "That Ellie and I have been involved in a couple of situations, before. And that I read a lot."

We two women had fallen accidentally into a reputation for nosiness where murder was concerned, and Ellie still regarded any snooping we did as merely a hobby. But I had a forensics text, *Practical Homicide Investigation,* on my bedside table.

"He believed it?" Wade asked. Broad-shouldered, with brush-cut blond hair and eyes the pale grey of a fog bank at sea, my husband had the kind of quiet patience I'd heard of but never managed to possess for myself.

"Seemed to." *Nux vomica,* the South American plant: a few in the medical literature had survived. Basically the stuff cranked the nerve impulses to the muscles up into the red zone and stuck them there. Its victim suffocated or died of exhaustion.

"The news people are here," I said, drawing the curtains.

Murder in Maine came in one of two flavors, mostly: guy vs. girl or two guys vs. a case of beer and a cheap handgun. But this was different, so the vans topped with satellite dishes lumbered dutifully up Shackford Street like elephants in a circus parade.

"What'd they tell you?" I asked Wade. A fire danced in the fireplace, birch logs piled on andirons with front posts cast in the shapes of leaping porpoises.

"That they think the body came up through the trapdoor from the cellar," he said. "Just like Colgate figured."

The volunteer fire department had arrived within five minutes, put the fire out in ten. The crackling had been pigeons' nests in the eaves, not yet the house itself, being consumed by flames.

"And the medical examiner was on his way back to Augusta from a meeting in St. John, so he stopped by and took a peek," Wade said.

"And?" I crossed my mental fingers.

"And they'd pin it down more at autopsy, but he thought Hector'd been dead between twenty-four and forty-eight hours."

"Anyone say anything more about that note in his pocket?"

Wade's usual target-shooting range was the favorite of many cops, so they'd hailed him in friendly fashion. But he shook his head.

"Nope. Only other thing I overheard was, the fire probably started in the wiring."

Not that anyone would yet have done a careful investigation, or even that there would necessarily be one, considering the fact that the wiring in the old place was probably ancient.

Wade surveyed the remnants of our meal. "That Will Bonnet's quite a chef."

"I guess." The remains of a brilliantly seasoned fish dinner were ready to be removed to the kitchen; Will had delivered it for no reason other than that he'd felt like cooking and thought we would like it. Unfortunately I'd run into some bones.

"Never know," Wade commented, "maybe he could make a restaurant go, here."

"Maybe," I said. "The numbers are iffy."

It was the thing I'd never been able to get through to my clients: maybe they *could* run a restaurant but without customers, so what? Summer people flooded into Eastport but on Labor Day, they flooded right back out again. As a result we barely had the year-round population to support the eateries we had, never mind diluting the mixture with any more.

Still, Eastport had put stars in the eyes of harder-headed men than Will Bonnet, and I had worse things to worry about than him pouring money into a nonstarter.

Upstairs a blare of guitar music exploded from Sam's room, got turned down hastily. Sam and Tommy had gone up there so Tommy could guide Sam deeper into the mysteries of the quadratic equation, Sam looking anxious as if he feared he might never emerge.

"Wade," I asked, "couldn't you try talking to Tommy? Get him to consider maybe just getting his feet wet in college?"

Wade looked regretful. "That's something he'll have to work out himself. For one thing, his mom needs the money he's earning. And as long as George is doing okay without extra schooling . . ."

"Right," I said, discouraged. I'd never seen anyone idolize anyone the way Tommy did George.

Except maybe me, in the old days when I was hanging out with Jemmy Wechsler. But this thought I pushed determinedly away.

"You heard Tommy's latest plan?" Wade asked.

"The alpacas?" I began picking up plates and silverware.

"Nope. That lasted twenty minutes." Wade started on the wine glasses and napkins. "Now he thinks he might go north, days off, pan for

58

gold. He heard what gold is worth an ounce nowadays."

"Somebody should tell him how much per hour," I replied. "Of hard labor . . . what is it, maybe a couple dollars a day?"

We'd done it once for a lark. If you can call freezing your tail off, getting wet and muddy and coming up with a teensy speck of gold dust anything like a lark.

"I wonder if George could," I persisted. "Talk with him."

"And say what?" Wade dropped napkins in the washing machine. " 'Go to school so you won't be a loser like me'?"

I turned, my hands still full of silverware. "George is no loser, we all know that. But Wade, he's not like you, either, he doesn't have a . . ."

Wade hadn't gone to college, but folks paid very well to get their antique guns restored. And in Eastport if you made a living on only two jobs, you were doing just fine.

". . . special skill," I went on. "He just cobbles it together, makes it work, but it's so hard. And now with the baby coming . . ."

"Yeah," Wade relented. He knew as well as I did how worried George had been lately, even though George would rather stick his hand in a fire than discuss it.

"George has already been asked to account for himself," Wade said.

"Really? By the police? And what happened?"

Nothing good, if Wade had been procrastinating about telling me. "Everyone else they asked cooperated or promised to, soon's they could get time, sit down and place themselves."

Because of the storm, I translated, and the hundred and one things they had to do to protect their livelihoods from it. But once the boats, engines and lines, bilge pumps and nets, lobster traps and dragging gear were all safe and accounted for, people who'd had run-ins with Hector would put some time aside, relate their whereabouts over the last day or so.

It was the sort of delay a Maine cop might be flexible about. But I didn't think Wade was talking about delay.

"Right." He read it in my face. "Cops weren't even being particularly aggressive. It was more like if someone's name came up they wanted to rule him out. And you know, a lot of guys who have work boats also have second mortgages on their houses, keep the boats running."

It was yet another reason why Hector was so unpopular, that he held many of those mortgages himself. And every year he got his greedy mitts on a couple of those houses.

"So that's why the cops had so many guys' names," Wade said. "They already went over to Hector's place, the door wasn't locked, had a gander at Hector's big black book. But like I said, most of the fellows were cooperative."

The book was famous. If your name was in it,

you owed Hector money. "But George," Wade went on unhappily, "was different."

"Sure, and the cops had *his* name because I told Colgate about him," I said bitterly. "Me and my big mouth."

Wade shook his head. "Didn't matter. Other people mentioned George, too. They didn't want to, but Colgate got it out of them somehow."

Yeah, he was good at that; small comfort. I ran hot water on the plates in the sink.

"But anyway," Wade went on, "that's not what I meant. What's different is, George said no."

A saucer slipped from my hand and broke. "He . . . but why?"

George didn't have any gear that might have been vulnerable to the storm's aftereffects. Weeks earlier at Will Bonnet's prescient suggestion he'd moved his own boat, fitted only to haul a few dozen lobster traps in season, to a more protected mooring out at Deep Cove.

"I don't know. All I know is that he isn't saying where he was for the last forty-eight hours or so. And he isn't saying *why* he isn't saying. His lip," Wade finished grimly, "is zipped."

Oh, brother: motive, method, and now what probably looked to the cops like opportunity. And once they get those three items corralled in a single suspect, cops don't go racketing around looking for *other* suspects.

Not on your tintype. The fact that in Maine life was all you could get for premeditated murder—

and if you fed someone strychnine, how could you say it wasn't planned?—was no consolation.

I dropped the saucer pieces into the trash. "So then what happened?" I asked Wade. "And how do you know this stuff, anyway?"

He'd already said it wasn't part of what he'd overheard, and I didn't think it would've been included in old-shooting-buddies small talk, either. "Colgate told me," he replied.

My uh-oh bells jangled like an alarm clock. "I see. Just out of the goodness of his heart he told you this?"

Wade shot a glance at me, then let it pass: the notion that maybe Colgate had been playing him for some reason.

"No. He wanted me to try getting George to reconsider. He's giving George time to think it over. Pretty decent of him."

My estimation of Colgate crept up a notch. He'd unnerved me with his interrogation skills back at Harlequin House, but in his place I'd have done just the same.

Or tried. "Not much time, though," Wade cautioned. "It won't even be up to him, soon. His bosses start asking hard questions, he'll have to get George's statement completed."

"That's a fine kettle of fish," I said, annoyed. "George and his stiff-necked . . ."

Pride, I was about to finish, still hoping that was it. He'd been the same way about Ellie's money, back when she'd had some; her small inheritance, so carefully invested, had evaporated in the accounting scandals that had helped pop the Wall Street bubble.

But just then I heard the boys coming downstairs so I didn't continue. Tommy talked with customers at the Mobil station every day and we didn't need this all over town right off the bat.

"Everyone okay at the boat basin?" I asked instead. "And the boats, are they all right?"

Wade nodded. "Guys were prepared. Scallop season coming, no one wants to be out of action during the earning time."

But despite my precautions, Tommy had over-heard plenty. And not for him the indirect angle when full-bore would serve. "Is George in trouble about Mr. Gosling?" he wanted to know.

Wade answered him frankly. "George could end up in trouble if he doesn't come up with a good explanation of where he's been and what he's been doing for the past couple of days. But he just doesn't want to, and unfortunately that's probably going to make them suspect him."

Wade believes that the truth shall make you free, while I tend more toward the well-balanced port-folio, healthy cash flow, and a decent credit record as instruments of liberation.

A shadow passed over Tommy's face, replaced by indignation. "That's nuts," he declared. "George wouldn't—"

"All this will be straightened out soon," I assured him.

"Yeah." But he didn't sound the least bit convinced. Then, "Hey, you know what?" He made a show of looking at his watch. "I gotta go. I just remembered I told my mom I'd help her, uh, clean out the refrigerator."

Sure, that was it. The phone rang, diverting me from what I had been about to reply: that Tommy shouldn't flimflam me, that I'd been flimflammed by the best and could see it coming a mile away. But later I was glad I hadn't said it.

Because I couldn't and didn't.

"A *search* warrant?" I repeated in disbelief. It was Ellie on the phone and she sounded more distressed than I'd ever heard her before. "Ellie, are you sure?"

Wade frowned over to where I sat in the telephone alcove.

"But I thought . . ." I went on.

What? he mouthed, and I waved him off.

"So did I," Ellie told me, her voice shaking. "That they were going to give George time. But with all the media attention—oh, God, there's a satellite van outside the house—I guess they had to do it right away."

So much for Colgate's help. I guessed the news vans and his bosses must've arrived simultaneously. And publicity plus bosses never spelled anything but C-Y-P.

Cover Your Posterior. Thus the decision would've

been taken out of Colgate's hands. "They're there now?"

"Yes," she said miserably. "Tearing through everything. They wanted to know where George has been working . . ."

So they would come soon enough upon Cory Williams and his pigs. And the poison. "Listen," I said, "call Clarissa Arnold and . . . no, wait, she's probably out of town."

Clarissa had been a prosecutor before moving to Eastport and switching to the defense side of her profession, so she was good at quashing the high-handed notions of police bosses. But she was also married to our police chief, Bob Arnold, and would probably be in Kennebunk now helping tend to Bob's sick mother.

"Will tried her," Ellie confirmed. "He's here with George, thank God. But yes, her answering service says she's away."

"We'll find her," I said. "Where else will they search?"

"I'm not sure. The truck, definitely, because they wanted to know where it was. They're going there, to the repair lot at the Mobil station, after they've finished in here and with the shed."

A mental picture of George's inner sanctum rose in my mind: a trim little wood-frame structure behind his house, furnished with a pot-bellied stove, a workbench, and all his tools.

"Are they going to impound the truck," I asked, "or search it there?"

"I don't know," she responded distractedly. Then her voice moved away. "Please, you don't have to . . . Jake, it's awful. Now they're going through the baby's things."

She was nearly in tears. I could only assume they had George outside, since otherwise he'd be after them with a brickbat.

"Ellie, listen to me. You let them search. Don't do anything and don't say anything. Just wait for us."

The boys were in the kitchen. Tommy must've realized the call was about George and stuck around. From their faces I could tell he and Sam had figured out what was going on and didn't like it. Tommy in particular looked ready to weep.

". . . come with you," I heard Sam say to him, but he shook Sam off and went out alone, his expression grim.

Wade pulled his jacket on. "We'll be there in a minute," I told Ellie.

With, I wanted to add, *our own brickbats.* But by the time we reached George and Ellie's snug little cottage overlooking the water, the searchers had entered the shed. There they'd found a can of powder. Helpfully marked POISON, its label emblazoned with skull and crossbones, it was immediately taken into evidence.

"It's been there for weeks," Ellie told me shakily. "George got it from Cory Williams, Cory wanted him to use it on the rats. George never really liked the idea but Cory kept at him so George finally got it over with, because Cory pays."

And of course George hadn't felt able to turn down honest work, or to tell Cory Williams how it should be done, either. If Cory wanted it some other way—a way for instance that included not having to buy a new substance—well, he was the customer. So George had used what Cory asked him to use and gotten on with the job.

Ellie's fingers laced worriedly together. "George was going to give it back to Cory as soon as they were sure the stuff really got rid of the rats. He didn't want it around here, not even out in the shed, once the baby came."

It had been around, though, and that wasn't even the worst part. The worst, or so I believed at the time, was when one of the warrant officers asked Ellie where George had been the night before, and she couldn't tell him.

"I went up to bed early last night," she began, controlling her voice with an effort. "He must've come in late. I didn't hear him. He's at work till eleven or later sometimes," she added.

She took a deep breath. "And when I got up this morning he was gone again. Out on another job already."

She didn't know what job. The police had already spoken with Cory Williams and learned that George hadn't gotten there until around nine. She only knew that in order not to disturb her, he'd spent the night downstairs.

He must have slept, she told them, on the daybed in the kitchen. He hadn't made coffee before he left, though, and there had been no pillows or blankets in evidence.

"He could have gotten his coffee at the convenience store. And George would make his bed, not leave it for me," she parried.

But when asked to say for sure that he'd been home at all the previous night, she couldn't. Whereupon a disbelieving George was put in handcuffs, informed of his rights, and driven away.

Then came the worst part.

CHAPTER 3

L et her talk it out," said my ex-husband Victor Tiptree. "I don't want to sedate her and she wouldn't let me, anyway."

I'd called him while the officers were still hand-cuffing George, and to his credit he'd come over at once. Now he tucked his stethoscope back into his bag, his hands moving precisely as befitted a brilliant brain surgeon, even one who'd given it all up for a remote general practice.

"And the baby's all right too?" I asked Victor.

"Absolutely. No reason it wouldn't be. Ellie's vital signs certainly aren't showing strain. Girl's got a constitution like a sixteen-year-old."

Which was only a bit younger than I was when I had Sam, and I don't remember feeling sixteen in the days before our son appeared. More like a hundred and sixteen.

"Changed your mind about the CPR class?" Victor inquired mildly. Trust him to get a zing in, whatever the situation. "Sam says you forgot," he added. "Maybe on purpose?"

I swallowed a retort: *The way you forgot you had a wife and baby son, back when you had so many girlfriends it was all you could do to keep track?*

If Victor had carved notches in his bedposts he'd have ended up sleeping on toothpicks. But I refrained; he'd come when I called, tonight, and done what was needed. And nowadays that was enough.

Mostly. "Finding the dead bodies was a distraction, Victor." Never mind that I'd forgotten his class *before* we found them, or that Victor's analysis was perilously close to being on target.

"Sorry if I missed a pearl of wisdom," I went on. I keep the peace as much as I can, but there's no statute of limitations on postmarital vengefulness. "We'll be there next week."

"Tomorrow," he corrected briskly. "What with the storm, so many couldn't come that I rescheduled it. I've called everyone."

So the class would be held on a Sunday morning, and never mind whether the change suited anyone else. If I had as much self-assuredness in my whole body as he does in his little finger, I would be Genghis Khan by now.

On the other hand, there's not much worse than an insecure brain surgeon. "Fine," I replied.

We were standing in Ellie's kitchen with its green enameled woodstove, bright woven rugs, and big oak table with a pitcher of red rose hips at the center of it. Ranged on the windowsills were a dozen quilted-glass jars of grape jelly, glowing royal purple.

"Nice," Victor remarked, glancing around. He

70

looked just like Sam: same hazel eyes, lantern jaw, and confidential you're-the-only-one-in-my-world smile. Sometimes that smile was the only thing that kept me from killing Victor, because Sam had it too.

A basket of kindling stood by the stove, a pine rocker and low footstool pulled up in front of it. Tucked into one corner was the white enameled daybed with a quilt spread on it. "I ought to try something like this," Victor said.

Victor's kitchen, in the big white Greek Revival house just down the street from mine, was about as cozy as the inside of a refrigerator. He paid ready lip service to style and comfort but rattled around his own old place like a marble in a box, trying and failing to solve the mystery of ordinary human-beingness.

Which was the other reason I didn't kill him: that he tried. From the table he picked up the papers the police had questioned Ellie about before they left.

"This," he said, "is strange."

I'd put the place back together from the mess the searchers had made of it. The baby's room, newly painted in pale yellow and white, smelled of garlic and tobacco; I had opened a window.

"Right," I said. "It's what's upset her most, I think."

Me too. I kept trying to understand those papers: that because of them everything was suddenly so much worse than I'd thought. Ellie's voice went on from the parlor: quietly, but the edge of hysteria in it was audible.

"Does it mean what it looks like?" Victor asked.

"I suppose so."

"Then how could they not . . . ?"

"I have absolutely no idea."

Together the pages comprised a copy of the last will and testament, prepared by a Bangor law firm, of Paula Valentine, George's recently deceased aunt. Jan Jesperson was listed as executor. The envelope they'd come in was postmarked a few days earlier.

The warrant officers said they had found two copies of the document in George's shed, and they'd taken one with them, Ellie insisting she'd never seen either copy before. Now I searched through the pages again, hoping I'd been wrong the first time I read them.

As I did so Will Bonnet came into the kitchen, poured a cup of mint tea from the pot on a trivet atop the stove, and returned to the parlor to offer it to Ellie.

"Come on, hon," I heard him telling her solicitously. "Drink a little of this."

Will was a kind man, I thought distractedly; his own elderly relative was lucky to have him. "It means," I told Victor, "that Gosling and Jan Jesperson didn't quite get the last laugh."

Not that it was any consolation now.

The opposite, in fact. "So all this legal stuff about trusts and predeceased and so on . . ."

"Victor," I cut in impatiently, "it means that

George inherits everything. His aunt left her estate in trust to Hector Gosling but only for so long as Hector lived. After that . . ."

After that it belonged to George. And if what I'd gathered about his aunt's net worth was true, it was a jackpot.

Her house was a gorgeously restored Victorian overlooking the harbor, with a fabulous bay view. Every tradesman in town had drunk from the well of its never-ending maintenance: plumbers and landscapers, painters and roofers, electricians and purveyors of custom-built windows, to name but a few.

And Paula paid in cash, which she'd gotten by unloading about a zillion acres of timberland back when the paper companies were buying instead of selling it. So there'd be liquid assets, too.

"You know," Victor said, "this might not look so good."

Like I said: a brain surgeon. "Right, and if he hung a sign around his neck saying 'I did it,' that probably wouldn't look so good either."

Because if George had known about this will before Hector died, he'd had a far better motive for murder than I'd feared.

Victor picked up his medical bag. "Look, I doubt Ellie will need me any more tonight. Call if she does. And . . ."

He eyed me suspiciously. "You did," he added thinly, "manage to remember to tell Sam you'd signed him up for the class?"

Ah, yes; there was the Victor we all knew and loved. If he hadn't bought his own house he could've moved into a wasp's nest. The other wasps would never have known the difference.

"I told him." It's amazing how well you can speak and bite your tongue at the same time, when you have as much practice as I do. "And Victor, *you* remember. You're not to talk about this."

As it was, the news of George's arrest would be a sensation and Ellie would be facing it soon enough.

He frowned. "You must think I'm a fool."

I smiled sweetly at him. "Thanks for coming. Really, Victor, it was awfully good of you. I appreciate it."

Sam says Victor is like an English muffin: butter lightly. Mollified, he went out into the darkness.

Standing in the doorway while he got into his car, I watched a skunk shuffling among the trash cans. George hadn't had time to bring the cans in before the police took him. Victor's headlights showed the skunk trundling away; George was so tidy, there wasn't a meal for a housefly in those cans.

Will was in the kitchen when I came back inside. "Hey, good job on those steps at Harlequin House," he said. "I was driving by and saw them."

"Thanks. But how'd you know it was me?"

"Well," he smiled, tipping his head, "the rest of the volunteers are a little shy with the hammer-and-nails stuff. You seem like the only one willing to bash something apart to fix it. I wish there were a few more like you."

"Oh," I said, pleased. Hardly anyone ever compliments me for bashing things apart.

"Actually, there are some other things that could use your attention," he went on. "I made up a list."

He pulled it from his pocket. "There's a window on the first floor that won't come out. The side trim needs a crowbar. And on the second floor, the ladies want to wallpaper over a hole. Could you maybe plaster it first? You know, just fill it so you can't put a fist through the wallpaper."

I felt taken aback. This hardly seemed the time or place for going over fix-up plans. But Will continued.

". . . washstand in the kitchen lavatory. I hate to say it but someone's going to have to take a sledgehammer to that."

He grinned winningly at me. "Seems right up your alley."

It was. But . . .

"Will, don't you think we should postpone the repair plans? Maybe until tomorrow? After all, with George being accused of a murder, I don't think . . ."

He was shaking his head. "No. Absolutely not. Everything can go on just as it has been, and in fact it should. Because look," he added as my face must have shown the doubt I was feeling, "George didn't do it," he said earnestly. "You know it, I know it, and pretty soon the police are going to know it, too. That they've made a mistake."

His shoulders straightened. "Tonight of course Ellie's upset and she needs us here, for support. But starting tomorrow, we all have to hold our heads up, and show by our behavior that we know how this is going to come out for George. That he's innocent, and that's all there is to that."

I have to admit his ringing endorsement went a long way toward making me feel better. "Yeah. I guess you're right. Okay, you give me the list and I'll see what I can do about it."

"Great. Maybe George will even be back in time to bash that washstand apart," he finished encouragingly, and went on into the parlor while I stood thinking about what he had said.

That George was innocent, and the cops would realize it. Of course, about the former part of the statement I was sure. I just wished I had as much confidence as Will did in the latter part.

Distantly I heard Will gently persuading Ellie into conversation, which I thought was probably a good thing. He had located Clarissa Arnold somehow, too. Now he was easing this waiting time for Ellie until Clarissa called back.

Alone in the kitchen, I looked around. The wood-stove burned steadily with a sound like tinfoil being crumpled. On the freshly waxed floor lay not a speck of ash or other mess. The fixtures gleamed, the windows glittered behind crisp lace-trimmed gingham tiebacks, and the appliances, counters, and cooking surfaces were so clean that Victor could have done surgery on them.

All George's work. Ellie said the only thing she wanted him cleaning was his plate but lately he hadn't been letting her lift a finger. Between that and his own jobs, dawn to midnight in his effort to earn enough to take care of the baby, I didn't see how he'd have had the time to do any bad deeds.

So why wouldn't he clear himself by revealing where he had been when Hector Gosling was murdered? As I joined the others waiting in the parlor for Clarissa Arnold's promised call, I had an unhappy suspicion that I already knew.

"Once upon a time," Ellie said slowly, in the age-old way that people have always begun telling stories: to quiet children, or to entertain the company.

Or to pass a terrible time. The lamps were dimmed in the small, low-ceilinged room with its worn Oriental rugs, polished brass andirons, and drawn curtains. Ellie sat in the big old overstuffed armchair with her feet on a hassock; someone— Will Bonnet, I supposed—had draped a shawl over her shoulders.

"Once upon a time, Harlequin House belonged to my great-uncle, Chester Harlequin, who after Benedict Arnold was probably the most disgraced man ever to live in Maine."

Her voice was weary. The telephone sat on a table by her chair. I willed it to ring.

It didn't. "In those days, Eastport was smugglers' heaven," she continued. "Whiskey or the ingredients to make it came over the border so fast, people joked they should call the St. John River the Mash-issippi. For sour mash," she explained with a wan smile.

Wade sat beside me on the loveseat before the fireplace. The room was warm but I shivered even with the fire blazing. Wade put his arm around me and I leaned gratefully against him.

"All the little coves and inlets around Passamaquoddy Bay, hundreds of islands, there's lots of places to hide things," Will Bonnet said. Ellie smiled wearily, letting him take this part.

"George and I used to explore 'em when we were kids, in his little boat. We'd pretend we were smugglers and Hopley Yeaton's men were chasing us in their cutters. When," he added, "George wasn't busy getting my tail out of some fool trouble or another."

"Hopley Yeaton," Ellie informed the rest of us, "was the founder of the Coast Guard. His house," she added to me, "is older than yours. 1812, I think. That red one across from the gas station. All its windows are broken out now," she added sadly. "Too bad."

Then to Will: "Remember the broken windows on Water Street?"

Will took the topic up unashamedly. "Yeah.

78

Broken by me. I was headed for juvenile hall after that, till George promised to be responsible for me. Said he'd make sure I didn't get into any more trouble."

He shook his head, recalling it. "Came down to the police station, George did, and swore to it, his right hand in the air. He wasn't more'n what, thirteen years old? And the amazing thing was, that's what he did. After that he was like my shadow."

There was a silence, all of us thinking about where George was now, until Will spoke up again.

"Kept me out of fights, George did. He'd beat a guy up just so I didn't have to, kids knew I had to stay out of trouble, they would do everything to try to make me mad."

Which probably accounted for some of the trouble George had been in back then, I thought, and Will confirmed this. "One time he took a kid down the street, smacked him till he blubbered, then stuffed a note in his pocket when he wasn't lookin' so his mom'd find it, when he got home. Bully, it said. Big, fat . . ."

His voice trailed off as something in our faces must have alerted him. I'd told Ellie about the note in Gosling's pocket and of course Wade knew, too.

"What'd I say?" Will asked, looking around helplessly.

"Nothing," Ellie replied evenly. "It's nothing, Will. I wish Clarissa would call."

We'd have gone down to the jail in Machias and

held a sit-in but the roads were still messy, and besides, Will said Clarissa had sent a message for us to sit tight, let her try to find out what the situation was and if she could do anything about it tonight.

I prayed she could. But the clock over the mantel ticked on relentlessly and no call came. "Does anyone know if the police've talked to Jan Jesperson yet?" I asked.

Will shook his head. "I'm pretty sure she's out of town. My Aunt Agnes was raising a big fuss the other day, wanting to see her."

He sighed. "Not that I like the idea, but she sees so few people. And if I'm there with them I doubt it could do any harm. Jan hasn't been answering her phone, though, and her car's gone."

Which was interesting. "But you were saying, Ellie, about your uncle," he turned the conversation back neatly.

"Right." With an effort, she gathered herself. I'd never seen her so exhausted-looking, so pale and nearly defeated. But even at Victor's suggestion she wouldn't lie down, and none of us wanted to try making her.

"Uncle Chet enjoyed nice things," she continued her story. "More than a big house, good furniture and so on, all of which he had. No, he wanted things he couldn't get just by being a country doctor. Big fish in a small pond, which is what it was here then. Busy still, but the boomtown days were over."

The days, she meant, of the early 1800s, when my old house and others as fine were built by men with so much money that they could hire architects and put up virtual palaces, homes as solid and beautifully proportioned as anything in Boston.

"And," she added, "he liked his cocktails, too. Chester was a good doctor, but what he was famous for—so famous that even today the old Eastport folks still tell stories about him—was money and parties. So it was no miracle he knew some of the men doing the whiskey-smuggling."

She paused, sipped from the cup Will had brought her. "Well, it wouldn't have been a miracle anyway. Everyone knew everyone in Eastport then, just like they do today. And those men knew other men, the ones running the smuggling, and the word got around, up the chain of command and eventually to the top."

A fireplace ember exploded with a sudden *pop!* I gasped, and Wade turned his pale-grey gaze slowly to me. *Steady, girl.*

But my mind couldn't stop racing with the implications of George's silence and the possible reasons for it, not to mention the conclusions that would be drawn from his aunt's bequest.

"Pretty soon Chester's big mansion—he'd never married, and for a while every girl in town hoped she'd be the one to get the chance to live in it—pretty soon his big house was turned into a hideout," Ellie told us. "And a hospital for gunshot

81

gangsters who got brought here from the city. It was a place they could recuperate and Chester could treat them without anyone knowing."

She paused. "And sometimes the house was a morgue. They say Chester took the bodies on the night ferry over to the mainland, paid the ferrymen ten dollars to keep quiet about it. And to help bury them."

I thought of my old friend Jemmy Wechsler, sitting somewhere in Federal custody. He knew where bodies were buried, too; some financial, others that had been living and breathing till someone decided they were a liability and had to go.

"The house got to be a social club," Ellie said. "Off the beaten track, and pretty in summer. Like a resort, they could relax. And at Chester's, it was parties 'round the clock. So the men brought girls there. You can imagine what local people thought of *that*."

Indeed; bobbed hair, bright makeup, and bare legs bouncing scandalously to the newest dance craze, the Charleston. But the images didn't replace my other thought: that someone had gone to a lot of trouble hiding those two bodies. Once eighty years ago, and again much more recently. So why put a note in Hector Gosling's pocket, then hide him where no one would ever read it?

"The town," Ellie said, "was all agog."

Nor could I duck another memory Ellie's tale triggered. I'd asked Jemmy once, unwisely, if it mustn't be just an awful job getting rid of the bodies. I'd been teasing him, knowing that he handled mob money but not what that really meant. I'd felt sure he had nothing to do with any actual murders.

Or rubouts, as the tabloids called them. Jemmy was eating a Philly cheese steak when I asked, and he didn't miss a bite.

"From what I hear," he said, chewing, "they put the body in somebody's bathtub. Somebody, he hasn't got any wife or kids to get too nosy. Run the shower, drain all the blood out before they chop it into pieces. Makes it neater. Easier all around.

"Not," he'd added, dipping his sandwich in ketchup, "that I would really know." Which was when I'd understood for the first time just who Jemmy's associates were.

Jemmy, who had no wife or kids to get inquisitive.

Now the Feds wanted to know, too, and if he told them (or if he didn't; his take on the witness protection program was dead-on in my opinion) Jemmy was mincemeat.

Ellie went on. "And sometime around then, Eva Thane dropped out of the picture. Just vanished. The woman," she added for Will and Wade's benefit, "that Jake and I found today. Her body."

She met my gaze and I knew what she was thinking: that we should have just done it. Walled them both up again and let the chips fall. She spoke again.

"She was a lost girl, Eva. A runaway from some little town, I suppose. Chester's girl for a while. Too wild for her own good was what people said then about a girl like that."

More recently too. My mom's folks, for instance, had said it about me.

"So when she disappeared people knew she wasn't around, but you couldn't say they missed her," Ellie continued. "No one was looking for Eva anywhere, probably. Not anymore."

I knew that tune as well, because I'd sung it myself, and if it hadn't been for Jemmy it probably would've been my swan song.

"So she was gone," Ellie said, "and who cared? But then . . ."

Her story drew me back to the cozy parlor where the fire was burning and the lamps were glowing and the phone wasn't ringing.

"But then, Eastport girls began disappearing."

Much later when it was nearly morning, Ellie's voice came out of the darkness. "Jake, did you know about what George said the other evening at Duddy's?"

I had decided to stay the night with her; that she'd agreed without argument let me know how truly frightened she was.

"Yes," I replied. She'd overheard the police

questioning George about the threats he had made against Gosling. Or anyway they'd have interpreted his remarks as threats.

"George doesn't always tell me what he's doing all day, you know. And if he's out late I don't ask where he was, necessarily. Why should I?"

We were in her kitchen, Ellie in the rocker pulled up to the stove with a blanket around her. I'd put myself in the daybed, not wanting to go upstairs when she wouldn't.

"Of course not," I replied. "I don't ask Wade, either."

Not always. For me it was a welcome sea change after having been married to Victor, whose whereabouts I used to obsess over. With Victor my suspicions had usually been inaccurate only in the sense that what he was really doing was worse.

"It's okay that you didn't tell me," Ellie said.

"I know. It'll get straightened out soon."

"Mmm," she replied, her tone expressing what I was thinking: *probably not.* Clarissa had called at last, but her message hadn't been what we'd hoped for. George was being charged with Gosling's murder. He would have a bail hearing eventually, Clarissa said, but we shouldn't get our hopes up.

Not that there was much chance of that. I'd wanted to question Ellie about the will; how *could* she and George not have seen it? One of them must have opened the envelope. But she'd been so despondent after talking with Clarissa that I hadn't dared return to the topic.

85

Or to the other thing bothering me; that if George wouldn't detail his activities it meant there was a hole in his time that he didn't want to account for.

"Local girls must've thought Chet Harlequin was glamorous," I said instead. "Fast money and easy living."

I didn't really expect the deliberate change of subject to distract her, but it seemed to. "And what else did most of them have to look forward to?" she agreed. "A mean little house, maybe a mean little husband. Hard work for the rest of their lives."

I drew the quilt around my shoulders. It was almost morning but neither of us had slept.

"They were young and wanted to have fun," she said. "Chester and Eva had screaming fights over the way he flirted with those girls, my grandmother used to say."

From her kitchen window I could see up the bay to Cherry Island, its red light flaring intermittently against the hills of New Brunswick, darker mounds against the indigo sky.

"Then one girl vanished," Ellie said, "and another. By the time the third one disappeared, town people were ready to burn Chester's house down with him in it. His gangster pals were long gone when the men went to drag him out of there, make him talk, whatever it took."

Of course they were gone, skedaddled at the first whiff of trouble like most crooks. The sky paled; suddenly the lighthouse at the tip of Deer Island materialized.

"But Chester wasn't there," Ellie said. "He'd lit out ahead of them. And in the attic they found the stabbed bodies of three girls. The ones who'd gone missing from Eastport."

Buddy Russell's little boat, the *Wahine,* puttered out into the channel on its way to the Deer Island ferry landing where he would begin readying the ferry for its first trip of the day.

"No one ever heard from Chester again," Ellie said. "They buried the girls and closed the house. And there it stood, with whatever happened inside just . . . soaking into it."

Brr. "I don't want to go back," I said.

Grey light filled the kitchen. "Me either. But we have to."

"Because we said we would?" Volunteer work in Eastport was as serious as a religious vocation. But despite Will Bonnet's urging I was having second thoughts about her involvement in the strenuous project, especially now. "Ellie, no one expects you to . . ."

"No." She got up and put the kettle on. "I still don't think Chester killed those girls, you know. He just ran because he knew they'd lynch him if they got their hands on him."

What the heck, I thought, let her ramble if she wants to. Or even work on that old house if it makes her feel better. Throwing off the quilt, I swung my feet down onto the cold floor, then yanked them back cringingly.

Ellie smiled, tossing a pair of knitted wool slippers

at me. The church ladies made them by the carload for benefit sales and we bought them dutifully; between the itchy wool and the bumpy stitches they were as comfortable as sacks full of sharp pebbles.

But the floor was so frigid I'd have happily worn footgear made of red-hot coals. Pulling them on, I continued, "So who do you think did it? Killed them. And Eva, too, probably."

"Someone who knew Chester well enough to make it look as if he had," she replied immediately.

"I don't know, Ellie, maybe your ancestor was the original Chester the Molester. He makes advances, they resist, he's got a screw loose, so he flies into a rage and murders them."

She eyed me over the bowl of eggs she was scrambling. She'd also gotten the coffee on, bacon sizzling, and slices of homemade bread toasting, while butter melted fragrantly in the skillet.

So much for *me* taking care of *her*. I pulled the quilt back up while I waited for the woodstove to begin radiating more.

"What's the catch?" She wasn't rambling. She hadn't been last night either, I realized suddenly. She was going somewhere with this.

"The catch," Ellie replied, "is what the *other* girls said. The ones who went to his parties and danced and flirted with him, but *didn't* vanish."

"Ah." She poured our juice: orange for me, the usual tomato-Tabasco-and-lime for her. In addition to her other qualities the woman had a galvanized digestive system. "And *they* said . . . ?" I asked.

She downed the juice. "According to my grandmother, they said he was a gentleman. Always made sure they got home safely and if anyone else bothered them he'd pitch a Chester-sized fit."

I looked a query at her as I dug into a breakfast fit for the linen-covered table of a swanky hotel. Ellie's perked coffee was infinitely superior to the lukewarm swill that drips from a Mister Contraption, and she'd put out real cream for it.

"Oh, did I forget to say?" She piled egg on a bite of toast. "Chester weighed—conservatively— about three hundred fifty pounds."

Oops, there went my image of a lithe, dark figure slinking through the night. In its place came a picture of a very fat man trying to overpower a series of strong young girls: *nope.*

"It's not easy to stab somebody," I said, beginning to be interested. "Not like they make it look in the movies. For one thing, a guy that size'll have trouble just getting close enough."

"Yes," she agreed. "And *that's* why you and I are going back to Harlequin House."

"Um, yeah." I drank more coffee, waiting for the caffeine to penetrate my brain cells. But it was five-thirty in the morning so they were feeling about as permeable as paint is to paint stripper.

In other words not very. "Uh, why is that, again?"

"Because," she repeated patiently, "someone *framed* Chester. Someone who killed those girls and *wanted* him to get blamed. Now why would you do such a thing?"

"So you *wouldn't* be blamed," I responded obediently, still not understanding. "So you could go right on living here free as a bird, only without . . ."

She nodded. "Without the person—or persons—you wanted to get rid of in the first place. Now, probably we cannot solve the murders of those poor girls . . ."

Trust her to put it that way: *probably*.

". . . although," she finished wistfully, "I'd enjoy clearing Uncle Chester's name too. But the main problem now is George."

Her green eyes met mine determinedly across the table. "The fact that now someone's done it to him."

Good heavens, so *that* was it. She wanted to *snoop*. "Ellie, just in case you haven't noticed lately, you're in absolutely no condition to—"

She ignored this. "What was Hector Gosling besides the most disliked man in Eastport?" she interrupted.

I looked down, noticed that she'd finished all her breakfast and was starting on my toast. "A real-estate speculator. And . . ."

"Right." Ellie looked triumphant. "*And* he was president of the historical society. So where do we go to hear gossip about him?"

90

Her technique was stellar: wave a cluster of antique murders in front of me, ones we *couldn't* solve, to get my nose twitching.

Then pull the old switcheroo. "But Ellie, we already know why people hated him. On account of sharp real-estate deals, and because Hector and Jan Jesperson were supposed to be swindling a series of helpless old ladies out of their . . ."

Personally I've never found elderly ladies to be helpless at all. They generally possess good genetics, excellent problem-solving ability, and a sharp umbrella or the equivalent thereof, aimed unerringly at the backside of any silver-tongued devil who is fool enough to try hornswoggling them.

But Gosling and Jan Jesperson weren't garden-variety silver-tongued devils. They were sharpies from away; she originally from Los Angeles, he a long-ago transplant from one of the western Canadian provinces, one of those places where land was only worth anything if you could grow something on it, not like here. And both had that odd, faintly forbidding air of professionalism, the sense you get from people who know things that you don't.

And what folks want when they're trying to decide what to do with their money or land, of course, is someone who knows. This I thought accounted for the success of the unscrupulous pair, whom George had begun calling the gold-dust twins long before his aunt even got tangled up with them.

"Hector and Jan's swindles are just the *fake*

motive." Ellie demolished my objection efficiently. "That's why *George* is supposed to have done it. What we need—well, one of the things we need—is the *real* reason."

"Mmm," I said uncertainly. "But let's not throw the baby out with the bath water. Oops, sorry, bad choice of words."

It wasn't, though; it made her eyes twinkle for the first time since all this mess had begun.

"Very funny," she said. "But I agree. We can rule George out without ruling out any of the possible motives. Because we don't *know* why Hector got murdered. Yet," she added confidently.

She finished the rest of my eggs. If I'd eaten that way when I was pregnant I'd have ended up looking like her Uncle Chester. But Ellie burned more calories just by breathing in and out than I could have if I'd run marathons for a hobby.

"So we go where they are," she went on briskly, as if it was all decided. Which I supposed it was; once she got going, she was as stoppable as your average freight train.

"The historical society members," she went on, "all papering and painting. And talking. Not just about Hector's longtime bad reputation, but about who might've started hating him *recently*."

Well, I supposed it was better than moping. She gazed at me expectantly, you should excuse the expression. Her mood was much improved, too, all the passive devastation of the night before evaporated now that she had a plan. And given the kind of news I expected we'd be hearing later, starting out on a high point did seem like good strategy, morale-wise.

"Okay," I conceded. "Right after Victor's CPR class we'll go over to Harlequin House and try to pick up some info."

By this I meant slog through a sea of useless gossip, a rehash of every old feud and vendetta since 1780 when the first settlers had waded to Moose Island at low tide.

"But that's it," I warned. "I'm not chasing around after any villains with you while you're getting ready to pop that kid out practically any second."

She smiled beatifically despite the fact that low tide was what most of that gossip was going to resemble. Still, if it made Ellie feel we were doing something useful I could endure it.

Before I left, she brought out a gift for me. "I meant to save it for your birthday or something," she said. "But I'd just like you to have it now." She held it out.

"Ellie," I said in surprise. "It's so . . . feminine."

I guess it probably says something about my karma that instead of a neat little purse with a spaghetti strap and space for a cell phone, I had a twenty-pound utility belt with a slot for a claw hammer. Plus safety glasses and steel-toed boots; the right shoes and accessories make the outfit, I always say. But now I had one of the aforementioned little bags and to my surprise, I loved it at once.

"Is it all right?" she asked anxiously. "I didn't know . . ."

"It's wonderful," I assured her. "I'm going to use it all the time. Thank you."

As a bonus she'd tucked a miniature flashlight inside, and as soon as I got a new cell phone—my old one was permanently on the fritz—I'd put that in there, too.

I hugged her hard. "Now you take it easy and I'll see you at the house. We'll soak those historical society members for every rumor, piece of gossip, and shred of innuendo they've got."

It drew another small smile from her. And we'd meant to go back anyway, to retrieve my tools.

So for her sake I managed a smile in return. But in my heart I was already thinking *bummer*.

Double bummer.

Which thought ended up being not only accurate, but damned near prescient.

CHAPTER 4

Around eight I left Ellie practicing her Lamaze breathing. Personally I thought breathing that rendered you unconscious was the only kind of breathing that could possibly be useful during what she was in for, but of course I didn't say so.

Instead I told her I'd meet her at Harlequin House, then began walking home, enjoying the fresh air. Early in spring in a burst of decisiveness I'd sold my old car, but then in a burst of procrastination put off buying a new one. Soon, though, I would have to do something about it, I knew as I hustled along through the chill morning. It was one of those brilliant days in late October when wind hides a razor in its pocket; the sun was warm, but any time now we would have snow.

The fish pier looked vacant without the two big tugs lined up against it. Beyond on the blue water, halfway to the Canadian island of Campobello, idled an orange-and-black freighter whose size put perspective all out of kilter. The few other boats out this early looked either too far away or impossibly small beside it.

95

I walked past the Waco Diner with its drifting smells of breakfast, Peavey Library with the cannon and the war memorial plaque on its lawn, and the sculpture garden and mulched chrysanthemum beds of the Motel East.

But then on impulse I turned left uphill toward the mansard-roofed structure where all the misery had begun.

Out front lay the cast-iron railings whose re-installation effort I had abandoned just after we'd found the bodies. More arms, or longer ones, were what I'd thought I needed then. Now, though, another idea struck me. And fortunately I had a flat-head screwdriver in my jacket pocket.

I still couldn't hold up the railing and reach the step treads at the same time. However, if something could hold it up for me . . . well, I didn't quite stand there shouting Eureka!

But almost. I'd left the screws in a neat little pile near the bottom step, and they were still there. Humming, I took three of them and put them through the railing's holes, not on a tread but where the railing attached to the front of the house.

Then I screwed them in and . . . presto, a railing holder-upper was born. Now that I'd had this inspiration I only needed about twenty minutes to get both railings back on.

When I was finished I backed away to admire my work, which was when I noticed something interesting: the bushes and whippy young trees in the unkempt yard, at the sides and extending back around to the rear of the house.

Thoughtfully I strolled around to inspect them. All along I had been wondering how someone got Hector's body inside. After all, it wasn't something you'd want to unload from right out in the street if you could help it.

And apparently the same new eyes that had seen how to repair that railing were still in decent working order, because now I saw how the body-delivery had been done. The whippy little trees, so flexible you could bend them flat and they would spring right up again, formed a solid screen. You could pull a car in here and haul a body out without being seen.

Then you could hunker down, hauling the body along, and get within a few feet of the front door—which you'd have unlocked in preparation—without risking discovery at all.

That last few feet would've been nerve-wracking, of course. But if you had the nerve to commit murder, last-minute anxiety would be just part of the cost of doing the deed.

From a distance the saplings seemed undamaged, upright and optimistic-appearing. But squinting closely I noticed their thin bark was scarred as if something had scraped against it.

A car's front bumper, for instance. And the earth was humpy not with actual tire marks but with enough depression to indicate that a vehicle had been there.

The police would say (a) that it was George's truck, or (b) that the marks meant nothing except that teenagers had been using this as a make-out spot.

But I didn't think so, because according to Sam the hot make-out spot now was overlooking Dog Island—not, he had added swiftly, that he knew this from experience—and as for George's truck it was junky but it was also very heavy; I thought it would have made much deeper impressions.

Not, again, that I expected police investigators to agree. So for now I decided to keep mum about my observation. It wouldn't help George, there was a chance it could hurt him, and anyway I had other fish to fry this morning.

Thinking this, I walked a few blocks farther south before turning onto a tiny street whose dead end overlooked the skeleton of the old wharf.

Here a steep bluff dropped to a narrow stone beach studded with rotted wooden pilings. They were all that remained of a steamship terminal where once you could set off on a voyage that might end anywhere in the world. But steam had followed sail into mass-transit oblivion; now the red bricks of the steamship companies' service buildings lay scattered among the wet stones, rounded to eroded lumps that from a distance resembled bloody fists.

At the end of the street stood a two-story frame bungalow with a tiny picket fence enclosing a small, well-kept yard. It was Jan Jesperson's house. I followed a narrow walkway around to the rear, noting that as Will Bonnet had said, her car was not there. But through the sliding glass doors of the deck at the back I heard music playing inside, and when I peered in through cupped hands I saw the light on her electric percolator glowing red on a counter in the bright, efficient-looking kitchen.

So it seemed she'd returned from whatever trip Will thought she'd been away on. Sitting down on one of the luxurious wrought-iron lounge chairs she'd set up on the deck, I decided to wait. Ordinarily this wasn't one of my favorite activities.

But I certainly couldn't have found a more pleasant spot for cooling my heels. Latticed screens baffled the breeze without blocking the wide water view, while glass-topped tables and teak planters of dwarf evergreens created a luxurious atmosphere.

It was all very nicely done. But after the night I'd had, if I sat too long I would surely fall asleep, so after a few minutes I got up again and walked around, ending once more at the glass doors which featured an unobstructed view inside.

Being a pharmaceutical-company rep had apparently allowed Jan to take good care of herself. Her taste included Thomas Moser chairs, a sideboard displaying an elegant collection of Bohemian glass, a harpsichord with the Bach Two-Part Inventions open on it, and a trio of large framed photographs on a far wall.

Ansel Adams, if I wasn't mistaken. Not too shabby. I tried the door, just experimentally. It slid open a crack, which on the one hand provided me with an interesting opportunity.

On the other, Jan would almost certainly be back any minute. People didn't leave coffeemakers on and music playing in their houses otherwise. She might've just run out to get a newspaper.

"Hello?" I slid the glass door open another inch. If I heard her coming in the front I could always slip out the back, and vice versa. Silence within, except for the music. "Anyone home?"

No one was. A laptop in sleep mode, thriftily plugged into the wall instead of running down its battery, popped to glowing life as I touched its display. Beside it on the table were two utility-bill envelopes stamped and ready for mailing.

"Jan?" Her tiny living area was a model of order, with more of the lovely, expensive Thomas Moser stuff, an Oriental rug every strand of which was softly immaculate, lamps made of ginger jars with pleated cream shades. There were some good lithographs and small, well-framed European oils on the walls.

I took a few more steps. The books on the shelves were recent; she liked A.S. Byatt, P.D. James, and Margaret Drabble, David Foster Wallace, and John Updike, too, but only when he was writing about golf. The music was Miles Davis, *Sketches of Spain* on an expensive-looking CD player set to repeat.

There was no TV. As I noticed this it occurred

100

to me that Jan might not be away. Instead she could be departed in the most final sense, and she could be around here somewhere.

And having come this far I supposed I'd better settle the question. What I would do if I found her I wasn't sure. Or if she came home and found me, upstairs in her house.

But neither of these things happened; a pretty white-painted bedroom and neatly made-up bed were all I found at the top of the stairs. In the bath was a businesslike collection of toiletries and a few patent medicines. No prescription stuff that I could see, and certainly no stash of pilfered heavy-duty drugs from her pharmaceutical-sales career.

A sound made me peek hastily past the white eyelet curtain in the bathroom window, but it was only a couple of seagulls in a quarrel over a bit of something one of them had dropped. In the linen closet: linens.

And she wasn't back yet. I was starting to think maybe she'd forgotten that coffeemaker, and the door. Maybe she'd gone out in such a hurry that she'd neglected to lock up.

Downstairs the CD player started in again on the "Adagio." The lamps gleamed and the tables shimmered, glass on the photographs reflecting shards of light from south-facing windows. It all had the clean, well-ordered air I always aspired to and could never manage.

But there was a hardness to it too; motionless,

nothing out of place. There wasn't any desk to rummage through and the few drawers I opened contained only domestic items: scissors, knives. At last I went back to the glass doors, feeling it was probably time to get out. I'd come to speak with her, hoping she might not be the icy villainess local rumor portrayed. Maybe something she said would give me a way to help George.

And by doing so, help Ellie. Secretly I thought of it as a sort of going-away present, because although she didn't know it and would have fiercely denied it had the idea been suggested to her, once the baby was born nothing would ever be the same again.

Selfish thought; I put it away with the many others I didn't like thinking lately. And at any rate wherever Jan had gone, it seemed she wasn't coming back immediately.

Outside, one of the seagulls grabbed the fallen morsel and flapped off, leaving the other poking disconsolately at the place where it had been.

Yeah, buddy, I know how you feel, I thought. Then, turning, I realized that something in Jan's house *wasn't* motionless.

The laptop screen. When I'd touched it, it had pinged softly and the screen had bloomed to life, showing the Apple icon. But after I'd left it there on the table it had gone on booting up. Now it showed a screen of labeled folders and a cursor, blinking provocatively at me.

So there I was, alone and uninvited in a

stranger's home. Before me lay, apparently, all the records of her private life; a folder marked "Bills" for instance, and one that said it held letters.

Let's see, now. I could respect her privacy, not to mention my own safety. She could walk in and discover me here any second.

Or I could go for broke. Moments later I'd opened a folder, clicked through the documents it contained, and found at least two reasons to make me envision Jan Jesperson jumping for joy when she learned Hector Gosling was no longer among the living.

Assuming she hadn't murdered him herself, a notion that was starting to look increasingly plausible. One of the documents, a list of Eastport ladies including Agnes Bonnet and George's aunt, Paula Valentine, also featured a schedule of dates and dosages of a variety of drugs. One of them was diazepam, better known as Valium.

Risky, I thought, to keep such a list. But if you had more than one scheme going you needed some kind of reminder as to who got what substance and when. And if what this schedule suggested was true, Hector could have implicated Jan Jesperson in at least one murder—Paula Valentine's—and possibly more.

But the kicker was spread out through the last documents I clicked open. One was a calculation of how much Valium it would take to kill a 160-pound human being, with or without the help of various amounts of alcohol. Was it coincidental that Hector Gosling had been average sized? He'd probably weighed about 160 pounds, which was no help in the strychnine department; still, I found it interesting.

The second document was Jan's last will and testament, in which she generously left the whole kit and kaboodle to "my good friend and associate Hector Gosling."

And the final item contained Hector's will, in language a near twin to Jan's. In it he bequeathed an even larger estate full of cash, stocks, bonds, real estate, accounts receivable, and other valuable doo-dads, to . . .

You guessed it: turnabout was the only kind of fair play these two had ever cared for. He'd left it all to his partner in crime, Jan Jesperson.

"The wills were dated the same day," I said. "And it looked as if each of them had e-mailed a copy of his or her own document to the other one."

Silence on the phone; I interpreted it as Clarissa Arnold's awestruck admiration for my intrepid sleuthing. I'd called her answering service and by a miracle she'd called me back at once.

"Which would've made sense," I pressed on. "Neither one of them could afford to have anyone else find out just how wealthy they'd really gotten."

I took a breath. "Because rumors are one thing,

but the size of those estates, the schedules of assets
. . . it would absolutely raise questions about how
they had gotten all that stuff. That's why whichever
one survived the other's death had to inherit the
loot. To avoid answering those questions."

I thought a minute more. "The probate records
would still end up in the public files. But by that
time interest would've died down. It wasn't perfect,
but it was the best possible way to try keeping a
low profile, under the circumstances."

Clarissa's silence continued. "Well?" I said at
last. "Don't you think this establishes some kind
of reasonable doubt? George wasn't the only one
with a motive. Or even the best motive."

Hector could have tried grabbing more by black-
mailing Jan. Or she could've decided to eliminate
any chance of his trying it. Then there was the
whole dosage-schedule thing and the notes on
how to kill somebody with Valium. I described
them to Clarissa. "Maybe she was planning to kill
him with Valium, then got hold of something even
deadlier and changed her plan," I concluded.

"Great," she responded skeptically. "And you
were planning on proving any of this how?"

Drat. Trust a lawyer to throw cold water on your
notions. If Clarissa's hard-headed practicality could
be dumped on forest fires we wouldn't need
Smokey the Bear.

"Well," I said, "maybe the court could subpoena
the laptop."

"Uh-huh. Because the defendant's friend saw it

while trespassing in the laptop owner's house."

Just then the refrigerator out in the kitchen quit humming and the light on the answering machine went out.

"Damn," I said.

"What?"

"Oh, not you," I told Clarissa hastily. The answering machine went back on and the refrigerator resumed humming. "I think the power just switched back from the generator to the Bangor Hydro grid, that's all."

"Oh. Anyway, I can't just have you testify to this, either. The prosecution would get the jury to ignore your testimony, because a) you've admitted you have no scruples since otherwise why would you sneak into her house and snoop, so they'll decide you're lying. And b) you're George's friend, so likewise."

She paused. "I'm assuming you don't have a printout of those files?"

"Nope," I replied, crestfallen. Damn it, I should have just grabbed the thing when I had the chance. "No printer. And I knew all that, what you said. I was hoping you'd be able to figure out a way around it, is all."

She replied doubtfully. "If there turns out to be any Valium in Hector's tox screens, I could try." Then she sighed. "Believe me, Jake, I know this looks good to you but you're a long way from anything that's actually going to be useful. And if Jan Jesperson gets wind of it, that laptop's going to end up somewhere no one can ever find it again and this whole discussion will be moot. So keep quiet, and I mean don't tell *anyone,* not even Ellie. I need to think about this."

With that she hung up.

Victor's CPR class was held at the Eastport firehouse, out on County Road next to the youth center. Behind the big metal prefab building loomed a sand pile already being heaped up for the coming winter. The tinny spatter of a radio scanner came from the tiny dispatch office as I passed it on the way in.

"Nice of you to drop by," Victor commented when he saw me, and of course I didn't smack him. Fortunately just then a pretty EMT-trainee flitted by and he forgot all about me.

I looked around, wanting to be here even less than when I'd walked in. A dozen blue exercise mats with life-sized mannikins lying on them had been placed around the room, and bringing a big rubber doll back to life wasn't my idea of entertainment.

Besides, I'd done CPR before—successfully—without taking a class. I'd just thought Sam might need backup for the reading part of the course, since naturally Victor refused to believe any son of *his* could have any learning difficulties.

Just then, though, Sam waved at me from across the room, indicating he'd partnered with another student whom I recognized from U. Maine functions. And since Sam's reputation for smarts at the practical end was well known, there would soon be a quid pro quo: Sam's partner reading aloud to him in exchange for help with the hands-on part of the program.

So I was redundant and on the point of taking off when a snatch of conversation caught my attention.

". . . gruesome," a young woman was saying to four others. All five wore nursing uniforms and name tags identifying them as Calais Hospital staff. The four listeners' expressions were alike, too: barely repressed impatience.

". . . stiff as a board, half tied in a knot, and that awful grin," the first one said with what seemed to me very un-nurse-like relish. "Like Dr. Sardonicus."

The others—not horror-film fans, apparently— glanced at one another. In their eyes I caught pity mingled with contempt, and the way they turned their backs on her was unmistakable, too: not our crowd.

"Hey," I said to the old-movie buff as she stared after them. Her badge said her name was Therese Chamberlain and from what she'd said I guessed she'd been on duty when Gosling's body reached the hospital. The ER in Calais would have been Hector's first stop on the way to the morgue in Augusta.

"You need a partner?" I asked.

She did, latching onto me gratefully as Victor started the class. He began with a ten-minute lecture on the rigors of resuscitating people whose hearts had stopped when they were—inconveniently and he seemed to feel also deliberately and spitefully—not in a hospital.

He also treated us to cautionary tales on why CPR was worse than useless when it was bungled: torn livers, broken ribs, and stomachs blown up like balloons were among the potentially fatal results of inept cardiac massage and rescue breathing.

Which didn't exactly make me want to learn these techniques officially. A sloppy paint job is about as far as I care to go in the bad repairs department, especially if I happen to be holding a current Red Cross certificate making me responsible.

But my new partner, a very skinny, dark-haired young woman with chapped lips and chewed fingernails, already knew real CPR and—this was the crucial part for me—could do it on the doll.

"Don't worry," Therese pronounced as we knelt on opposite sides of the floor mat. Called Resusci-Annie, the rubber model was anatomically designed so you could practice all the maneuvers of bringing a nearly dead person back to life without risking the opposite by practicing on a live one.

"I'll walk you through it," Therese told me. "It's easy after you get the hang of it."

Right, and tightrope walking was probably easy too when you'd been at it for a while. But if you put a foot wrong you'd only be killing yourself.

"You'll probably never have to do it in real life anyway," Therese added.

Famous last words. But it was after all only a rubber doll. "If you can do it, why are you here?" I asked her.

Therese shrugged, wincing at the hard concrete floor under her bony knees. If there was an extra half-ounce of flesh on this girl anywhere, I couldn't see it.

"Renew my certification," she replied, pushing on the doll's forehead and pulling on its chin. Its neck arced sharply up into what seemed an uncomfortable and possibly even crippling angle. I mentioned this hesitantly.

"Pine box is uncomfortable too, and it's where the victim's going, you don't get that airway open," she replied.

Tough little nut. She pinched the doll's nose and blew into its mouth. The rubber chest rose with a whooshing sound.

She swabbed the doll's mouth with an alcohol pad. "Now you."

She had sad pink-rimmed eyes and bad skin. "Mostly everyone here," she informed me, amplifying her answer to my earlier question, "is a cop, EMT, or a nurse. Couple college students," she added, gesturing at Sam and his partner. "You have to keep taking these courses to stay certified if you are on a health-care job."

"Oh." I assessed the doll. At least I wouldn't be in danger of lacerating its liver.

"What'd the cops say when they brought Gosling in?" I asked, trying to sound casual and hoping she'd forget I hadn't been part of her audience earlier.

"That they knew who did it."

Around us other students were blowing into dolls' rubber lips, compressing their rubber chests, and shouting the CPR formula's question at them. "Annie, are you all right?"

The dolls didn't reply. "How did they know that?" I asked Therese.

Steeling myself, I followed the other students' example and tried to inflate our doll's lungs. No good; it was like blowing against a brick wall.

"Here," Therese said. "Like this."

She pulled sort of *up* on the jaw and sort of *out*. I tried again without result. Apparently when I'd done it in real life I'd just had good luck. Unlike now, until finally:

"All right, Annie," I snarled. "Do you want to die? Because if you don't, you'd better cooperate."

Then I *pushed* on the doll's forehead and *yanked* on its jaw, meanwhile pinching on its nose and jamming my lips to its hard, inhuman-feeling mouth. Whereupon to my surprise my exhaled breath rushed easily into the doll's rubber lungs.

111

"Hey, you did it," Therese congratulated me. "Now press on the chest like this."

She demonstrated, meanwhile going on with her reply. I got the feeling she didn't often have anyone to talk to.

"The cops said everybody they'd questioned so far had named one guy, this George somebody? As the guy who wanted Gosling dead? But no one wanted to? Name him, I mean?"

Somewhere, Therese had picked up the tic of ending nearly every sentence with a question mark. And now that she'd strayed from a topic about which her profession made her feel confident, the tic was surfacing. Ellie called the question habit an insecure person's way of making sure you agreed with whatever they were saying, before going on. I just found it annoying.

I didn't like the information Therese was giving me either. If lots of people named George as the man with the motive, even reluctantly, there'd be a few who would do it in court, too. The whole fiasco was closing around him like a trap.

Correcting my cardiac massage position, Therese put the heel of my right hand on the lower third of the doll's breastbone. "You want to squeeze the blood out into the vessels, not break a rib and push the sharp end into the victim's heart," she lectured me.

Great. Not only was George in even hotter water than I'd realized, it was starting to look as if any dying person I might encounter would

112

be better off taking his chances with St. Peter.

"Didn't anyone mention anyone else who might have wanted to kill Hector Gosling?" I asked. Because it was still a case of the more reasonable doubt the better.

"Like I said, no one *wanted* to mention anyone at all, from what I heard," Therese replied. "But when the cops asked a direct question? Who wanted Gosling dead the *most*?"

She put her own hands on the doll's chest and pushed. "It was this guy George whoever whose name kept coming up."

I wanted to ask more but the class was nearly over, Victor strolling around to observe how the students were doing.

"I hope you're not planning on meeting a nearly dead person, Jacobia," was all he said when he got to us.

Me, too.

But as was true of almost everything that overlapped my life with Victor's: drat the luck.

"He kept blathering on about how crucial everything was, how dumb it would be to do it wrong, and he kept adding unappetizing details," I reported indignantly to Ellie later when we met in the parlor of Harlequin House.

I opened a fresh trash bag. If we wanted to hear gossip we couldn't just grab my tools and go; we had to hang around.

Meanwhile I was dying to tell her about Jan Jesperson, but I couldn't. Clarissa Arnold was a friend, but she was also a tiger when her instructions weren't followed.

I turned my mind from the topic. "Such as," I went on, "the fact that you're not only giving the person air, with rescue breathing. When you blow into their lungs you're also removing excess acid from the body by way of what he called waste gases."

I swept up yet another dustpanful of sawdust and dumped it into the bag, along with some wood splinters. "Which is just the person's exhaled breath," I added.

Put that way it didn't sound so bad, but Victor's commentary had not made doing actual cardio-pulmonary resuscitation seem attractive in the slightest. Which I supposed it wouldn't be; the details of my own last try had faded mercifully in my memory.

"Apparently if the victim's blood stays too acid you can't resuscitate them at all," I continued. "As if their heart seizing up like an old engine isn't *enough* of a problem."

I dumped more sawdust into the bag. "Not that you can do anything about *that*, either. The acid, I mean."

Ellie listened patiently as I vented the nervous energy I'd absorbed in the firehouse. Most of the professional medical folks and paramedics had been weirdly cheerful, as if eager for a shot at a real tragedy; between that and my newly acquired merit badge in housebreaking over at Jan's place, I was jazzed.

"In the hospital they give a medical version of bicarbonate of soda to treat the extra acid." I scraped up another dustpanful of scraps. "But who except ambulance drivers goes around with any of that?"

The bag was full; I twisted the top. "I think he just told us so we'd know how futile *our* efforts are likely to be."

Ellie made a noise of assent. "Anyway," I continued, "mostly what *I* learned is, the doll's lips taste like rubber and rubbing alcohol. *Bleaggh.*"

The taste wouldn't go away and neither would the disaster we'd made of the Harlequin House parlor. It was early afternoon, we'd torn out everything that had to go, and sunshine streaming in lit up every chunk of plaster, rag of torn-off wallpaper, and scraped, sanded, or otherwise paint-denuded patch of woodwork.

"What a mess," said Ellie as she contemplated it.

Or I think it's what she said. To keep her little passenger safe from toxic materials she wore a yellow paper jumpsuit that covered her from neck to ankles, rubber gloves, and a green-and-black respirator that made her look like a bug from outer space. Paper boots and a hair-covering paper cap completed her outfit.

But even through all that I could tell she had

her game face on. If anyone here knew anything at all about Gosling's murder, she meant to discover it.

And so did everyone else. The police were finished with the scene examination, the smoke smell from the near-disastrous fire of the day before had been aired out, and the house was full of volunteers with rumor on their tongues and fresh scandal on their agenda. Many of them came shamelessly up to Ellie, angling for new info, and I'm sure I couldn't have been as patient with them as she was.

"You poor thing," crooned Siss Moore, her eyes glittering. "Have they really *charged* him? And what happens next?"

From the hall where a lunch was being set up came an alert silence. Enquiring minds wanted to know. Ellie stopped shoveling plaster bits into a trash bag and pulled off her respirator.

"Well," she began slowly.

There were a dozen tasks in progress in the rest of the house: floor sanding and woodwork stripping, doorknob replacement and tin-ceiling (in the kitchen) patching, replacement of sections of the wainscoting in the library, and even repairs to the dumbwaiter from the butler's pantry up to the second floor.

But it all stopped dead as everyone within earshot waited to hear how Ellie would answer.

She paused another moment. Then, "I'm not sure," she confessed.

A little exhalation of disappointment went through the old house, an *oh!* of gratification denied.

"A lot of court hearings," she added. She was a genius at answering politely while revealing nothing. "It's all very confusing."

No kidding. Speaking of rumors, I hadn't passed on to Ellie what Therese Chamberlain had said, either. It was just more gossip, this time filtered through hospital shoptalk. And I had already decided not to pass on bad news unless it was news we could do something about.

Meanwhile Clarissa had spoken to Ellie that morning, too, to let her know George's bail request had been denied. It was what I'd expected; it's rare for someone to get bail on an actual murder charge. But then Clarissa had added something else, that I hadn't expected. George had instructed that no one be allowed to visit him, not even Ellie.

I supposed it was understandable; who wants his pregnant wife hanging around a jail? But it put an awful crimp in Ellie's effort to stay upbeat, one she was attempting to get over now by pursuing her snooping plan with even more determination.

And that meant listening to everyone. "If the police want to arrest somebody for poisoning Hector Gosling, they should try that housekeeper of his, Ginger Tolliver," Siss Moore sniffed.

A recently retired high school teacher, Siss was

a black-haired woman with big teeth and an authoritative manner. "I knew her in school, she was a man-chaser then," Siss went on. "And I wouldn't put it a bit past her."

Dumping an armload of peeled-off wallpaper into my trash bag, I turned to Siss. "You don't mean she was after Hector?"

Siss made a face. "No. Of course not. It was some fellow Hector found out about, started coming by the house. Sweet on Ginger, or so he said. Until Hector noticed it and put a stop to it. Some sailor off a ship," she sniffed disapprovingly.

"How'd he do that?" I asked. "Stop it, I mean. And why?"

But Siss didn't know. Evidently if Ginger wanted something, that was more than enough reason why it should have a stop put to it, in Siss's opinion.

"That girl never had any use for the advice of her elders," Siss finished, "and look what she's come to."

I didn't know what she'd come to and was about to ask. But Siss went on talking. "At any rate, Ellie, I'm sorry for your trouble, but I must tell you, you belong home in bed. In my day, women didn't go out in your condition."

In your day they didn't vote or own property either, I was on the verge of retorting. But before I could, Siss bustled off to position her rain cloud over somebody else.

A few minutes later, though, she was back, and

this time she cornered me. "How is my young friend Tommy Pockets?" she wanted to know.

"The same," I told her. "Working, trying to make money."

Siss looked regretful. "I'm afraid I pushed him too hard in school. When I go by the gas station Tommy's never the one who pumps. I think," she confessed, "he's trying to avoid me."

According to Sam, that was the situation with half the students in Eastport. "Tommy has responsibilities, you know." Something about the urgency of her interest made me want to defend him.

"That's a cop-out," Siss replied tartly. "A reason not to try." But then her face softened. "Although not in Tommy's case, perhaps. Well, tell him I said hello."

Her gentle tone reminded me: nobody's all bad. But then as if deliberately to dilute the effect, Siss added a postscript.

"Don't forget," she snapped, "what I've told you about that Tolliver girl."

"So, was I right?" Ellie murmured a little later as we stood six newly removed window sashes against the wall. From there they would be worked on by whoever was in charge of reglazing them; not, thank goodness, *moi*.

But Harry Leonard, a local WWII veteran who lived on the mainland in a brand-new manufactured home that required no maintenance at all, wasn't burned out on window glazing. He bustled in, spied the windows, and whipped out his cordless putty-removing tool, and if I had one I wouldn't be so burned out, either, I thought.

He set the tip of the tool along one pane, pushed a button, and *whirr!* A whole strip of old putty turned to powder and fell out onto the floor.

Bzzt! Another strip went. Harry was like a kid with a new toy. A *great* new toy; in less than a minute he'd removed one pane and was starting on the next.

I resolved to purchase one of these gadgets for myself, as I took Ellie aside.

"One suspect, coming up," I replied cheerfully to her question. Because I had to admit she *was* right; the Ginger Tolliver story was worth pursuing. Maybe it wasn't as good as what I'd discovered about Jan Jesperson, but there was no such thing as too many other people with good motives.

I propped up the final window and after that we wiped down all the parlor's other surfaces with a dust mop and a second time with a tack cloth, dumped the rags and cloths into the trash bags, and tied the bags' tops.

"Okay," I said, pleased in spite of myself. "Now we're ready to make an even bigger mess."

Because much as I didn't enjoy being in Harlequin House, now—the little room where we'd found the bodies yawned darkly at me, its repaired door ajar—I do like the part of a job when the prep work is done and the debris all cleared. The labor of priming and finishing is still to come, with its trials and missteps. I once painted an entire wall before I realized I was doing it out of the wrong paint bucket; to this day that bedroom has three satin-finish surfaces and a glossy one. But for a glorious instant the old Harlequin House parlor seemed cleansed of its past.

"Jake, look." Ellie's voice came from the little chamber I'd begun calling, in my own mind, the dead room.

"Ellie, what the heck are you doing in . . . Oh."

She'd shoved the old red rug aside and lifted the trapdoor that Trooper Colgate had told me about. I could just glimpse the top rung of a ladder leading down. She put a foot on it.

"Ellie, don't you dare! We don't know what's down there. Or if," I added, eyeing her shape, "you can get back up again."

She'd taken off the goggles and respirator again. "All right." She stood back a little. "You go."

Sheesh. If there's anything any higher on my hit parade of hideousness than an old wooden ladder, it's one leading down into an area I know nothing about, other than that it's *very* dark.

"Ellie, there's a door to that cellar in the back hall. With nice safe steps leading down. And a handrail."

"I know that. But there's also a dozen people out there. I'm sure they'd all like to follow us down, mill around and ask lots of questions, maybe mess up items of interest we might discover."

I sighed, tried again. That ladder looked awfully rickety. "The cops must've looked at the cellar already."

She made a face. "Sure, and all we have to do is say please, they'll tell us everything we want to know about it, is that it? I," she pronounced caustically, "don't think so."

The ladder vanished into the velvety blackness about three rungs down. Furthermore, unless you happen to be an agile person it's not easy stepping onto a ladder from above.

I am not an agile person. But I felt very guilty not telling Ellie about Jan or Therese. And I *was* curious.

"Oh, all right. Just give me your hand." I positioned myself beside the ladder and stepped down sideways onto it.

Nervously at first, and then a little more confidently; old it might have been, but that ladder *felt* solid enough. Also the cops had likely used it too, and it hadn't collapsed under them.

Turning my mind from the possibility that they'd weakened it just enough to set *me* up for the big fall, I continued down.

"Maybe this was an escape route for the criminals when Uncle Chester was here," Ellie theorized from above.

"Or even earlier," I said. Because another human cargo that got transported through this part of the world, years before some genius realized that the way to make money on booze was to forbid it, had been slaves.

Escaped slaves headed for the freedom of Canada. "Hand me a flashlight, will you?"

Gripping it, I aimed it first at a dirt floor and a granite foundation like the one in my house. Hand-adzed beams, massive old cistern, lots of unpainted shelves along the walls, and . . .

"Gah!"

"What is it?" Ellie's face appeared worriedly in the square of light above me.

"Nothing." A moose's head, stuffed and mounted, hung on a wooden post, its glass eyes reflecting the flashlight's glow.

"You think George is hiding something, don't you?" she said in a different tone, after a moment.

"Ellie, I'm starting to think he's being set up just like you said. The strychnine, the note on Gosling's body, the paperwork from his aunt's attorney . . ."

"I'd never seen . . ." she began insistently.

"I know. I believe you about not knowing about the will. I also know you're not in the habit of locking your doors. Anyone could've put those papers in your house. But my point is that if George would say where *he* was, none of it would matter."

I peered around some more. "The only way George could be set up like this is if someone knows he's got something *else* he needs to keep secret, so he won't say what he *was* doing. And *that's* what I'm worried about."

I stepped off the ladder. "So yes, I do think he's hiding something but at this point I have no idea what. You're sure *he* had no idea about any inheritance from his aunt?"

"I'm sure. Believe me, I would know. *And* I'd remember."

"Yeah." From upstairs came voices, purposeful footsteps, and the *whap!whap!whap!* of someone using a nail gun.

"Yeah, I'm sure you would. Do you think he'll call you?"

The plan *had* been to visit him and impress upon him that in this case silence wasn't golden. Instead it was fool's gold.

"Sure," Ellie replied. "He'll just sit for a while waiting. But when it dawns on him that he's really stuck there . . ."

That he wasn't in Eastport anymore, where everyone liked and trusted him. George might not have been the brightest bulb in the chandelier, but the light he shed was warm and steady. Her voice trailed off sadly. "Then he'll call."

The flashlight picked out an ancient coal furnace, a few shiny black cinders lying around its door. Behind it was the old coal bin. Into it deliveries of the fuel had made their entry via the coal chute.

"Jake?"

A complicated system of pipes and valves connected an old boiler to the heat and hot water

124

systems. Brick arches spread the weight of the chimneys that, before central heating, vented the stoves and fireplaces.

"I'm here." Small rooms as far as possible from the furnace would've held hung meats, fruit and vegetables canned and stored up against the winter, and root vegetables, carrots and potatoes and parsnips, laid away in sand.

I took a few more steps. Nothing but another old cellar like mine. In fact I was willing to bet there was a . . .

Yep. I found a switch string and pulled it; a bulb snapped on. My heebie-jeebies nearly vanished as the darkness went away.

But they didn't vanish *completely*. Ellie's voice came down through the trapdoor hole.

"This wasn't always a secret room," she reasoned. "You could go through the door in the parlor before it got plastered over."

"Uh-huh. But what was it for?" Then it hit me.

"Ellie, are there *marks* on the floor up there? Out in the parlor, in front of the mantel where a stove would stand, if there'd ever been one? Can you see where maybe its feet were?"

She went away, came back swiftly. "Yes," she confirmed. "And there are char marks on the floor, too, from embers. And screw holes in the wall here, big ones. A pulley, maybe, to haul up a coal scuttle?"

She'd followed my thought. Why bring coal all the way around up the cellar steps when you could haul it up through the floor?

125

"Maybe that's why the trapdoor's here. And when Chester redid the house he got rid of the stoves, put in the furnace."

"He had an art collection," she remembered aloud. "Gone now, of course. But once he didn't need coal upstairs maybe he had the door plastered over just to get more wall space?"

Good enough. Even without an art collection I'd been sorely tempted to jettison my old cast-iron radiators; between them and all the fireplaces, there was barely enough clear space for furniture.

"Fine. So the next puzzle is, how did anyone know this room existed? Someone, I mean, who put Hector in it not long ago?"

"Well, if you were in the cellar just snooping around and you saw that ladder standing there, wouldn't you figure it must go somewhere?"

I'd already thought of that. "Which means the ladder wasn't there. If it had been, Eva's body would have been discovered sooner. By, for instance, whoever redid the electrical work."

I aimed the flash at the ceiling and the wiring snaking over it. Contrary to my earlier belief, it *was* modern insulated stuff. "This is new. The historical society must have had it redone when they bought the house," I said.

Which suggested another question. Why had there been a fire? For a while after we'd arrived today an electrician had been here examining the place, but nothing dangerous had been found.

"If the ladder had been there when the wiring

was installed, someone would've been curious enough to climb it," Ellie said.

"Uh-huh. That's what I mean. It suggests that the ladder's placement here is more recent. Close the trapdoor, will you?"

She complied. The cellar ceiling was a jumble of old boards and beams. Even with the light on, without the ladder to clue you to it the trapdoor was practically invisible.

"Darn," I grumbled as Ellie opened the door again. I was getting a clearer picture, now, and it wasn't pretty.

"Somebody went to a lot of trouble to find that room," I told her. "Someone who was looking for a good place to put Hector's body. Whoever it was, once they found that trapdoor, they placed the ladder and hauled Hector's body up. And then . . ."

"Left the ladder on purpose." She finished my sentence.

"Uh-huh. They hid him, but they wanted him found. It makes sense of that note in Hector's pocket, and it confirms the idea that someone's setting George up. But . . ."

Dragging Hector in through the front door of Harlequin House still bothered me, though, even after my efforts at rationalizing it to myself. Too dicey, secrecy-wise. Could there be some other way, I wondered?

Standing on tiptoe I pulled on one of the boards nailed over the coal chute's opening, at the top of the old wooden coal slide. The board came off easily, as if it had been removed before. "Ellie, I think Hector *slid* in."

That accounted for the grime on his face and clothes. Then, somebody had hauled the body up the ladder into the room. All of which argued for a plan, especially the part about leaving the ladder like a big wooden arrow: *this way up.*

But there was one other possibility. I climbed the ladder again, moving quickly. The less time I spend on one of them the less chance there is of my departing it in, shall we say, an unregulated manner.

The police could have stood the ladder against the trapdoor themselves, when they were in here. But they hadn't; at the top I found two big nails toenailing it in place. And the last time I looked, cops weren't carrying claw hammers on their utility belts.

Someone else had wanted to make very sure that ladder stayed there; wanted it so that one way or another somebody working on the well-publicized rehab of Harlequin House would be likely to find Hector dead.

All of which was still theory. But I had a bad feeling as I clambered crabwise from the ladder's top into the little room.

The feeling got worse as, getting up, I found myself staring into the face of a person who would actually rather be found dead than clambering anywhere. It was the patronizing face of Sally Crusoe.

"Intrepid," she murmured. Her ultrarefined tone always made me want to stick my thumbs in my ears and waggle my fingers at her.

"I came to let you both know that we have a small luncheon prepared for everyone here today," Sally continued, "in case either of you wish to partake."

Her look registered my disheveled condition; I'd managed a shower before the CPR class, but on essentially no sleep I still felt like the bottom of a birdcage.

"Jacobia, dear," she began once Ellie had gone to inspect the food. Warm aromas were drifting in; they smelled delicious.

"It's probably not important," Sally went on, touching a manicured hand to the back of her hair. The gesture was meant to let me know she was uncomfortable with what she was about to say.

Which was nonsense; due to her entire nervous system having been replaced by the Social Register, Sally wouldn't have been made a bit uncomfortable if she were drawn and quartered, a plan I heartily approved.

Also, she thought everything she said was important. "Spill it, Sally," I told her. "I'm busy."

That she was speaking to me at all indicated that she wanted something, and I was constitutionally inclined not to give Sally anything she wanted.

"Well." She steeled herself prettily. "I don't know if you know this. Or if Ellie does."

I waited.

"But Jimmy Condon, who used to work for me until he stole all that firewood . . ."

Whereupon I nearly shut her down right then and there. Jimmy Condon was a well-liked local man whose business was cutting big woodlots for other people, selling the wood, and paying himself from the profit. The terms of the deal were spelled out: what got cut, what was to be left, and what the owner received.

"Care to get to the point?" I suggested.

People around here operated on margins so thin you could read the newspaper through them, and Jimmy was no exception. His mistake had been taking the trash wood from Sally's woodlot. It was stuff so small no one else would want it or so full of pitch it would turn your chimney into a tar pit, so she'd have had to pay to get it hauled away otherwise.

She bridled faintly. "That wood wasn't in the contract," she insisted, sensing whose side of the argument I was on.

Right, it hadn't been. Still, she'd been fine with it until she found out Jimmy used it to boil maple syrup at his little farm, where he also sold vegetables, eggs, goat's milk, and pumpkins.

Then she'd raised hell. It wasn't, she'd protested, for his personal use, as she had believed; it was for a *business*, and a pretty successful little business at that. There was, as she had told anyone who would listen, a *principle* involved.

The principle being that she could no longer imagine Jimmy's family huddled around the fire she had so charitably provided, a picture I was sure she'd summoned up on a regular basis, with herself as the benevolent lady of the manor, gooey with *noblesse oblige.*

Anyway, Jimmy had ended up buying the wood to stop her bad-mouthing him—a woodman with a crooked reputation might as well go pound sand—and that along with the next year's poor sap yield had put him out of the maple syrup business.

Which was another reason I so disliked her. "He was about to be ruined by Hector Gosling," Sally said. "Jimmy, I mean."

"Really. What makes you think that?"

My first reaction was that Sally just wanted to finish Jimmy off. Everyone knew what she'd done to him, and no one appreciated it; suggesting he might've had a bone to pick with Hector would make him look worse and her somehow better, she probably imagined.

But then I thought again, because Sally's patrician nose was exceptionally good at sniffing out news. "How could Hector've done anything to Jimmy Condon?" I prompted her. Because Jimmy could be as innocent as the day was long and still deliver a heaping helping of reasonable doubt over to George's side of the table.

"You'll have to ask Jimmy," she replied primly. "Or you could talk to Maria. She's out there now with Will Bonnet helping him prepare lunch. I

131

shouldn't," she added, "be telling you this much."

Which meant she'd probably extracted the information from her husband, a loan officer at the bank. Meanwhile I'd forgotten that Maria Condon was a historical society member; my, what an interesting connection, I thought, suddenly hopeful again.

"Jacobia." Sally stopped me as I moved away from her.

I turned back to find her gazing at me, wearing as usual a skirt and sweater set, stockings, and low heels, her pearls and makeup flawless and her white hair beautifully combed into a style that had been *au courant* thirty years earlier.

Chin up and shoulders back. Tummy flat; I'd have bet any money she was wearing a girdle. She looked, I realized all at once, lonely as hell.

"I hope it turns out all right for George," she said softly. "He's a good man."

I believed she meant it; even a stopped clock, and all that. But she'd been sealing her fate since moving here from Newport, Rhode Island, two years earlier, bringing along with her a down-the-nose gaze for anyone not meeting her standards. People just didn't like, as George would've put it, the cut of her jib.

So I couldn't help feeling a kind of sympathy for her. But I didn't have time—and let's face it, later I wouldn't have the inclination—to begin trying to exhume Sally from the grave she'd dug herself into.

"Thanks," I said, and left her alone in the ruined parlor.

In the next forty minutes I had jobs of my own to do, but I was also constantly being summoned to a remarkable variety of others. Intervening at the last instant before the power saw was applied, I saved an old panel door from being chopped off at the bottom; that lopped-off half-inch would've kept it from sticking, but would also have prevented the door from hanging straight ever again. Instead we rehung it on new hinges; afterwards it swung smoothly, unmutilated.

Next I wandered out to the kitchen where a very nice young man thought roofing nails would do for securing a loose corner of the kitchen linoleum, the venerable old kind that was actually made from canvas and linseed oil. Hastily I went to Wadsworth's Hardware store for a bottle of white glue and pressed it into the young man's hands, confiscating the roofing nails.

Finally I snatched a can of latex primer from a woman who, looking doubtful, was about to paint the insides of some first-floor window wells. Also, she hadn't scraped them; apparently she hoped latex primer would hold down the old loose paint chips.

Unfortunately, latex primer won't even hold itself down when painted onto anything but indoor locations. In a window, you might as well use a child's tin of watercolors. So I put a chisel to the old paint chips, which practically fell off, vacuumed them up, and gave some oil-based primer to the woman.

"Here," I told her, thinking I was being a little pushy. "You'll like the result much better."

But the gleam in her eye said she didn't think I was pushy at all. "Thank you," she said, wielding the paintbrush with new energy and beaming with the lovely zeal of the newly converted. It is remarkable, I have noticed, how the right tools can improve a person's mood.

At last I got away for lunch, which in its own way turned out to be remarkable, too.

Visitors to Eastport think an unending supply of fresh fish must be among the culinary delights of the place. But fish come in seasons and are in addition very heavily regulated; cod, for instance, once a mainstay of the fishing fleet, is so strictly controlled that the men are obliged to throw back much of what they haul in.

Somehow, though, our newest culinary genius Will Bonnet had gotten some cod, and from it he'd made the most delicious codfish cakes I'd ever tasted; fresh, delicately seasoned, gently crispy, and wildly popular with the historical society members.

"You like?" He stood behind the steam table he'd set up to keep them hot, wearing a white apron and a tall white chef's cap.

"Oh, indeed," I assured him through a mouthful.

In the wide hall of the old mansion where people stood refreshing themselves after their labors, approving comment about these delicacies had nearly managed to replace talk of Hector's murder.

"You must be feeling sandbagged," I told him as I selected asparagus from a dish positioned over a warming candle.

"You uproot your life to come home and save your Aunt Agnes, turns out someone steps in, does the job for you," I continued.

Two perfectly good non-George suspects had just been handed to me on plates, neat as the ones set up here to present deviled eggs spiced with locally made mustard, sweet-pickled baby carrots stuffed with hot peppers, and tiny steamed potatoes with butter and parsley, still in their tender jackets.

But I wanted more. Specifically I wanted Will's own problems with Hector Gosling and Jan Jesperson given a thorough airing. Because if this all dragged on as long as I had begun fearing it might, I could imagine wanting Ellie to be able to depend on him.

And I couldn't want that if I didn't trust him completely. He got my message, though, and to my relief he stepped up to it promptly and frankly.

"Yeah, I guess that's how it would look. City boy goes home, worried he'll have to haul his inheritance out of the villain's clutches. Or worse, that he won't be able to."

He slid cod cakes onto another plate, accepted

compliments, handsome with that cleft chin and curly black hair. You could see him greeting guests in his own restaurant.

"Might make the guy mad," Will admitted. "Truth is, though, those two did me a big favor."

He looked past me to where Ellie stood chatting with Maria Condon. His eyes softened at the sight. "Man, is she a trooper or what? She doing okay?"

"Sure. Reasonably." I hadn't had the chance to tell Ellie what Sally had said about Jimmy Condon, and now seeing the two women together I thought Ellie should be running a psychic hotline.

But then I realized from their body language that the small dark-haired woman had buttonholed Ellie, not the reverse. Maria spoke urgently, moving her hands in the quick, intense way that was among her trademarks, the other two being a razor-sharp tongue and a grip on a dollar that could make the eagle scream.

I scanned the crowd for Jan Jesperson. Cozily, she was the historical society's vice-president under Hector's leadership. But she wasn't here, and for that I was grateful. To get away with so much for so long I thought she'd have to be as sensitive as a cat's whisker; I didn't want her picking up any vibes from me.

"George," Will said wistfully, still watching Ellie, "is one lucky guy."

Yes, I thought sarcastically, except that he's in jail. "You were saying Hector did you a favor?"

Across the room Will's Aunt Agnes sat quietly on a folding chair, gazing wide-eyed at the people milling around her. She looked up confusedly each time another one stopped to greet her.

"Yeah." Will watched as she accepted a glass of sherry, then busied himself with the serving implements again. "But what you're really asking is something else," he went on as he worked. "And to answer the gist of your question, I was in Boston the night before last."

He waved at the cod cakes. "It's where I got the makings of those, the fish and seasonings." His eyes met mine calmly. "I can show you the receipt if you want."

He was right; it had been precisely the gist of my question, and I liked his straight answer.

"Or," he added without a hint of rancor, "you could talk to the people I saw there. Some business I had to take care of."

I liked his not being offended by my curiosity even better. "That's okay, Will," I said. "I appreciate your candor. But what did you mean about Jan and Hector doing you a favor?"

He shrugged. "I came back here thinking they were about to make off with my inheritance," he answered. "But that Agnes, she used to be a sharp cookie and even though she's failing some now, she was way ahead of me. Way ahead of them, too, it turns out."

He angled his head in her direction again. "Set up her will so she couldn't change it without my input, insisted on giving me power of attorney. Lawyer said she told him she didn't want to be made a fool of, if she ever got too far gone to notice."

Which now it seemed she had. The people speaking with her wore the sad smiles of visitors who expect not to see you again, or not to be recognized if they do.

"I don't get it," I told Will. "That means you never had to come here at all. It was all a waste of . . ."

"No." He waved his spatula at Agnes. "Just look at her. She raised me, you know, after my folks died. And she must have been going downhill to begin with or it was like George said about his aunt, she'd have never given Jan or Hector the time of day. So who'll take care of her now if I don't? Until I arrived I had no idea she was so fragile."

Almost the first thing he'd had to do was put a wheelchair ramp on her house. Still, she was lovely in an old-lace way; somebody picked up her fallen napkin for her, and the smile she offered in return would've broken a tax-man's heart.

"And now George," Will finished grimly. "He's going to need a pal, too. I mean even more pals than he's already got."

He raised the warming candle under the asparagus. "I owe him big-time after all he's done for me. So anything he needs, I mean it, all Ellie has to do is ask."

I'd have said something appreciative in reply but just then two things happened. The asparagus dish exploded with a startling *crack!* like a rifle shot. And somebody upstairs began screaming.

CHAPTER 5

So what's the deal with funeral-home franchises, anyway?" I asked. It was evening and Wade was plying me with whiskey sours.

"Can I have it my way? Let's say I'm a car mechanic, can I get shot up with brake fluid instead of embalming fluid?"

I'd never seen a woman with a knife in her chest before, and I guess he thought a few drinks might ease the experience for me.

It hadn't. "How about super-size, do they give you a roomier coffin? And cremation, there's a hot topic."

Sam and Tommy were in the dining room working on $ax^2 + bx + c = 0$, which if it doesn't equal anything I frankly don't see much point to. Will had taken Ellie home, saying he'd return to stay with her for a while after he settled his aunt. After that, Wade and the boys had teamed up on the dishes, shooing me into the parlor.

And a few blocks away the police were again swarming over the crime scene that was Harlequin House.

"Any idea how long she'd been there?" Wade asked me gently.

"A while." I shook my head, seeing it again: Jan Jesperson's body folded knees-to-chest, arms at her sides, wrapped a couple of times around with packing tape and tucked in a closet the cops hadn't noticed the first time they'd examined the house.

The closet door had looked like just another of the upstairs hall's oaken wall panels, without any handle or mark suggesting there had ever been one. Jan's body had been found when somebody leaned casually against the wall and fell in on it.

The knife had pinned the note to her chest: GUILTY.

After the first scream, the historical society members had reacted to the discovery in a variety of ways: running, shouting, staring, weeping, and in a few cases, fainting. Only Ellie had looked grimly pleased for the merest instant, since if by chance Jan had died *after* George was arrested . . .

But no such luck. I'm not going into the grisly details, but despite the coal dust she'd been heavily smeared with only a fool could have failed to comprehend that Jan had been dead for days.

As I should have suspected at her house. People might leave their coffeepots on, or music playing. But they wouldn't leave a laptop full of incriminating files out in plain sight unless they had departed in an awful rush.

Because, for instance, they'd been lured out. "You're sure the laptop is ruined?" Wade asked me.

It was the first thing I'd thought of, once I understood whose corpse had been found in that closet. "It's toast. When the power went back over to the Bangor Hydro grid, there must've been a surge."

I'd hotfooted it over there praying I could get in ahead of the police, and I had. But Jan hadn't been using a power-surge protector. All that could be coaxed onto the machine's screen was a grey-and-white crosshatch pattern that meant the contents were fried well beyond anything I could do to resurrect them.

"What'd you plan on doing if you did get the files?" Wade asked.

"Don't know," I replied morosely, getting up and following him into the kitchen. "But it's beside the point now. And I didn't have time to root around in her place looking for backup disks. Assuming she even kept any."

Angry with myself, I managed a final swallow of whiskey and dumped the rest down the sink. "Wade, *why* is George doing this? What secret could he have that would *possibly* make him think it's better to . . ."

"Get blamed for murder?" Wade shook his head. "Don't know."

"If he just came out and *said* where he was . . . and it's such a *cruel* thing to Ellie. Every bone in her body wants to go and see him but . . ."

"But instead she's letting him do it his way?" He wrapped me in a bear hug, smelling as always of salt water, fresh air, and the lanolin he used to keep the weather from cracking his skin.

"Maybe he knows Ellie trusts him, Jake. Maybe he knows if he explained his reasons, she would agree with them."

"I don't see how." I pressed my cheek against his flannel shirt. "You don't suppose he'll let this go on all the way to trial, do you?"

Or to prison. Awful thought; I banished it quickly. My ears were ringing. "You got me drunk so I'd be out of action for the evening," I accused him.

"That's part of it," he admitted. "Just seems like your coil could use some serious unwinding."

Because of my funeral-home rant, he meant, although I don't know why that was what pushed me over the edge, finally, that Hector's autopsy was done but he wasn't coming back to Eastport to be laid out and buried. Instead he'd gone at his own premortem wish to an outfit in Rockport, owned by some business pal of his with a string of them all over the state.

"Once upon a time when you died, the people who took care of you afterwards had known you their whole lives, and you'd known them," I said mournfully.

"Yeah." He spoke into my hair. "When my mom died, my sisters went over to the funeral parlor and did her hair, and painted her nails with that special polish she liked, that pearly stuff."

Inside the bear hug it was safe and peaceful, just our two hearts beating. "The rest of us waited at home," he continued. "Drinking hard, not talking about it until my sisters came back."

Wade's two sisters lived far away now, one in California and the other in the port city of Valdez, in Alaska. That was the way it seemed to happen with families in Eastport. Some stayed; others went, and either did or didn't come back.

"But it's true," he added, "I wouldn't mind you just hanging around here tonight. I've got to go out."

"On a Sunday night?" I pulled away from him. When he said *out,* he meant on the water, and though the storm had passed us by its effect out there still included gale winds and eight-foot swells.

"Yeah. Coupla more freighters waiting, we gotta get things back on schedule or we'll have boats lined up to Finland."

Wade piloted the ships through wild currents, hull-smashing granite ledges, and the chaotic winds with which the entrance to our port is well furnished. But first he rode a tug out to where the behemoths idled and climbed aboard on a metal gang or in the case of less-well-equipped vessels, a dangling ladder.

"Well, if you've got to, you've got to." I looked around our kitchen, all shining clean with its floor freshly swept, counters wiped and sink Ajaxed.

Wade had done it all after he and the boys had finished the dishes, in between ferrying whiskey sours to me. Now he squeezed me hard, let go. "Home tomorrow night, maybe."

I nodded. Women in Eastport had been sending their men out to sea for two centuries; a stiff upper lip was a bred-in facial feature around here.

I faked mine. "Okay." The dogs got up, Monday shoving her black Labrador head under his left hand, Prill her fake-ferocious red Doberman noggin under his right.

"They'll take care of me," I said. As guard dogs the pair were as useful as a bowl of marshmallows but they barked at strangers and since the strangers didn't know they were in danger of being licked to death by happy goofballs it worked out.

"Just be careful," I said, handing Wade his work duffel, an old dark-green canvas one he prepacked for journeys like these.

"I will." Sensing Wade's departure, even Cat Dancing stood up on top of the refrigerator, raked the kitchen with her cross-eyed glare, then curled to sleep again.

Now *there* was a guard animal; I once reached blindly into a closet and a cranky Siamese came flying out like a cartoon buzz saw. George said if you tied Cat Dancing to the end of a stick you could use her to trim hedges. But burglars hardly ever climb onto the refrigerator so we were reduced to loving Cat unconditionally, as we would if we had, say, a Tasmanian devil for a house pet.

Wade hugged me hard once more. Then, because time and tide really don't wait, he was gone.

Which left me in an ocean of silence. But

shortly thereafter in the dining room someone pronounced a curse word, and after it a worse one.

Much worse. "Sam?" I called. "You guys okay in there?"

"Fine, Mom." And then in an urgent whisper to Tommy, "C'mon, man, what's the matter with you?"

I peeked in and saw them together, Sam in jeans and a hooded sweatshirt, gazing with mellow patience at the page of equations he was working on. And Tommy with his carrot hair, round freckled face, and the jug ears he kept threatening to have pinned back.

"Guys, when you're done, lock up and lights off, okay?"

Tommy glanced up, pencil in hand. The circles under his eyes were purplish half-moons; his forehead was sheened with sweat. His usually ruddy complexion was a sick green, the color of old cheese.

Sam caught my look of startled inquiry and shot me a warning glance. *Don't ask.*

So I didn't. Instead I went upstairs, so boozy and exhausted I could scarcely see straight; later I heard Sam let Tommy out and go around the house shutting things down for the night.

Too bad I couldn't shut my brain down as easily. My whiskey buzz was gone, leaving that wide-awake-but-too-disorganized-to-do-anything about it feeling. Without Wade there beside me eating ice cream and rereading an old Tom Clancy novel—better than a sleeping pill, he always insisted—the big bed was lonesome even with both dogs on it.

And I couldn't stop seeing Ellie's expression when we first found Jan. She'd managed to hide her exultant look from the rest but I'd caught it; the awful relief of someone given a reprieve from disaster.

It reminded me of what my alpaca-raising ex-client had said about the money business and why he was getting out. His colleagues were getting Botox shots, he'd explained, to enforce their poker faces, abolishing the subtle changes that might otherwise queer a pitch or sink a deal.

The sweaty palm and killer gut-clench had been my personal gruesome twosome, back in the old days; there's a drug you can take to get rid of both, I happen to know.

But around here, Botox wasn't needed. Like the stiff upper lip, the flat, tight expression that had replaced Ellie's short-lived happiness was bred in the bone. It hid the hurt of losing a job or missing a boat payment; in her case it covered the pain of George's sudden salvation being snatched away just as suddenly.

I'd have done anything to fix that pain, to wipe it away with something like the equivalent of cosmic Botox. But I couldn't; not for her or for my old buddy Jemmy Wechsler, sitting somewhere now with the idea of salvation little more than a bitter joke.

Instead I paged through my forensics textbook—I'd made it into possible bedtime reading material by razor-blading all the photographs out of it—pausing to reread carefully any item about estimating times of death. What I needed was something that might put George's absence outside of the time range the medical examiner had given for Hector's demise.

In other words, a forensic fluke. But I couldn't find any. Degree of rigor mortis obviously wasn't a help, since strychnine poisoning induced the mother of all rigors. Stomach contents were useless; the victim ejected them while succumbing. Livor mortis, the pooling of blood after death, was unrewarding; the poison in question wasn't a blood thinner and would be unlikely to derange the process. Nor did it alter the time it took for the corneas to cloud, as far as I could discover.

Which left body temperature, which I guessed must be how the medical examiner had made his estimate; that and the fact that no advanced decomposition had yet begun. As it would have now that the sealed room had been opened; another day or so and the body's condition would have begun deteriorating severely.

Firmly I averted my imagination from this eventuality and picked up Wade's Tom Clancy novel. If you focused your eyes just right and kept turning pages determinedly, the book was perfectly readable.

At nearly eleven the phone rang, and I answered it.

The next morning I stood at the upstairs hall window as the day exploded into a glory of blue and gold, the last few yellow leaves on the maples backed by the indigo water of Passamaquoddy Bay. Jemmy used to call such views "Kodak moments," in the same wry way he might say "government expert" or "family values."

Or "witness protection." And like Jemmy I had my own pocketful of wry. But something about that sky, its pitiless clarity, sent me unexpectedly back to another bright day many years earlier.

My mother's body was found in the ruins where she died, or it wasn't; burnt to ashes and blown off on the wind.

Or not. Victor says I tell it a different way every time. Wade says I can expect to go on being blindsided by it, painfully and at odd moments, for the rest of my life.

He says it will be different every time.

While I was standing there Sam came out of his room. "So who was on the phone last night?" he asked me.

"Ellie. I'm picking her up in a little while." I turned away from the Kodak moment. "What's up with Tommy?"

He grimaced, heading for the shower. "Don't know. Something sure is bugging him. George, I guess. Or maybe it's Perry again."

"Perry Daigle?" I asked, startled.

Tommy's last name had been Daigle, too, until he changed it to avoid being linked with his notorious uncle. "I thought Perry was in jail."

"He is. But it's on another DUI and this time the judge gave him ninety days. So he's hassling Tommy's mom for money, get a lawyer to help him out."

"Hmph. What Perry needs is help putting a gun to his head."

I didn't usually say such things in front of Sam. But Perry Daigle was about as worthwhile as your average sewer germ, in my opinion. He'd broken a bone in Tommy's mother's face and had put a scar on Tommy's forehead with his ring, a big gold signet.

Sam rubbed his jaw thoughtfully. "Yeah. I guess Tommy was hoping for more action from George, in the Perry department."

It was George who'd persuaded Perry that it would be an extremely good idea never to lay a hand on Tommy or his mother, ever again.

"And George had been driving Tommy to work in the mornings, too," Sam went on. " 'Cause Tommy's car needed a new fuel pump and he's still saving up to buy it."

I nodded. Tommy's car, with its custom mufflers, *oo-OO-gah!* horn, and raccoon tail flying from the radio antenna, was a well-known vehicle in Eastport. "So maybe that's it," I said. "Losing his ride and so on. Which reminds me—can I borrow yours today?"

"Sure," he agreed, "I won't be needing it." Both of us thinking it would take worse than walking to work, to wipe the smile off Tommy's face.

"Oh, and your father called," I said. The crack-of-dawn phone call was another of Victor's charming habits. "He wanted to know, are you still on for dinner with him tonight?"

Victor had wanted to talk about other things, too, but I didn't mention them. Besides not waxing violently sarcastic in front of Sam, I tried keeping him out of the dead-body stuff as much as possible. One of us hip-deep in it was enough.

"Yeah," my son replied with a rueful laugh, "I'm still on. Which one you think he wants to talk me into going to this time, Princeton or Cal Tech?"

Victor had never abandoned his dream of Sam's attending what Victor termed a *real* college. Luckily, Sam's own self-esteem was robust enough not to suffer from his father's pep talks.

"If he offers to pay for either one, come and talk to me," I said. "We'll work something out."

"After I pick myself up off the floor," Sam agreed. Somehow Victor's ambitions for his son always included silver platters.

Without warning Sam changed the subject. "I wish Bob Arnold were here. I'm kinda worried about George, myself."

151

"Nothing Bob could do now." Me, either; not about George or whatever was bothering Tommy. Not until I knew more. So instead I got started on the project Ellie had lined up for the day.

Which was chasing a wild goose.

"Listen," I said to her an hour later, "what if we get all the way out there and then you decide to have the baby?"

We were driving toward the mainland, over the long causeway with the bright, blue-green water spreading away on both sides, the racing waves whitely foam-topped.

"I'm not deciding anything, the baby is," she replied from the passenger seat. "At this stage of the game, anyway."

I didn't tell her that in my experience "this stage" lasts forever. Let her keep her illusions; she'd find out the reality soon enough.

"And it's not coming for a while," she added, "no matter what the doctors say. Why should it? Everything's just ducky where it is. Why give up a good thing?"

Berries still clinging to the mountain ash trees stood out like blood clots against their leafless branches in the fields on either side of the road. Campaign signs for upcoming elections clustered in the dry grass next to ones for a hunters' breakfast at the Grange Hall.

"Will stayed late last night," I observed. She'd

waited to call me until after he went home.

"Yes. It was okay, though. After dinner he went over and got the truck. The police were finished with it."

From the Mobil station, she meant, where George and Will had taken it when it wouldn't start. Two days ago, but it felt like two years.

"And he put some shelves in the spare room for me. Just . . ." She raised her hands, let them fall. "I think Will's lonely. His aunt, I guess, is not very much company. I didn't mind."

Past the causeway I took a left and slowed for a hay-wagon lumbering along behind an antique tractor, the bales on the wagon swaying hugely every time the wagon went over a bump. Around the farmhouses, meadows had been cut, gold stubble sticking up in geometric grids like the pattern of a patchwork quilt.

Canada geese arrowed overhead. "I still don't see what you expect to accomplish with this trip," I told Ellie. The wagon turned off. A couple of cars had lined up behind us, in the rearview.

She shrugged. "I'm not sure either. What's wrong?"

I looked in the rearview again. "Nothing. I thought . . ."

But the car that had seemed to be following turned off too. Not one I recognized.

"Just because people's names come up in rumor doesn't mean they'll say anything helpful," Ellie conceded.

But that was her plan. Because rumor had touched on Jimmy Condon and Ginger Tolliver in relation to Hector, she meant to visit both of them and see what, if anything, we could glean from them.

"It was all just talk about them maybe having reasons to want Hector dead," she admitted. "But it's also all I've got."

She sighed. "And you never know, maybe they will turn out to have hated Jan Jesperson, too."

I thought choosing interview subjects based on their names having come up in idle chatter was about as likely to pan out as selecting them by throwing darts at a telephone book. Still, she had her heart set on this.

"So it's a fishing expedition," I said. "Fine, I get the picture. Look for the turn, will you? It's been a while since I've been out this way."

The road meandered prettily between old homesteads, each with its barn, rail-fenced garden, and row of apple trees. Sheets and pillowcases strung on wash lines bloused out in the cool breeze, gathering the scents of balsam, sweet woodruff, and new mown hay.

"There," Ellie said. But I'd already spotted it, a collection of buildings very much like the others we'd passed but polished looking, somehow. More disciplined; near the trim farmhouse an old maple with a last crimson leaf still clinging to it presided over the immaculate yard.

I turned onto the crunchily pea-graveled drive

past a sign that read Saltmeadow Farm. A dog the size of an elk got slowly up from the front porch and stood there, eyeing us measuringly.

My fingers tightened on the door handle of the car, which I had unwisely exited prior to scanning the area for carnivores.

"*Grr*," said the dog, narrowing its eyes with interest.

"Oh, grr, yourself," Ellie said, waving a hand dismissively as she strode toward it.

"Ellie? I think . . ." The dog leapt from the porch, traversing the lawn in a couple of long, slavering bounds. "Ellie!"

I love dogs; just not the possibly murderous ones you tend to meet in strange dooryards. The dog kept snarling, growling, and threatening right up until the moment it stopped short in front of Ellie.

"You big faker," she said, ruffling its ears, and went on toward the porch where Maria Condon had come out, wearing a red corduroy smock over a navy turtleneck, scuffed clogs, and navy leggings with a patch in one knee.

"Ellie, it's you. I didn't recognize you at first. Somehow yesterday you didn't look so . . ."

"Huge." Ellie completed the woman's sentence without rancor. "All those protective work clothes covered it up some. But don't worry, I'll be back to my normal size soon."

Another illusion I'd failed to dispel. I'd gotten back to my own normal size right around the time my son picked up his first marijuana cigarette.

That he'd done it right in front of me, with the defiant flair only a twelve-year-old dope fiend can really master properly, may have accounted for the sudden, complete, and terrifying loss not only of my appetite but also most of my mind for the next couple of years.

"This is my friend, Jake Tiptree. I don't think you two met yesterday. Jake, Maria Condon," Ellie introduced us.

Maria had a thick brunette braid, dark eyes, and the remnants of the deep summer tan she'd have gotten working in the big garden that lay at the end of the mowed yard. The small hard muscles of her arms were visible even under the turtleneck sleeves. A boy of about five with bowl-cut blond hair and red cheeks came out onto the porch behind her.

"Hello," Maria said to me. But then something changed in her eyes as she looked from me to Ellie and back. "Porter, go back inside, please."

Silently the child obeyed. I wondered what Maria had used to instill such instant, protest-free compliance. But it went with the perfect orderliness of the place, the trim painted and the porch swept and the ruler-straight rows in the garden. No weed ever grew there, I'd have bet; it wouldn't dare to.

"You're here about Hector, aren't you?" Maria asked. "Because of what Sally's been saying. I told you yesterday she's a troublemaker. And I know the kind of thing you two get up to," she went on.

156

"You want to know if Jimmy could've killed him, maybe Jan too. My husband," she added pointedly to Ellie, "instead of yours."

Ellie didn't duck the accusation. "You're the one who brought it up to me, that Sally was bad-mouthing Jimmy again and that you wanted a stop put to it. Well, if we can rule Jimmy out for sure, that will put a stop to it." Then she looked around curiously. "Where is Jimmy, anyway?"

Maria bristled. "In the woods. Despite that horrible woman's slander, people do still hire him."

"So *was* there trouble between Jimmy and Hector?"

Something flickered in Maria's dark eyes. "He didn't do it," she declared flatly.

"How do you know?" I asked.

Brass tacks being a game two can play at. If she started in on the old "he was here with me the whole evening" story, I'd do an about-face on my earlier opinion and start thinking maybe he had done it.

But instead Maria faced Ellie. "I know in the same way you know George didn't," she replied. "Because I know *him*. And I know you, too, Ellie. I can't believe that you'd want to make Jimmy a scapegoat."

A real goat looked up inquiringly from behind a rail fence. Past his enclosure lay a tranquil pond, yellow corn stalks, and a pumpkin patch with big orange spheres thickly strewn among the already-withered vines. The cultivated land ended at a stand of hardwood, maple and oak interspersed with dark-green cedars.

"No," Ellie agreed at last. "I'm not looking for someone to blame. Please, Maria, I need your help. And," she added, wincing a little, "I could stand to visit your bathroom, too, if it's not too much trouble."

So maybe it was an unorthodox way to get invited in. But it worked. "All right," Maria said grudgingly. "I guess you'd both better come inside."

There was nothing fancy or new inside the Condon house, just orderly efficiency and the sense of grim, constant making-do. Besides the usual appliances, the kitchen held a slant-topped desk where Maria had apparently been paying bills when we arrived. A fat stack of them remained on the spindle.

Maria led us through into a chilly parlor. "Okay, here's the deal," she said when she'd sat us down. "If Gosling got away with his scheme we'd have lost everything. And it looked to me as if he was going to. To Jimmy, too."

I blinked at her frankness; she saw it, shrugged impatiently. "You want the truth. And we have nothing to hide," she explained.

Um, maybe. "That woodlot you saw is for sale," she went on. Beyond the animal pens and garden, she meant; that forest.

"A hundred acres, you could cut a little every

year, open it up right so the little stuff grew big," she continued. "Keep it going forever if you knew what you were doing. And Jimmy does."

"Tree-farm it," Ellie said comprehendingly; Maria nodded.

"There's regulations on what you can cut, but Jimmy knows how. You wouldn't make a lot of money but it's steady. Enough to make the payments on the land, plus taxes and a little extra."

I got it. "Collateral."

She shot me a swift glance. "Exactly. We do have a decent down payment, so pretty soon we could borrow against *that* land. Again, not much, but . . ."

She turned toward the kitchen where the little boy was about to put a half-eaten apple into the homemade compost keeper.

"Porter, if you're not going to finish that apple, leave it on the table so Mommy can wrap it for you. You can eat it later."

Waste not, want not. But I got the sense that here that philosophy was taken to the extreme. "And the next loan, it would be enough for a down payment on another piece?" I hazarded.

Another nod from Maria. "Beyond the first, another parcel of land also with excellent wood on it. We had it all planned out."

"You mean you did," Ellie pointed out, and Maria flushed faintly.

"Jimmy," she agreed, "wouldn't buy a package of gum unless somebody held a gun to his head."

She gestured around. "His truck is older than George's, and every stick of furniture in this house is second- or third-hand."

She said it proudly but something about it didn't strike me quite right; she was too intense about it. "So you make the money plans and Jimmy goes along with them," I said.

Her face revealed that I'd hit home; Jimmy's contribution to this little operation was a snappy salute.

And of course cutting the wood. I thought a moment. "The hard part was probably getting him around the idea that you're a better money manager. You being the woman, I mean."

Might there be friction between them about it? If so, Jimmy could've felt pushed to prove something about being an equal member of the team. But Maria wasn't having any.

"You know what? He's a better tree cutter than I am. And if I can't get Porter to go to bed, he can. And—"

"Okay, I take your point. Everybody does what they do best." But privately, I still suspected that Jimmy was also pretty good at pronouncing the phrase, "yes, dear."

Maria nodded. "I milk goats better," she added, which struck me funny. But when I glanced over, she wasn't smiling.

"It must have made him nervous, though," I suggested, probing. "Thinking about all the things that could go wrong."

If one of them got sick or had an accident, the little extra that greased the wheels of their plan would vanish. I doubted they had health insurance either, or if they did the deductible was bigger than their yearly income. And I certainly knew better than to think they had the luxury of disability protection.

In other words, Jimmy and Maria were swinging in the breeze and praying that the wind blew fair.

"He worries about it," she admitted. "Taking loans and using other people's money to get ahead. But it's the only way," she insisted urgently. "You can't stay even, I kept telling him, although you might feel safer if you do. Unless you go forward, you fall back."

I regarded her with new respect. If I could've slapped that fact into the heads of half of my clients back in the city, we'd all have ended up wealthier.

Somehow Maria had figured it out for herself, though, that life is risk. The only choice is, are you the taker or the taken?

"We had to get the land for the collateral, but also for the income. To help make," she explained, "payments on this house."

Yeeks; riskier than I'd thought. "That's where the first land down payment came from? Second mortgage on this place?" An even scarier thought struck me. "Not from Hector, I hope? The second mortgage, that is."

"Uh-uh. I'd never have talked Jimmy into that,

even if I'd wanted it." Maria's small, determined chin lifted. "No, it was the bank. Preliminary approval and the deal was all made. A lady down the road owns the acreage and she had agreed to sell to us."

Uh-oh. "An elderly lady," I hazarded. "No family. And the land, if you didn't buy it, would've ended up in her estate."

"I suppose," Maria said slowly. "I don't think she'd been planning to sell it until we asked her."

"The money would've been there, though," Ellie objected, "in the woman's estate, if they *did* buy it." Catching my drift: that Hector could as easily have swindled the old woman out of the cash.

"Yeah, but who knows what kind of rackets he had going? What happened next?" I asked, turning back to Maria.

"Hector told the lady that it would be worth more if he got it zoned residential for her, put in roads, and parceled it off for house lots. Which we could've done, too," she added. "But we didn't want to."

The child had fallen asleep in a shabby armchair, thumb in mouth. "We thought someday it could be Porter's."

A worthy objective, but they were way out on a limb. They needed to buy more land just so they could hang onto the house they were living in.

"So the lady started to back out," I said. "Listening to Hector's advice and waffling on the deal she'd made with you and Jimmy."

162

"And the trouble was, we didn't have anything in writing," Maria confirmed. "And that was where things stood when Hector . . . Well, you know more about what happened to him than I do."

Maybe. And maybe not. This was shaping up to be a much more interesting situation than I'd expected.

"Where was Jimmy?" Ellie spoke finally. "Last Friday and on Friday night."

According to what Victor had told me that morning, the autopsy in Augusta had confirmed the medical examiner's original estimate for Hector's time of death: twenty-four to forty-eight hours from the time the M.E. had first seen the body

Which meant George was still firmly on the hook. "Out at the sawmill in Cooper during the day," Maria replied evenly. "Bird's-eye maple, he was having it cut for a furniture maker in Rockland. It had to be just so and he stayed till the end, to make sure that it was."

"He didn't leave for lunch or anything like that?" But the moment I'd said it I realized how foolish it was.

She shot me a look. "I make his lunch. It's a twenty-mile drive to a lunch place from there. It's not like they've set up a McDonald's in Cooper, you know. And it's cheaper."

Of course. "Okay, so then what?" I asked her. "How about in the evening?"

She bridled, not liking the close questioning. Ellie put her oar in efficiently.

163

"Look, Maria, if you want Jimmy ruled out of it, just tell us where he was, that he couldn't have been somewhere else killing Hector, that's all."

Ellie had her best don't-mess-with-me face on, and she was using her stop-screwing-around-with-me voice to go with it. And for someone who resembled a storybook princess—even one with a watermelon in her middle—she could be very persuasive.

Maria gave in. "He was at the boys' clubhouse, playing poker."

"Boys' clubhouse?" I looked at Ellie, who shook her head at me minutely. *Never heard of it.* "You mean like no girls allowed, swear an oath to get in, that sort of thing?"

"Yes, sort of." Maria seemed embarrassed. "It's Truie Benoit's place, do you know him? Truman, that's his real name. Anyway, Truie has a barn behind his house. Has a woodstove, an old icebox with a case of shorties in it, the guys go there in the evenings to play cards and smoke cheap cigars."

"So that's where Jimmy was? Playing poker with the boys?"

"Yes." She nodded firmly. "I know he was there all evening because I dropped him off and picked him up. I needed the truck, there was a craft fair to get ready for at Porter's preschool."

"Well, there you have it, then," I said to Ellie. "That's where Jimmy was, so I guess we'll know what to tell Sally Crusoe next time she tries to say otherwise."

"Mm-hmm," Ellie concurred. She was rising with an effort. "I guess we will. It's a good preschool, then, is it?" she asked Maria disarmingly. "Because we are already looking around for one."

I happened to know that Ellie meant to keep her child out of school for as long as possible, having herself been packed off at the earliest legal moment. But there was no sense letting Maria know we didn't believe her; thus the distracting small talk.

She got up, picked a few dead leaves off a geranium. "Oh, yes. Porter loves it. Don't you, honey?" The little boy wandered in sleepily to lean against her, clutching her skirt.

"We trade goat's milk and vegetables for his tuition, and firewood in the winter," she went on. She cupped the dead leaves in her palm, probably for deposit in that compost keeper. Heaven forbid a shred of organic matter shouldn't be recycled. But her hand closed tensely around the leaves and you could sense the relief coming off her in waves as she walked us to the door.

Minutes later we were backing out the driveway, me feeling anxious to go home and waste a bread crust or something just to prove that I could.

"I'll bet she makes them eat their potato skins," I grumbled as we reached Route 190 and I signaled to turn back toward Eastport.

"Yup," Ellie replied distantly. "Go the other way, okay?"

It was nearly noon. "Ellie, don't you think you should . . ."

"Rest?" She snapped the word out. "No. Because it's almost lunchtime. What do you think they serve for lunch in jail, Jake? Baloney and cheese? Stale chips, instant coffee?"

At home George got a cooked lunch, say a hot turkey sandwich with stuffing and gravy. Piece of pie, maybe, and fresh coffee.

A car pulled up behind me. It was the one I'd thought might be following us earlier, a beat-up old black muscle car with a big mismatched front grille and a crack in its tinted windshield, its plate too smeared with grime to read. I didn't care for it. But when I turned left toward Route 1, it went the other way.

Ginger Tolliver's place lay beyond the Route 1 intersection, way up a side road at the far end of Boyden Lake. It was a long drive, deep into the countryside, and Ellie looked pale.

I pulled over, meaning to take her home.

"Please," she said quietly, putting a hand on my arm.

So I didn't.

CHAPTER 6

How'd *you* know Maria was lying?" I asked Ellie as we drove up the winding two-lane that led toward Ginger's place.

"The gambling part, of course." To our left a river bubbled merrily over gleaming rocks; to the right, boulder-studded fields spread uphill to a row of windbreak cedars.

"I can go along with the woodstove and the icebox full of shorties," she added. "As long as Jimmy didn't bring any of the beer or a single stick of firewood."

"Yup. That's what I thought. And unless they were playing for bottle caps Jimmy wasn't gambling. Maria would as soon toss dollar bills out the window and you can safely assume he doesn't have a dime that she doesn't know about."

"And three fellows betting aren't going to let a fourth in just for fun," Ellie concurred.

"How about the part about Maria dropping him off and picking him up, though?"

"That she was at a craft fair meeting?" Ellie shrugged. "I don't see any problem, there. Or with the fact that Jimmy could have borrowed one of the other guys' cars. If I tell my friends I was supposed to be with them, I was. You know how it works."

"In other words same story as for Jimmy: I was with *them*. Just a different set of people backing it up for each of them."

The road made a snakelike set of wiggles through a sunlit stand of hardwood, the leafless branches gleaming pewter-colored.

"The minute Sally started telling her latest story, you can be sure Jimmy and Maria's pals closed ranks around them," Ellie went on. "A wealthy lady from away implicating an Eastport boy?" She snorted softly. "Now that word's starting to get out about when Hector died, Jimmy's buddies and Maria's, too, will swear on a stack of tide charts that Jimmy and Maria were with them Friday night. Make Sally look like as big an idiot as they can. Which," she added, "shouldn't be difficult."

Ellie didn't care for Sally either, since what she'd done to Jimmy she could as easily have done to George. It was a class thing, that the peasants shouldn't eat so much as an apple from a tree without getting the landowner's permission.

"They'll make Sally look foolish for implying that Jimmy could've killed Hector," I agreed. "But it also screws *us* up."

A woodcock ran out from the underbrush and paused at the gravel edge of the road, eyeing us brightly. With a ridiculously long bill and plump body atop long, sticklike legs, it looked more like a carved bird than like something that lived in nature.

"Because they *did* have a motive," I added. "If they don't buy that woodlot and Jimmy doesn't start managing it quick—"

Cutting on it, I meant, and selling contracts, too, for wood to be cut from it later—

"—they'll lose their house," I said. "And my problem with the whole thing is that Sally's b.s. comes in so handy for them."

"Because we don't know if their story might be to cover their tracks on Hector or just a hit-back at Sally's gossip," Ellie agreed. Then she frowned suddenly.

"What's the matter?" I pulled over, startling a wild turkey into emitting a loud *gobble!* and strutting into the sumac bushes.

"Nothing." Tiny beads of sweat glistened on her forehead.

"You swear, Ellie?" I peered closely at her. "Because I'm telling you, if you have this baby out here in the woods I'll . . ."

Well, I didn't know what I would do so I didn't finish the threat. She mustered a weak smile.

"Swear. I said it'll be a while. I'm just uncomfortable."

"Yeah." I pulled the car back onto the road. "When I was in your boat I started asking Victor for spinal anesthesia at about thirty-six weeks."

Actually by that point he'd been threatening to inject the stuff into my brain. There's a chance the nubile X-ray technician he was dating at the time might've added to my distress, too.

"I hope this kid doesn't turn out like Victor," Ellie murmured. "I mean precocious like him."

"Awful thought." Victor had finished college at thirteen and medical school three years later. He'd been the youngest first-year resident his hospital ever had; if anyone complained, they were going to make him get a Ph.D. first, then return to hands-on medical practice.

But no one did complain. Even back then, Victor could charm the birds out of the trees.

When he wanted to. "Don't worry, though," I told Ellie. "There's not much chance it'll turn out like Victor. Mutations like him only happen every billion or so years."

She managed another smile. Then: "Jake? How much does it hurt? To have the baby, I mean. Tell the truth."

I thought a minute. "Pain's not what you'll remember."

She glanced at me, scenting evasion. But I saw no point in scaring her since after all there's no bail-out option. If there were I'd have taken it seconds after I reached the delivery room. I'd have taken heroin too, if any had been on offer.

On the other hand, it's evasion that scares *me*. And Ellie could smell it a mile away.

"Look," I relented. "It hurts like a son of a bitch, okay? It really does. But the instant it's over you won't care. Trust me on this, you won't."

170

I was about to go on. But as we reached the road leading into the woods I thought maybe she didn't want to know about the heroin-desiring portion of the program after all.

Because all she said was, "Turn here."

Hector Gosling's ex-housekeeper Ginger Tolliver turned out to be a tall Nordic beauty with masses of braided yellow hair pinned in complicated fashion atop her head. In a red-and-green reindeer sweater and green stretch pants, her appearance suggested skiing and other strenuous winter activities.

Or it would have except that her left arm ended in a hand so unusual that it was impossible not to look at it.

"Car accident," she explained when we'd pulled up into her drive and gotten out. Her place was a trailer on a woodsy cleared spot, with a lake visible through the trees behind it.

Ginger's hand was a sort of claw fashioned out of the thumb joint, working pincerlike with what remained of the scarred palm.

"It's okay," she added, seeing my embarrassment when she caught me staring. "Everyone always wants to know."

She wore a built-up shoe, too, that didn't entirely correct her spine's curvature. Her ice-blue eyes had tight lines at the corners and her mouth betrayed a burden of chronic pain.

Victor would've had a team of specialists lined up in about ten seconds. "Can't they do some kind of . . . ?"

"Surgery?" A brief, bitter laugh. "I've had enough surgery. Besides, I don't have any way to pay for more."

She limped ahead of us into a screened porch. "The surgery that might help," she told us, "is experimental, according to my benefits administrator. And when Medicaid pays, Medicaid calls the tune."

We followed her onto the porch. "Sit," she said brusquely, waving at a pair of plastic lawn chairs alongside hers. "I was out here relaxing. But soon I have to go to a job interview."

My surprise must have shown on my face. She gave me a "d'oh" look. "Well, what do you think? Hector's dead, isn't he? So I need a new job. I'm not going to retire on a pension, that's for sure."

"Actually that's what we wanted to ask you about," Ellie put in. "Hector Gosling being dead."

Another look, this time a little less friendly. A yellow cat jumped onto Ginger's lap and settled there.

"Yeah, I didn't think you two were selling Avon," she said. *And especially not you,* her look added to me.

Hey, not everyone can resemble a Viking goddess. It was cold on the porch so my lips were probably pale blue against my ghost-white skin. Any tan I get during the summer fades promptly, any makeup I try stands out like paint on the side of a barn, and my hair probably looked as if it had been styled with an egg beater.

"Poor kitty," Ginger told the cat. "But you're staying out while I'm gone or you'll claw the furniture."

The cat meowed as if in grudging acceptance of this dictum.

"Anyway," Ellie said, "we heard Hector wasn't very nice to you."

From the screened porch you could look downhill fifty feet through the birches and some huckleberry shrubbery to the water. A pebble path led to a rickety dock.

"No. He wasn't," Ginger agreed placidly.

The place was so backwoods-beautiful, it wasn't obvious at first how desperately poor it was. There was a burn-barrel for the trash, a fraying clothesline with a few rusty pins clipped to it for laundry. Thick sheets of plastic had been affixed with nails and cardboard furring strips to the trailer windows to save on heat.

"Hector broke up a romance?" I probed. "Because that's what we heard. It's what people are saying. Siss Moore, for one."

Ginger turned to me, her astonishing blue eyes suddenly full of angry tears. "Well then, it must be true."

She got up. A cane leaned by her chair but she either didn't see it or wouldn't use it in front of us. "When I was in school Mrs. Moore wanted to take me under her wing. She picks someone every year, a deserving candidate."

She gave the last words a bitter twist. "Starts sticking her nose in their business. 'You're smart, you should do so-and-so.'"

Staring at the water lapping the dock pilings, she went on. "But if you didn't take her advice she turned on you. I've heard that later she wised up, figured out why some kids avoided her."

The way Tommy was avoiding Siss Moore now, I remembered. "Anyway," Ginger added, "she got it right about what Mr. Gosling did to me. As if he hadn't done enough."

I wanted to ask about the "enough" part. Enough what? But she hurried on. "His name was Mark Timberlake. We were going to be married. He's in the merchant marine."

Head high, voice steady. Ginger wasn't the type who enjoyed letting you in on her private troubles. On the table beside her chair were a stack of chess books and a little chess computer, a wooden flute and a leaflet that promised it could teach you to play, and a big tapestry knitting bag.

It was the gear of a self-sufficient and intensely private person. "Then what happened?" I asked.

"And then Mr. Gosling got to him. He said Mark wasn't good enough for me, kept at me to change my mind, do what he said and end the engagement. All he really wanted was to keep me working for him. He could tell Mark didn't like him, wouldn't have wanted me to stay in the job."

"But you wouldn't break the engagement. And you didn't quit before you got married because . . ."

Another laugh, harsher this time. "Because what if it ended up turning out I didn't get married? Jobs don't grow on trees around here, in case you haven't noticed it. And for me it's always twice as hard because people don't think I can work."

She waved the ruined hand. "Or if it's a company they can't afford me on their insurance. It's not what they say, of course. They're not allowed to discriminate against me. But they do it anyway. They just tell me some other reason. Everyone does what they have to do to survive, right?"

Interesting comment. "Including you?"

Sam was considering a stint in the merchant marine. For the right type of person, working aboard the big freighters offered a solid career and a harsh but not impossible existence. You could climb the promotion and pay scale, and the job offered excellent benefits. The downside was that you were away most of the time, your loved ones just snapshots in your wallet. For newlyweds in love it would be terribly difficult.

But Ginger hadn't said she loved him, had she?

She hadn't said that. "How did Hector 'get to him'?" I asked.

She frowned down at her shoes: one ordinary sneaker, one big complicated piece of machinery. "I don't know. I got a call from Mark, all worried. First he wanted me to marry him right away and

175

when I wouldn't do that he did a sudden turn-around, said maybe we'd better call it all off. I hung up on him before he could say anything even worse. Like maybe he never really wanted to. Or at least not enough."

Ellie had been silent. She spoke up now. "What makes you think that Hector had anything to do with it? Couldn't it be that this guy just . . . chickened out?" Her shoulders moved helplessly as Ginger and I looked at her. "Hey, it happens," she said.

But Ginger's face denied this. "You'd have to know Mark. He wasn't . . ."

She turned back to me. "I know what you were thinking. I saw it in your face. You think I didn't love him. But it's not true. I did. I just wasn't brave enough to give up the job in advance, because I couldn't believe it."

Her inability to credit such good fortune remained in her eyes; that and the new pain of realizing she'd been correct to proceed with caution. "I mean, I couldn't believe he loved me. And," she finished briskly, "it turns out he didn't. He caved in to Hector, and if he would do that he's no good to me."

A car pulled in. The driver, a woman, remained behind the wheel. "That's my ride," Ginger told us as it arrived. "To the new job interview. I have to go."

She pulled on a battered old sheepskin jacket. I'd seen it in the thrift shop in Eastport a few weeks earlier.

"The jacket looks great on you." It did, too; some people redeem their clothes, and Ginger was one of them. The messed-up hand and leg were just things she carried around; in every other way she seemed one of the healthier and more resilient women I'd ever met.

And among the best at facing hard truths. She beamed briefly at the compliment. "Yeah, huh? And it's warm. Okay, I'm coming," she called toward the waiting car when its horn tooted gently in summons.

"How exactly did Hector scare your boyfriend off?" I asked as she moved away from us. Because I thought she did know. Two young lovers, telling one another everything as lovers tended to do . . . it didn't make sense that she wouldn't.

Her gait, the kick-forward-and-lock stride of the practiced prosthetic-wearer, was painful to see. Not for esthetic reasons; the woman was too damned gorgeous for her looks to be spoiled by that. But it hurt. You could see it in her face: every step shot a zing of anguish through her.

"What'd Hector have on him?" I persisted.

She stopped, her back still turned to me. Her torso shifted under the reindeer sweater, to ease itself in the brace I suddenly realized she must be wearing.

"I don't know," she repeated stubbornly. "I just know it was something. And Mr. Gosling must have known that it would work, because the day after Mark broke off our engagement Mr. Gosling didn't try to make *me* break it off anymore. He just didn't talk about it, so I knew he knew already. And . . . he had the look on his face."

She didn't have to explain. I'd heard somebody say once that Hector Gosling's *gotcha* look was like the face of an evil tomcat after it had just finished eating up all the canaries. He looked especially satisfied, the person had gone on to say, if they were your *favorite* canaries.

The person being George. "Anyway, I have to go," Ginger said. She made her way to the passenger side of the car, a white sedan with the name of a local health agency on the door.

"How'd Siss Moore know about it?" I asked.

"Mr. Gosling probably bragged about it," Ginger replied at once.

Bingo; that was Hector, all right. "Mark hasn't been back? You haven't seen him or heard from him since the phone call?"

By now I was convinced of one thing, anyway. Ginger hadn't hauled Hector from where he'd been killed, up a ladder and into a hidden room. She had enough trouble just hauling herself around.

"No. I haven't heard from him and don't want to. I won't put myself in the position of being let down again."

She got herself into the car and slammed the door hard as if to punctuate her final statement. It backed out the drive and was gone, leaving us standing outside Ginger's beat-up trailer.

Which turned out to be her mistake. For all her I'll-do-it-myself-dammit demeanor, the grit and solitariness that must have been at times terribly lonely, even her caution in love . . .

For all of that, she was too trusting.

She had believed that once she left, we'd go too. Wrong.

"Listen, you got me out here," I told a reluctant Ellie as I fiddled with the lock on Ginger's door. "And now that I am here, there's something I want to know."

It was the kind of setup that if you turned the knob from inside, it unlocked: a safety feature unless you were a burglar.

But if you were one, it was a convenience feature. I pulled the oblong plastic tab that held my movie-rental bar code from my wallet and weaseled it in between the door and the doorjamb.

"And she's not coming back soon, so stop worrying about it," I said. "That girl wouldn't miss a job interview if someone cut her other leg off."

Ellie glanced nervously around the trailer's clearing, gold leaves carpeting the raggedy grass areas and more floating down. The silence was amazing. Only the rippledy-slap of waves against the dock broke the autumn serenity.

"Jake, we're breaking into her place, for heaven's sake. We can't just . . ."

179

"Baloney and cheese," I reminded her, "on Wonder Bread. And it's jail food so it's *processed* cheese. With a packet of yellow mustard. Those potato chips are rubbery and the instant coffee is barely lukewarm, with that white powder floating on it."

Ellie's face hardened before I finished speaking. "Just get the damn door open," she told me.

I wiggled the plastic bar-code tab again. There was a metal strip over the opening between door and frame but it had been pried at in the past, maybe before Ginger owned the trailer, so it offered the lock-set no protection.

The lock popped with a soft *chuck!* and the door swung wide.

"In like Flynn," I announced. "Come on."

Ellie followed and I shut the door behind us, noticing that the yellow cat had slipped in too. "Now, where is it?"

I looked around at the toy-sized sink and stove, the box refrigerator, a tiny seating area, and a bath hardly bigger than an airliner restroom plus a curtained sleeping bunk at the rear.

Where was the damned computer? Of course she would have one, I'd concluded after seeing the chess-dedicated one on the porch, and despite the cost I was willing to bet she was online. E-mail and chat rooms are the default social life of your standard Lonely Guy.

Or Girl. "There." I located the very basic but serviceable machine in the corner of the small living area, fired it up, and clicked the dial-up icon. A minute later a list of recent e-mails scrolled down the screen.

"Okay." There were a bunch from someone named Mark. I doubted there were two important men named Mark in Ginger's life. Ellie watched over my shoulder as I moved the mouse across the pad and clicked on the most recent e-mail, dated the previous night.

Before I could read it, though, a noise came from outside. It could have been the wind rustling the few remaining leaves in the birch trees or someone on the gravel path leading down to the dock and the lake.

But it wasn't. It was that damned little white sedan that I'd promised Ellie wouldn't come back, turning into the driveway.

I stabbed the power switch on the computer, grabbed Ellie, and we booked out of there so fast that by the time the car made it to the clearing we were in my own car with the engine started.

"Forget something?" I asked as Ginger got out of the sedan. Hey, the best defense and all that.

She eyed us both questioningly. "My job application. I left it in a desk drawer. Did you want something else?"

Translation: *What the hell are you still doing here?* But I'd learned long ago from Jemmy Wechsler what to say when my hand got caught near the cookie jar.

Never apologize; never explain. "No. We were just leaving."

Ginger stood watching as I backed around the sedan and out the drive. I was nearly to the paved road when she finally turned and went on into the trailer.

"Did we lock it on our way out?" Ellie asked me.

I headed back toward Eastport. "Uh-huh."

"Okay, then. Maybe she won't notice."

"That we were in there? Oh, she'll notice."

I drove a little faster. Ginger said she hadn't heard from this Mark guy she'd been engaged to. But she had, and though she couldn't haul Hector's body around, he probably could.

Now I needed to find out what Hector Gosling had held over Mark Timberlake, and when Mark's ship had last visited Eastport.

"I don't see why she should notice," Ellie objected. "I know you didn't shut the computer down. So it'll go through its disk-checking routine when she starts it again. But maybe she'll just think *she*—"

"Shut it down wrong last time? Maybe."

I'd done it myself: snapped the switch off absent-mindedly, not going through the steps the computer instructions prescribed. And I'd been surprised the next time I turned the computer on to realize I'd made this error.

"But that's not how she'll know. Think about it, Ellie. What's the last thing you saw just now?"

"Oh," she said. "We let . . ."

"Right. So we know she lied. But she also *knows* we know."

Because the last thing we'd seen as we backed away from the trailer was the grin on the face of the cat that Ginger had left outdoors.

Sitting in the window, licking its paw, behaving for all the world as if it belonged there. *Inside.*

Damn.

On the way home Ellie said she was okay, but she looked just awful. "Look," I said as we got into town, "you've got to rest. I know you feel you need to do more, but—"

"I'll make you a deal," she interrupted. "I'll rest if you do something by yourself."

It occurred to me that maybe I wasn't the only one thinking about how things would change once the baby was here.

"All right," I said. "What?"

We drove down Washington Street past the massive granite Post Office building, turned left. "I want you to talk to Jimmy Condon and ask him where he was on Friday night. Get him by himself and ask him, and where Maria was, too."

"And he'll tell me because . . . ?"

"Because you'll tell him you're asking for me."

I glanced at her, surprised. "Ellie, is there something I ought to know?"

We pulled up in front of her house. "I went to

high school with Jimmy," she said. "And that's all I'm going to tell you now, because I promised him I never would."

She looked down at her hands. "But he'll probably tell you. Find him, Jake. We have to know if we can rule Jimmy and Maria out or not."

Exasperation took hold of me. "Ellie, what if Jimmy just lies? There's no reason to think he'll tell me the truth."

"Then you'll know that. Jimmy's got a ticker-tape across his forehead, what he thinks in words of one syllable on it. You'll know."

"Okay," I said reluctantly. "I still don't get it, but if that's what you want . . ."

"It is. I'd go with you but I can't. Because you're right, I really do have to lie down." She put her hand on my arm. "We already know Ginger's not telling us the truth. I want to find out if we have to go after Jimmy too. Or instead."

Her face said she hoped we didn't have to investigate her old friend any further. It also said clearly that if she didn't decide to get horizontal soon, her body would make the decision for her.

"All right," I said a final time, and sat there watching to make sure she got inside the house. Then I drove away.

But I couldn't find Jimmy immediately because I'd told Victor that I needed to see him that afternoon and he'd said he'd come. So I went home to wait for him and when I got there, the message light was blinking on my phone machine.

Oh, terrific. I pressed the message button.

"Ms. Tiptree, this is Assistant U.S. Attorney Peter Farrell in New York. I'd appreciate your contacting me at your earliest convenience."

My outgoing message didn't mention my name. So Farrell knew who I was, where I was, and probably also what I was. Or at any rate what I'd been back when Jemmy Wechsler and I were a Gotham duo.

The call confirmed what I'd been expecting, that my name had come up in Jemmy's case. And the last time I looked, prosecutors didn't phone people to ask if they'd like to appear for the defense.

So just as I'd suspected, the choice Farrell had lined up for me was clear. I could testify against Jemmy and walk away. Or I could fail to cooperate and let the government try to build a second case.

Against me. Which by itself might not be so bad; I'd always been careful to stay on the right side of the law myself. So they wouldn't have a lot of leverage to turn me against Jemmy.

But that wasn't the problem. The problem was that compared to my father, Jemmy Wechsler was small potatoes.

Pondering this I hauled my tools and a fresh tin of paint stripper up two flights of stairs to the third floor. I couldn't hear the door from there but I would know if Victor came in; the hairs on my neck would bristle like porcupine quills.

185

My work area was a big whitewashed room with no curtains, just a wall of bare windows facing south. A paneled door lay flat across two sawhorses in the pale yellow light; over the course of a few days I'd put two coats of stripper on it already, removing most of the many coats of paint it had gotten in its lifetime.

But to keep your hands busy during a session of thinking, there's nothing like yet another application of paint stripper so strong that if you spill some, it will eat a hole right through the floor.

I popped a CD into the player I kept up there. Golden light washed the room as k.d. Lang's smoky voice drifted into it.

"Save me," she sang as I opened the paint stripper and began applying it. But you could hear in her voice she wasn't expecting much action on her request.

Me, either. Slopping on the paint stripper, I realized again that in the getting-saved department I was running on empty.

In the old days it would have been easy. I'd have called one of my fat-cat clients and pulled in a tiny favor. Doctor, lawyer, Indian chief; Jemmy had led them all into my plush-carpeted reception area where they'd sat with their hands in their laps as if waiting for a session with the dentist.

After the introductions Jemmy would slip into the shadows again, eliminating the embarrassment his presence might cause if anyone saw them

186

together; these guys couldn't afford even a whiff of scandal and Jemmy was a snootful. Only the hope of a solution to their money troubles could have gotten any of them onto the same city block as my mobbed-up friend, much less into the same office.

In short, Jemmy knew everyone. But only I knew that fact, and I never told. For one thing, no one would've believed me; if for instance I linked him to the scion of one of the nation's most celebrated clans.

Or to the scion's . . . well, never mind which relative it was, but when she told me how much that little gigolo had gotten out of her I'd nearly fainted. Then I'd called one of my other clients; forty-eight hours later, the money had been recovered and the gigolo was in jail on unrelated charges.

But that was in the old days when the lips of the fellows I dealt with were greasy with the fat of the land. The only thing they'd feared was anyone learning how they'd met me at all. And because they feared so little I needed my own protection against them. Who knew when one of them would try to use me for a bargaining chip somehow, in some deal I didn't want to even try imagining?

So in the eye of the pyramid on the dollar bill framed on my office wall, there was a camera. It took a snapshot of everyone entering my office with Jemmy, recording an association they'd have denied with their dying breaths. My stash of old mug shots couldn't help me now, though.

Revealing that I had them might get Jemmy out of a jam—I knew for a fact some of my old clients had leverage in Federal circles—but for me it would already be too late. Federal investigators interested in me would've taken note of the people around me, too, whether I was cooperative or not.

So it was obvious what I needed to do. I just wouldn't enjoy doing it. Telling my fugitive father, I mean, that he had to go. Leave Eastport, maybe see me again and maybe not.

Hit the road, Jack. And the sooner the better.

"Rat poison really only comes in two varieties," said Victor an hour later.

I already knew this. But I'd asked him over here to get some information from him, and when you want information from Victor you have to listen to what *he* wants to say, first.

And at the moment due to recent local events he was hot on poisons. "You've got your coumarin-based compounds, warfarin, the blood thinners. Animal leaves the premises searching for water. Dies outdoors."

He had another swallow of wine. "Then there are convulsants. Strychnine's one. You've got to catch 'em within minutes of their ingesting the substance. People, the accidental poisoning cases, I mean."

More old news. But he was getting up a head

of instructional steam. No sense knocking the train off the track.

". . . Catch 'em fast, charcoal lavage. You pump a slurry of the charcoal into the gut, it absorbs some of the poison. Pump it out again, support all the vital signs meanwhile, maybe you've given yourself half a chance. But . . ."

He wagged a warning finger at me. Once upon a time if he'd done that I'd have bitten it off.

But he had been on a fairly decent run of behavior recently. So I just thought about biting it off.

"But it's not often a strychnine victim even makes it that far. Strychnine gets absorbed fast," he continued.

"Is there an antidote?"

He shook his head. "Treatment's supportive. Anticonvulsant drugs, try to keep 'em alive until basically the stuff's excreted and the effect wears off. Which," he added, "is why it's become a registry-only substance."

I raised an eyebrow, which was all he ever needed. He moved along in his lecture, which was what *I* needed.

"The bottom line is, you've got to be registered to buy or use it," he said. "But there used to be products you could buy."

He refilled his glass. "I saw this case back in the city once, kid got hold of an old mole-bait from back in the fifties. Mole-Gone, I think it was called, and it was for putting into mole burrows in gardens and parks and so on."

189

He frowned, remembering. "I guess it had been sitting in a cabinet for years and the kid just found it. The trouble was, the bait was made by mixing strychnine powder with peanut butter."

He drank. "That was one we didn't have a happy outcome on."

When Sam was a small child he'd associated the skull and crossbones from poison labels with a cartoon character he enjoyed at the time, called Happy the Pirate. And when I learned of this I went a bit overboard in reindoctrinating him. As a result, for years he was terrified not only of pirates but also of parrots, eye-patches, hoop earrings, and anything else that buckled even the faintest swash.

Funny the things that pop into your head when you're sitting with the only other person in the world who remembers them, too. Time to change the subject.

"Do you know Ginger Tolliver?" I asked.

Ginger was an attractive young woman who lived in the same time zone as Victor. So it was highly unlikely his babe-radar hadn't registered her. But probably he knew Ginger for another reason as well.

"I met her today," I went on, "and I'm curious. She seems quite pain-afflicted. Mostly from her back, I guess, even though it's the thing that shows least."

The taut, controlled lines of her face rose in my mind. Just looking at her, you knew she was in

190

the kind of chronic pain that would have most people incapacitated.

"Yet she says she has to work. So I wondered . . ."

Victor was nodding. "She's disabled, just based on her pain," he confirmed. "I did the physical. Prescribed her the painkillers too, but she won't take them."

I blinked. This was more information than I'd expected him to offer, based on patient confidentiality.

"It's no secret," he added, understanding my look. "Ginger told me I could shout it from the rooftops if I wanted. If maybe it could help her disability case. But it hasn't."

I sat down, poured my own glass of wine. It was always good to have something in the emotional bank account with Victor. The memory of ten friendly minutes, for instance, so that next time he morphed into Doctor Doom I wouldn't strangle him on the spot.

"So she's not on disability," I mused.

"Too young, and she was out of work for a couple years after the car accident. So she doesn't have enough credits."

Enough calendar-quarters with the minimum income, he meant; it was the other thing besides a work-preventing ailment that you needed in order to receive Social Security disability payments.

"Criminy," I said, "can't work so you can't collect,

can't work so you can't qualify to collect. Don't you hate that?"

He nodded and for a moment we were unified in dismay. I used to see these problems all the time when I worked pro bono for an agency back in the city, and Victor faced it regularly at his clinic.

Then I thought of something else. "How did the car accident happen?"

He looked surprised. "You didn't know? Ginger's mother used to be Hector Gosling's secretary. They were on the way to a title search in Machias, Ginger in the backseat."

Uh-oh. Was that another motive rearing its ugly kisser?

"So he was behind the wheel that day?" I said. "And I guess his driving skills couldn't have been much good, even back then."

Stories abounded of Hector driving in the same damn-the-torpedoes manner in which he did everything else, with complacent disregard for any obstacle in his all-important way.

"Coming into Whiting, that long set of curves?" Victor said.

Whiting was a village on Route 1 about halfway to Machias. In its vicinity, thirty-year-old drivers did seventy and the seventy-year-olds did thirty, which to my mind was like putting the tortoise and the hare in a face-off and giving them bazookas.

"Passed on a curve," Victor said. "Hit a town

truck loaded with sand. Surprised me that Ginger would have worked for him."

"She has trouble getting work at all. Maybe Hector's the only one who'd hire her? Off the books, too, I'll bet, so she's not getting any benefits or Social Security contributions."

"Could be. And from what I've heard of Hector Gosling that's a situation he would enjoy."

"It is obvious how much she hated him. I thought it was on account of him getting between her and her boyfriend."

But now her lasting injuries from the accident provided yet another reason. "What happened," I asked, "to Ginger's mother?"

"Dead at the scene," Victor replied.

Correction: two more reasons.

"Hector was about to ruin Jimmy Condon's life, and he'd already done a number on Ginger's," I told Will Bonnet later when he stopped in to borrow an extension cord.

He was headed to Harlequin House to clean up some debris the other volunteers had left. Finding Jan Jesperson's body instead of only hearing about it, as with Hector's, had put a damper not only on lunch but on the historical society's enthusiasm for the fix-up project.

With Will were two other helpers he'd found. One was skinny and scraggly with dirty-blond hair in a ponytail and front teeth that stuck out like a pair of half-raised light switches; the other was beetle-browed and obviously not the sharpest pin in the cushion.

"Hey," Will told me, "that's good. That means George isn't the only one who really hated the old guy."

I was putting pieces of leftover pot roast through a grinder to make shepherd's pie. Wade wouldn't be home tonight but Sam would—his father, not surprisingly, had backed out on their dinner date— and Tommy was staying too. Now the boys were in the dining room switching Sam's gears from algebra to geometry.

And I still had Jimmy Condon on my agenda, all of which made me wonder why I'd ever thought moving to Maine would be a stress reliever.

"Yes, it provides other motives," I agreed with Will. "What it doesn't tell us is who else could've got hold of something as difficult to buy as strychnine powder."

That was the other information Victor had supplied on his visit; that in addition to confirming the time range of Hector's death, the autopsy had also confirmed the cause.

The scraggly helper with the ponytail had been slouched in the hall, studying his boots. Now he perked up. "Half a' the old barns an' sheds around here prob'ly got a can of it stuck away," he said, "from back when you could buy it legal." This guy looked as if he had a passing acquaintance with old barns and sheds, likely from sleeping in them.

194

"George got his from Cory, the guy with pigs," Will added. "Cory identified the can, he told me. Had it out in *his* shed."

"Yeah," the scraggly guy put in. "Cory didn't like the idea, using it himself. Scared of it. But you know George."

Right; everyone did. If he thought he could earn an honest dollar at it, George would pack his pockets with nitroglycerine.

The beetle-browed guy spoke up. "Old man Gosling had some."

I turned, surprised. "How do you know?"

Massive shrug. "Did yard work for him. Went in for a drink a'water, saw the can, his garage shelf. My name's Ronny Ronaldson and I can read," the fellow added to me with soft pride.

"I'm sure you can," I responded, not knowing what else to say. His happiness at this accomplishment seemed to spur him on.

"You remember," Ronny added to the scraggly guy, "when Jimmy Condon was findin' work for me. That's when. Jimmy," he finished ponderously, "he's a good guy. Cuts down trees."

"Yes." So Jimmy might have known about the poison, too, and Ginger probably would have because she also worked in Hector's house.

"That reminds me," Will told me. "I need to get hold of some syrup of ipecac. You happen to know where I can get some?"

"Um, yeah," I said. Before I'd so cruelly abolished Sam's love for the skull-and-crossbones character,

I'd put a bottle of ipecac in every room in the apartment.

"Because," Will explained, "I'm making a first-aid kit. With Agnes, you never know what might happen. I want to be prepared."

Back when Sam was at the stage of putting everything in his mouth and if possible swallowing it, ipecac had made sense; it caused your stomach to eject whatever you'd eaten. And Agnes did seem to be regressing to the toddler stage.

"Drugstore," I said to Will. "It's over-the-counter stuff, you won't need a prescription for it. But if you don't mind a secondhand bottle you don't have to buy any. I've got some."

Two bottles, actually. Despite Sam's having become much more choosy about what he ingested, Victor had sent them to me along with many other first-aid supplies soon after we had moved here. He also sent me a dozen roses with the heads cut off, but that's another story.

"Take one," I told Will, waving at the tin box on the shelf in the hall. "If I need two bottles I'm in worse trouble than any first aid can fix, anyway."

He helped himself, then hoisted the orange coil of heavy-duty extension cord on his shoulder. "Come on, guys, if we want to get out fishing yet today, we'd better hustle it up."

Then, turning to me, "After I finish up at Harlequin House I'll be taking a look at one of the storefronts on Water Street."

For his planned restaurant, he meant. Ellie said it was all he talked about when he was with her. Personally, I thought if he couldn't keep bones out of his fish and dishes from exploding over warming flames, Will might want to go slow in the doing-it-professionally department.

In addition, that is, to my other doubts about the project. "After *that,* we're going out fishing," he concluded.

"On," the big slow guy informed me delightedly, "a boat!"

Will smiled. "Yeah, Ronny, on a boat. George's been letting me borrow it," he added to me. "And Ellie says it's okay with her, so . . ."

He shrugged. "Hey, I gotta reward these guys somehow. Tell Ellie I'll check in on her later, will you?"

"Fine," I replied, just as happy to see the three of them go. I still had the vegetables to chop for shepherd's pie and somehow I didn't think doing it with a steak knife was going to meet Will's food preparation standards, dish explosions or no dish explosions.

But just then Tommy came into the kitchen, maybe for a soda or some milk. It could have been anything. Whatever he'd wanted, though, he didn't want it anymore once he'd spotted the scraggly guy.

"Hey," the guy said lazily, his close-set eyes narrowing in sly recognition. "How're ya' doin', kid?"

"Okay." Tommy's face looked suddenly carved of stone as he turned and walked out.

The scraggly guy chuckled. "Kid don't like me. Thinks he's better'n everybody, is that kid's trouble."

He pulled a cigarette from the off-brand pack in his shirt pocket. "Don't light it in here, please," I said automatically.

He shot an unfriendly look at me, then tucked it away. "Kid had better be careful when his uncle gets out," he observed.

Perry Daigle, he meant. His voice took on an ugly edge. "All Perry wanted was his stuff out of the house. He shows up, that kid there goes and calls the cops on that bogus violation-of-protection beef the old lady's got goin'. Next thing, Perry's got ninety days on a DUI he had pending. You want to tell me that was accidental? Wasn't fair. Perry's all right."

All of which reminded me of the charming company George must be enjoying, locked up with Perry and a bunch of other roughnecks as bad or worse.

"Come on, guys," Will said hastily with an apologetic glance at me. "Better get a move on. We don't want to be out on that bay after dark if we know what's good for us."

He urged the other two out ahead of him. "Sorry about that," he said when they were gone. "Weasel's kind of a jerk."

"Weasel? Perfect name for him." I was annoyed.

Will shrugged. "Wesley's his real name. Wesley Bodine. Don't worry, I won't bring him around anymore."

He really seemed sorry. So I accepted his apology and he left, too, promising to return the cord to me as soon as he finished with it.

Then I returned to my original project: grinding up the pot roast. But shortly thereafter I heard an astonishing *thump!* from the dining room, and a half-sobbed curse.

Rushing in, I found Tommy alone, cradling his right hand. And from the bloody mark on the old gold-medallion wallpaper I knew what must have happened.

He'd slammed his fist into the wall. For Tommy, it was an unthinkable outburst. "Hey, you okay?"

"Yeah. I'm great." He sank into a chair, dropped his injured hand into his lap, and with the other hand began sullenly drawing on a scrap of cardboard with his protractor. The point hadn't yet gone through the cardboard into the table but it was about to.

"Watch out for the tabletop," I cautioned him gently.

In response he snapped it closed one-handed and dropped it into its small black fake-leather case. It was the kind of kid he was, that he still had his high-school math-class protractor in good order and in its original box.

"Anything I can do?" I asked. His knuckles were ballooning.

He shook his head. "They should keep him in jail a hundred years. But they're so *stupid,* they'll let *him* out."

Perry Daigle was himself so dumb that in his defense on the assault charge he'd told the judge how Tommy's mom needed someone to keep her in line now that her husband was dead.

Tommy's father having been no prize either. Sam appeared in the door with the book he'd apparently gone to fetch. "Hey, what happened?"

"Tommy's had a little mishap. Get a towel with some ice in it, please," I said.

Take your time, I added with my eyes. Sam nodded and went.

"But they'll put *George* in jail," Tommy went on grievingly.

A thought struck me. "Tommy? Do you have something to tell me? Maybe *you* know what George was doing when Hector was killed?"

He shook his head mutely, turned his tear-streaked face to me. "No. I don't know what he was doing; I wish I did."

He knew something, though; that the world was a hard, unjust place where the good guys didn't always win. I wasn't sure why the people who'd already absorbed that information always seemed to be the ones getting new lessons forced on them.

People like Tommy, for instance, with his sociopathic uncle eternally poised to deliver a two-fisted refresher course and the one guy who'd always been in Tommy's corner locked up, unable to help.

Because George was refusing to alibi himself. And the biggest question was still . . . *why?*

CHAPTER 7

It was late afternoon when I finally set off to find Jimmy Condon, crossing the causeway and turning south on Route 1 in the already fading light.

Purple shadows gathered along the east side of the road as I reached the turnoff to Cooper and began the long winding climb uphill past houses, sheds, and barns. Some places had the cabs of eighteen-wheelers parked in their driveways; others featured homemade signs advertising smoked salmon, lawn mower repair, or quilts.

Past the corner store in Meddybemps, the road turned sharply and crossed the old railroad right-of-way. The last locomotive was no more than a memory now. A few hundred yards later the rusty blade of a bucksaw nailed to a tree stump marked the dirt rut leading up to the mill.

When I pulled in, Jimmy Condon was coming out of the old red trailer that served for an office. Whole trunks of trees in a pile higher than the trailer made a wall on one side of the yard, while the cutting apparatus made a boundary on the other.

If Will Bonnet looked like the Hollywood version of Paul Bunyan, Jimmy was the ox, a massive man with a big head, enormous shoulders, and hands the size of Ping-Pong paddles. But he wasn't so big, I noted automatically, that he couldn't have fit through that trapdoor in Harlequin House.

I got out of the car, bending to pat a yellow dog wiggling up to me in happy welcome. Jimmy pulled his gloves off and came over too.

"H'lo, Jacobia. What brings you way out here?"

"Hi, Jimmy," I replied, remembering what George said about him once, that he was the kind of guy who made "simple" into a compliment. Hard work and straight answers were Jimmy's stock-in-trade; for one thing, he wasn't equipped for anything else.

On the other hand, if Maria was the brains of the pair, Jimmy was the heart. "I came because Ellie asked me to," I told him.

The sun was on the horizon, pouring red-gold light onto the carpet of sawdust covering the yard. No sense wasting time. "She said if I told you I was here on her behalf, you'd tell me what I need to know."

His brow furrowed. "She did, huh? You talked to Maria yet?"

"Yes, Jimmy, we did. Maria says you were playing poker with your friends on Friday night, and she was at a school thing."

Jimmy received this information impassively.

203

"Uh-huh." You could see the gears of his mind turning over slowly as he lined up what he should say. "That's right," he offered at last.

"But Jimmy," I went on, "Ellie says that might not be so."

His eyes met mine, gentle but implacable. "I don't remember. If Maria says that's what happened . . ."

"Jimmy. She's in trouble, Ellie is, and I'm trying to get her out of it. Her and George both. But I'm not interested in getting you into any. Now, Ellie wouldn't tell me anything about why she thought you might help her. She says she promised you she wouldn't."

His lips pressed together. Then he said, "Yeah. Ellie keeps promises. She always did, even back in school. You could talk to Ellie."

"I know. And what I'm telling you is, I keep them too. Exactly the way Ellie does. Whatever you were doing, as long as it doesn't have anything to do with Hector Gosling, I'll never tell a soul. But Jimmy, I need to know. Ellie needs to."

He looked away. "Please, Jimmy," I said.

He didn't like it. But the mention of Ellie had set other wheels turning in that big head of his. "You better come inside."

In the trailer all vestiges of domesticity had been stripped away and replaced by pure, uncosmetic functionality. Insulation strips covered the walls, holes knifed in it around the windows. The floor was plywood stained black in the traffic areas, chairs and a table rejects from a landfill. A utility lamp on an orange cord was the only light.

Jimmy waved a big hand at a rickety wooden chair; I sat. "You can't tell," he impressed heavily upon me. "Maria doesn't want it getting around. She says it would be real bad for business." His gaze darkened. "She'd be mad, she knew I told."

"All right. Then she won't find out." If, I added mentally, it's not George's get-out-of-jail-free card.

"Ellie tell you about when that Sally was spreading all her stories? Said I stole from her?" His chin thrust out mutinously.

"She told me. But what about it? And what's that got to do with . . ."

"Maria got mad then too. Said I was dumb. Said I should've known better. But it was only scrap wood."

His eyes met mine in appeal. "No one else had use for it."

"I understand." The dog had come in with us; now it put its muzzle in Jimmy's lap, its tail wagging anxiously.

He smoothed its head. "I didn't know what to do. But back in school I used to ask Ellie and she would tell me. So when Maria wouldn't stop being mad . . ."

The light dawned. "You asked your old friend what to do."

He nodded in misery. The light streaming in

through the windows went suddenly grey as the sun dropped below the horizon.

"Ellie said wait a while, and if that didn't fix it, maybe Maria and me should go to, like, a marriage doctor," he told me.

"A marriage counselor." At that, all became clear. "So you suggested that to Maria?"

Oh, you big lummox, I thought. You big brave lug. Going to a marriage counselor for a guy like Jimmy Condon would've been like sailing off over the horizon to an unknown world.

And his buddies would have a field day with it. "Uh-huh. She wouldn't, but then I found a free one. In Ellsworth, far away, so nobody would find out about it."

"And that's where you and Maria were on Friday."

He nodded, and it began to make sense. Not only was marriage counseling dandy gossip fodder, Maria would also have another reason for keeping it quiet. Partnerships have a harder time getting business loans if the lending institutions think the partners might be breaking up.

"Yeah," Jimmy said. "We were there. Maria's real mad about the land deal we might've lost, too. Said if I hadn't dragged my feet on it, Hector never would've had the chance to put his oar in."

He sighed heavily. "Started out early, got back pretty late. Bring a cold supper along, so we don't spend on anything but the gas, and Porter sleeps most of the way, so that's good. I don't know," he added stolidly, "if it's working."

He stood up. "I'm not as smart as she is. That makes it hard for her, I guess."

A racehorse hitched to a plow horse; no, it probably wasn't easy. But as Ellie had said, Jimmy did have a ticker tape across his forehead; he was telling me the truth.

He pulled his gloves back on. "She figures she made a mistake marrying me. Going to try to make the best of it now that we have our boy. But it's not easy being what somebody is trying to make the best of."

"No. No, I suppose it's not."

Or eating your potato skins while you're doing it, either, I thought as I drove away. All in all, it was a sorry little peek into someone else's life that I could have done without, and as I headed home it only emphasized what, unhappily, I already knew: that behind the drawn curtains of the warmly lit houses I passed, anything could be happening.

"Hey, you know George," Sam said later at the dining room table. "He probably just thinks it's nobody's business where he was or what he was doing."

He dug into the seafood casserole, chock-full of scallops, shrimp, and other tasty morsels. "Wow, this looks great. Thanks, Will."

I picked a piece of crab shell from between my

teeth as unnoticeably as possible. It was eight in the evening, the house was full, and we weren't having shepherd's pie after all because Will came back unexpectedly from his fishing trip laden with provisions for a seafood feast. And apparently he'd made other stops along the way, because you couldn't catch oysters in Passamaquoddy Bay and you surely couldn't hook beluga caviar.

Clarissa Arnold took a sip of her champagne, another of Will's contributions to the meal. "Well, if that's it," she replied to Sam's theory, "he's being a fool."

Clarissa looked as usual as if she'd stepped from the pages of *Lawyer's Quarterly:* low black heels, straight black skirt that ended chastely at the middle of her slim knee, a silk cable-knit sweater in a dark shade of old gold, plus a cashmere jacket.

"They're not messing around," she added, meaning the state people arraying themselves for George's prosecution. "I'd say he has very little delay time before this gets bumped up to Superior Court. And at that point I won't be able to yank him out again, like a rabbit out of a hat."

She looked around at us. "George needs," she emphasized, "to speak up for himself."

"Does he know that?" Ellie asked. She was drinking ginger ale; me, too, in sympathy with her. "Really *know* it?"

An impatient frown creased Clarissa's forehead. "I've spelled it out for him in terms even a child could understand."

Her own little boy was still in Kennebunk with his dad and their extended family; she'd only come up for the evening to talk with Ellie, bring her up to speed.

"If Bob were here . . ." I began.

"No," Clarissa said firmly. "I'm sure he'd be pleased by your faith in him, Jacobia, but it would take someone bigger than Eastport's police chief to fix this. George doesn't only need a character reference. He needs an *alibi*. And it still looks like he's the only one who can supply it. Because—"

"Because he's protecting someone," Will Bonnet cut in. "That's it, isn't it? George is keeping his mouth shut on account of someone else."

There was grit in the stuffing of the clams casino. But Will had worked so hard to prepare this dinner—even people in bad trouble needed nourishment, he insisted, and he wanted us to keep our strength up—that I ate them anyway, chewing carefully so as not to fracture any fillings.

Ellie nodded emphatically. "George would rather choke on his own spit than betray a friend. I'll bet you're right, Will."

"But Ellie," I objected. "That makes no sense. With the baby coming, or even without, you don't believe he'd go to prison just so a murderer could go free, do you?"

"No, no. Of course he wouldn't protect the actual murderer." She waved a toast round loaded with caviar to make her point.

She'd said she wasn't hungry but the stuff was

209

so delicious she ended up eating it, and some casserole too, a little pile of crab shell and other inedibles heaped at the side of her plate.

"But obviously George was with *some*one, doing *some*thing. And if that someone could get in trouble for whatever it was . . ."

"He doesn't want to put some other guy in the soup. So he's waiting for the guy to speak up. But if he does, this guy maybe catches some sort of rap, himself?" Will asked thoughtfully.

Sam took a bite of casserole, winced and extracted something into his napkin. "That sure sounds like George, all right," he said, after having a sip of water.

"I wish I'd been around that night," Will went on. "If I had, we'd probably have been together. But no, I had to be in Boston on business," he castigated himself. "Wasn't even a big deal . . . hell, why did I have to pick *that* night?"

"What business?" Tommy Pockets inquired interestedly, which was encouraging. He'd been silent all evening.

"Talking to a guy about supplying fish for the restaurant," Will replied genially.

That again. But hey, it was his money. "And picking up the ingredients for all this while I was at it," he went on.

Including the imported caviar, I supposed, tiny beads of glorious subtlety that popped with a sweet-salt burst. I felt guilty eating it, knowing it cost a fortune, but I couldn't resist. For one thing, it had no grit or shell bits in it.

"You left Agnes alone?" Ellie asked Will. Trust her to think of this. In response, he looked properly embarrassed.

"I shouldn't have, probably. But the guy I needed to see was on his way out of town. And Aunt Agnes sleeps through the night. Turned out okay, but I did feel kind of bad about it."

"Next time ask one of us," Ellie suggested kindly, and he agreed to.

"Can we get back to the subject here?" Clarissa interrupted, still focused on George. "If he is protecting someone, he needs to figure out whose tail he wants caught in the door. His own or someone else's, whose ideas of loyalty obviously don't match his."

I couldn't think of anyone whose loyalty matched George's, except maybe all the Knights of the Round Table put together.

Which brought me to a new thought. "There might be another possibility," I said slowly. "Maybe he thinks we'll straighten it out. Ellie and me."

Once it was out of my mouth I thought it could actually be true. "We've done it before," I added a little defensively, at Clarissa's skeptical look. "Snooped around in deaths that were, um, unexpected, and been able to figure out . . ."

"Whodunnit?" This was news to Will, clearly. "Wow, you mean you two . . ." He looked at each of us. "Hey, I'm impressed."

Clarissa wasn't. "Whatever." She brushed the notion off. "What I'm saying is that if something else factual doesn't come up, he's going to trial for it."

"But," Will objected strenuously, "it's all circumstantial as it is. There's no witness to say—"

"Right." She batted his remark away, too. "But they've got strychnine out of George's work area and they've got people who heard him say he'd gladly murder Gosling if he could find a good method. And he had a motive to kill Jan also, since George thought she and Hector were in it against George's aunt together."

She took a breath. "Jan was probably strangled, by the way. The knife was postmortem. Marks on her neck, not extensive but they were there according to the preliminary medical report."

She paused, thinking. "I'm going to have questions for all of you individually as we go on. But for now, just for my own reference, when's the last time anyone here saw Hector Gosling?"

Sam looked blank. "Don't know. Not for a long time."

An odd expression flitted across Tommy's face in the moment before he spoke. "Last week, maybe? At the gas station."

I hadn't seen Hector at all lately but Will had. "Friday at around two," he said without hesitation. "I was headed out of town, he was on his way in. I might not have noticed it was even him, but he was passing some other guy on a curve, I had to pull halfway onto the shoulder." Will grimaced. "Bat out of hell as usual, and that big

212

ugly kisser of his hunched over the steering wheel," he said.

Ellie spoke reluctantly. "I haven't seen him. But he called me. The day before we found him. Around three in the afternoon."

About the time George had gone off everyone's radar. I turned to Ellie in surprise. "You didn't tell me Hector'd called you. What did he say?"

She bit her lip. "I didn't want to tell anyone. And I don't know what he wanted. When I saw it was his number on the caller ID box, I picked up the phone and put it down again. I didn't say anything to him, and he didn't get the chance to say anything to me. He'd already said plenty."

"He'd called before?" But of course he had. The foul-mouthed harangue was among Hector's best-known conversational strategies.

Will was already nodding agreement. "Harassing them. He'd been doing it awhile. Telling George he'd better stop talking about him or else, George told me. Not specific threats, just playing the heavy as per usual."

I'd been a victim of it myself once, after opposing Hector's plan to build a cinder-block dwelling for the residents of the poor farm, and turn their current pleasant spot into high-rent condos.

"It just wasn't something I'd wanted to complain about," Ellie told me in explanation. "George either. And I never connected it with . . ." Her voice broke.

"So Hector was alive until then," I concluded. "But it doesn't really matter because it's the time *afterwards* that George won't talk about. And unfortunately under these circumstances saying nothing is almost as bad as confessing."

Clarissa's nod was grim. "Almost. They'll eat him alive. I'm sorry, but all they need is to get past reasonable doubt. And the doubt so far is pretty *un*reasonable."

"Unless you know him," I said.

"Unless you know him," she agreed, but her tone made clear how little help she expected from that.

She got up. "Thank you, Will, for a lovely dinner." She had eaten almost nothing but managed to move things around on her plate so it looked as if she had.

"Tell him I said to stop," Ellie said suddenly.

We all turned to her. "I mean it," she told Clarissa. "Tell him I said I don't care what it is. I want him to say what he was doing the other night, and who can back him up on it. And I want it now."

Clarissa eyed her appraisingly. "You know," she said slowly, "that might actually work."

But I noticed she didn't say she would try it. Instead, she stooped to embrace Ellie. "Anyway, I'll let you know what happens. I will," she repeated, "do all I can."

"Best to Bob and his mom." Ellie's smile held back a flood of tears. She would weep when she was alone.

In the hallway Clarissa pulled on her coat while Sam and Will began clearing the plates and glasses. Ellie still sat at the dining room table with her fingers pressed to her lips.

"You didn't sound eager to have us poking at it," I said to Clarissa. "I mean, in case Ellie's ultimatum doesn't work, why not try finding out a little more about what might be going on?"

Clarissa didn't look at me, pulling a pair of fake-fur-trimmed galoshes onto her feet. "What are you going to find, though? It's what worries me about Ellie's idea, too. Think about that while you're digging around, Jake. I have client confidentiality to fall back on, but given your reputation around here you need to be aware that you're almost certainly going to be called to testify."

"Oh." I took a step back. "I hadn't thought of that."

Ellie couldn't be made to testify for the prosecution. She was George's wife. But I had no such shield. If we found anything that incriminated George further instead of clearing him, I might have to stand up in court and say so.

She went on. "Look, I didn't want to say this at the table. But he was desperate, Jake. The two of them get along all right on their income, when it *is* just the two of them."

Out in the kitchen Tommy had begun questioning Will about the caviar. ". . . fish eggs?"

Mutter of assent from Will, as I caught Clarissa's

drift. "But with the baby coming, it's different," I said.

"Uh-huh. Kids're expensive. I ought to know, most of what I earn goes to cover it. Anyway, I'm still hoping I can get him off this without incriminating him in something else. So I think I'll hold off on Ellie's idea for a little while."

Tommy's voice again, astonished: "*How* much a pound?"

Will replied, "You bet. I just read an article in the paper, some guy tried to bring in about four hundred pounds. But those fish are beluga sturgeon, endangered. The stuff's restricted. Anyway, the article said the shipment was worth two and a half million."

Tommy's amazed intake of breath was audible all the way to the hall, as was what Will said next.

"Now let's change the subject, okay? It's not polite to talk about what somebody's gift is worth," he added gently.

Which was what that caviar had been: Will's gift to us. But it was the money talk that reminded me of another matter.

"I'll get the check to you tomorrow," I told Clarissa. Her retainer, I meant; it was a cinch Ellie wasn't going to be able to pay it.

Meanwhile Tommy had cottoned onto the profit possibilities of caviar. "Man, if you could smuggle in a couple of those fish, you could raise 'em and make . . ."

Will cut in. "Hey, wait a minute. That kind of

216

thing will get you in big trouble. Stick to what's realistic. *And* legal."

"Just make sure whatever you come up with doesn't put George more behind the eight ball than he already is," Clarissa instructed me, and seemed ready to say more. But Wade interrupted us. He came up the back steps, worry plainly visible on his face.

"Clarissa," he asked, "you heard anything from the jail?"

As he spoke, her beeper whirred and she went to take the call in the phone alcove without answering him.

Wade shrugged his jacket off. "Heard it on the scanner just now when I was coming home," he told me. "Call for EMT service down to the county jail, code blue."

The scanner in Wade's truck was always on and code blue was the highest summons level for the ambulance. Clarissa returned from the phone alcove, her expression so alarming it made my heart pump icewater.

"What is it?" Ellie wanted to know. "I heard you talking on the phone about . . ."

Sam and Will came too, Tommy behind them. "What's going on?"

Clarissa answered. "There's been an incident. George has been injured. They're transferring him now up to the Calais hospital. Your ex-husband's on his way there," she added to me.

"You mean because Victor's on call," I said evenly.

217

"At the hospital, for emergency room admissions. Not because . . ."

Not because he's a brain surgeon; please, I thought.

"Someone hit George with something. Part of a bed frame, they think. Something heavy," Clarissa said.

"Oh, my God!" Ellie swayed. Will caught her and led her to the kitchen, helping her to a chair. I heard him talking calmly to her, his low voice a steadying rumble.

I couldn't believe it. "Why? Who attacked? Is George all right?"

"I don't know, some local guy, and he's unconscious." Typically, she answered my questions in the order I'd asked them. "They don't know yet the extent of his injury. I'm going up there and if he comes to, I'll try to get a victim statement."

"Won't the county prosecutor do that?" I asked her.

"Yeah, the D.A.'s sure going to rush up to Calais on account of maybe one jailbird cracked another one's skull open."

She stopped. "Sorry, I didn't mean that the way it sounded. Anyway, I'll keep you posted," she finished, and went out.

Something in the stars must have shone a troubled light on a lot of people that night. Will Bonnet needed to go home and get his aunt settled, so Wade, Ellie, and I drove up to the hospital.

218

But after we pulled into the lot surrounding the sprawling low building and went inside, I saw Ginger Tolliver being helped painfully toward the orthopedics clinic by the woman who'd been driving the white sedan earlier at Ginger's trailer.

Ginger's face was twisted in some fresh anguish, overlaying her regular misery. The health aide, or I guessed anyway that's what she was, grabbed a wheelchair from the row of them near the entry and wheeled Ginger toward the ER treatment area. Then at the corridor leading to the pediatrics area we ran into Maria and Jimmy Condon with Porter, whose cheeks were even redder than when I'd seen him last; the little boy wept fretfully with fever.

No one stopped to talk. All of us were too intent on our own grim errands for conversation. But I saw Jimmy give Ginger a familiar wave as if perhaps they'd met here before.

"Busy night," I remarked as Victor led us in.

"Not really," he replied. "You might be surprised how many of your friends and neighbors wind up here in the evening." He gestured back toward the lobby as he spoke. "Pain gets worse at night, kids get sick. Condon kid's been in a lot lately. Only place in a hundred miles for medical care at night. Anyway, here we are."

George's room was the nearest to the nursing desk so he could be observed constantly. A guard stood silently by the door. Ellie gasped when she saw George, his chest rising and falling with the cycling of the respirator. Half his head had been shaved, and a thin tube emerged from a patch of adhesive tape on his scalp, connected to a monitoring device.

And I'd been a brain surgeon's wife long enough to know what it all meant. If the trip from the jail to the hospital had been much longer, George wouldn't be here at all.

Ellie gripped his hand. It didn't grip back. "He's sedated," Victor explained. "He had a subdural hematoma."

Rough translation: after the injury George had developed a sort of blood blister on his brain.

Ellie had gone very white. Now she braced herself and said, "Will he be all right?"

"There is every possibility of full recovery," he replied. "I have evacuated the hematoma and stabilized his ICP."

Intra-cranial pressure. It's amazing how much you can pick up just by listening to people. Back when I still thought he walked on water, Victor would describe his surgical procedures, complete with every single retractor, sponge, and hemostat.

I took him aside as a nurse with a glass syringe went in to draw some of George's blood. "What's the deal?" I asked.

"I'm not sure. Smack to the skull. Couple of neurological signs I'm not too keen about." He looked unhappy.

"Brain damage? You mean permanent brain damage?"

He angled his head to where Ellie still stood by the bed. "I don't see why. But the truth is that I just left the ICP monitor in as a precaution. He should be waking up by now, only he isn't. He's fully comatose and has been since right after the injury."

"Oh, God." It was another thing I'd learned when I was with Victor; sometimes for reasons that no one has been able to figure out, comatose people don't wake up.

"What are you going to do?" I asked. "Wait and see, or . . ."

Will Bonnet came down the corridor with Tommy right behind him.

"CAT-scan him again later," Victor replied. "In twenty-four hours I'll reassess. If I were anyone else I'd be transferring him."

To a bigger hospital with better specialists, he meant. But Victor was the better specialist. And he'd furnished the Calais hospital with enough gear and trained so many of its nurses that if brain transplants could be performed anywhere, he could have done them here.

"What happened?" I asked the guard posted by George's door when Victor had gone. "Was there a fight?"

"No, ma'am." The guard shook his head. "Way I heard, another fellow clobbered him. Ready to hit him again when a supervisor ran in, broke it

221

up. Guy by the name of Daigle."

Perry Daigle. Tommy's uncle. My jaw must have dropped a foot. And the look on Tommy's own face was dreadful as Ellie and Wade came out.

Will went to Ellie's side immediately. "He'll be fine," Will said. "George's a hard-headed little son of a bitch, Ellie, you know that. He'll be just fine."

He offered his arm. "Come on, I'll take you home."

"No!" She looked alarmed. "I'm going to stay here. He," she insisted, her voice breaking, "wouldn't leave me."

Fortunately, Victor returned at that moment and stepped in. "Ellie." He seized her hands. "I'm going to take care of him. And there is absolutely nothing in this world that I won't do to make this come out right."

His eyes held hers. "Do you believe me?"

She nodded shakily; of course she did. When he wanted to, Victor could persuade the stars down out of the sky.

"Now, what do you think he would say if he knew you and the baby were here, worrying and getting exhausted, maybe even making yourself sick?" he asked her.

She bit her lip. When she spoke it trembled. "He'd be angry, wouldn't he?"

"That's right." He let her hands go. "Now, I won't be going anywhere. If anything changes, anything at all, I'll call Jake up and she'll call you. All right?"

Reluctantly, she nodded at him. "All right."

Thanks, I mouthed at him. Victor may be the world's biggest jerk most of the time, but he's magic with patients and their families.

Will had wandered gloomily away; now he returned. "I guess I don't need to go in again," he said. Then another thought struck him.

"Listen, maybe I should get the locks changed on Harlequin House. What do you think? It's kind of after the fact, but right now everyone in the historical society's got a key and . . . I don't know. It's just, who knows what else'll happen?"

It was a good idea. After agreeing to take care of it he turned back to Ellie. "Now let's get you home."

Another excellent plan; Wade's truck would be a tight squeeze for the three of us. "You two go on," I said. "I'm going to make sure the charge nurse has all our phone numbers."

Ellie's eyes yearned back into George's room. But in the end she went, Tommy remaining stubbornly just outside George's door.

At the nursing desk I recognized Therese Chamberlain, the nurse from Victor's CPR class. Wearing a rumpled uniform, her hair messily pulled back from her pale, picked-at face and fastened with bobby pins, my partner in rubber-doll resuscitation looked even more washed-out and exhausted than the last time I'd seen her.

"Long night?" I asked.

She shrugged dispiritedly. "We rotate shifts. I

223

drew short straw for the night shift, I guess. No one asks, they just stick me wherever there's a hole in the schedule."

She frowned at what I'd had her write. "Isn't he the one they think did the murder last Friday night?"

Near the main door on the far side of the lobby, Will was helping Ellie put her coat on. Ginger Tolliver passed them on her way out, as the Condons attempted to wrestle a screaming Porter back into his jacket.

Will looked back over his shoulder at me, flashed me a grim thumbs-up sign, and guided Ellie through the heavy glass doors exiting to the parking lot.

"Yes, George is the one," I said guardedly. Maybe she didn't like taking care of accused murderers. I didn't need a nurse with a chip on her shoulder to contend with, too.

But that wasn't it. She glanced around to be sure no one else was near enough to hear. "And you're the ones. You and her."

She angled her head minutely toward the doors Ellie had just exited. "I've seen your pictures in the paper. You're the ones who are so . . ."

"Nosy," I finished for her. "Is there something you wanted to say to us? Or me? We will of course keep whatever you want to tell us confidential."

If we can, I added silently. All's fair, and all that.

Therese looked down at her bitten fingernails. "Yes. That he couldn't have done it."

"Well, of course not. George wouldn't hurt a—"

"No, I mean I *know* he couldn't."

My heart thudded. "How? You mean you actually . . ."

Her look of fright cut me off. "No more here." She glanced at Tommy, so still and silent outside the door to George's room that I had completely forgotten about him.

He turned away, hands stuffed into his pockets, as Therese pushed a bit of paper at me. "This is my number. Call me before noon tomorrow. After that I sleep. You won't be able to wake me."

Wade came back in, giving me a brief glimpse of the parking area and of Ellie and Will. The darkness outside made the glass opaque, their faces a near-subliminal flash against something dark blue that I couldn't quite distinguish. Then they were gone.

Tommy shuffled unhappily over to stand with Wade as I took the scribbled paper from Therese. "But can't you . . ."

"No. And don't tell anyone." With that, she strode into the conference room behind the nursing desk and closed the door.

"Oh," I said to the empty air. "All right."

But it wasn't. For an instant I debated going in there and dragging Therese Chamberlain out by her unkempt hair.

Instead, I crossed the lobby to join Wade, leaving

George with his chest slowly rising and falling mechanically, his heart drawing a thin green line on the cardiac monitor screen, glowing in the dark.

CHAPTER 8

The next morning Wade lured me into riding the Deer Island ferry with him by telling me we needed some time together to work on our relationship.

"You've been browsing those magazines at the beauty parlor again," I accused him. The haircutting place we both favored was unisex but its reading material wasn't.

"Ayuh," he replied as we drove down Water Street toward the ferry. But I could tell he had some other reason for wanting to talk with me alone.

Downtown, it hit me for the first time how suddenly summer had ended. Under the grey sky the shops had a shuttered look. Most were already closed for the season. The few bright banners remaining hung woebegone over deserted sidewalks, and cars with Maine plates were the only ones around the diner and Post Office.

There was something I wanted to talk over in privacy too. "Wade, do you think Tommy's acting . . . I don't know. Strange?"

"Sure." Wade pulled the truck down the ramp to the parking area at Halpert's Cove. A granite cliff rose straight up from the water opposite a dock piled high with hundreds of lobster traps.

"He's worried as hell. We all are," Wade continued as we got out of the truck.

"I guess. He'd do anything for George."

The *Island Hopper* was already waiting, diesels idling, her flat rectangular deck damp with spray. Because it was early and not in tourist season anymore, we were the only two passengers aboard when the vessel cast off.

"I don't know, though," I told Wade. "I've seen Tommy in a lot of moods. One way and another that kid's had plenty to contend with in his life. But I've never seen him look . . . secretive. As if his conscience were bothering him."

We leaned together against the rail, a light chop slapping and the wind seeming to blow right through me. The streets full of houses rising behind the waterfront diminished swiftly to picture-post-card size, the breeze freshening as we got out into open water. Land seemed suddenly far away.

Wade snugged an arm around my shoulder as we hit the current and the ferry's engines revved. "Maybe Tommy feels he should've done more to help George somehow. Kid that age, he might have a kind of unrealistic idea, what he can really accomplish."

"Maybe." Across the water the low outlines of the salmon pens moved on the waves. In the under-water enclosures, thousands of the fish were raised on a scientifically devised diet, then harvested like chickens or heifers. That, I imagined, was what had given Tommy the idea of raising sturgeon.

I still thought he looked worried about something he'd done, though, not something he hadn't. But I had little more than an uneasy feeling to go on so I dropped the subject.

Ahead lay the massive whirlpool, Old Sow, its power merely hinted at by the small round upswellings called piglets swirling on the surface of the water. "Lots of freighters in the last few days," Wade commented, gazing at them.

"Could Ginger's boyfriend have been on one?" I asked.

We'd been over it all the night before when Wade and I got home from the hospital: Ginger and her ex-fiancé Mark Timberland, the Condons, the poison on George's workbench. And the nurse, Therese Chamberlain, still a wild card but I hoped somehow a promising one.

"Nope," Wade replied. "Talked to him this morning."

I turned to him, astonished. "How'd you manage that little miracle?"

"Called around, found the company he works for, pulled a few favors. He's in California, I got him on the phone. That hadn't worked, I'd have tried the union halls. But I didn't have to."

"They keep lists? Of every single person working on the freighters?"

"You bet. Think about it, Jake. If anything happened . . ."

Sobering thought. "If the vessel went down or had some other disaster, like a fire or an explosion, they'd need a list of the people on board for the casualties report," he added.

I leaned hard against him as we crossed over the whirlpool, deceptively calm on the surface but surging below.

"First thing I learned, he wasn't around when Gosling died, or Jan, either. His ship was in transit and he was on it."

I didn't know whether to be happy or sad. It wasn't a good feeling wanting to get George out of a jackpot by getting some other person into it.

"Had quite a talk with the kid," Wade went on. "Once he knew who I was, Mark was pretty interested in talking with me."

"And he knew who you were because . . ."

"Didn't, at first. But his first mate does. I've met him a few times out here." Wade waved at the channel where the big boats traveled between Deer Island and Campobello.

"So I had the mate call him first, introductory-like. I think it being the middle of the night out there sort of lent a bit of urgency to the whole thing, too. And it turns out Mark wants a career in the merchant marine. So he had a few questions about the tests he'll be taking for that, how to approach them."

Every so often it hit me that Wade had a whole life I knew almost nothing about, one that he led out on the water. "So we talked about it a

230

little," he went on. "Then I asked him the question."

"What Hector Gosling had on him?"

Wade nodded. "That's right. And he told me the answer. But I am afraid you're not going to like it at all."

"Why?" A couple of porpoises arced greenly out of the water and submerged again. "How would whatever Hector had on Timberlake have anything to do with me?"

"He's dyslexic. That's the kid's big secret and old Hector knew it."

"You're kidding me! That's all? How would Hector know that, anyway? And . . . what's the big deal? Sam's not making a secret of his dyslexia."

"Sam's not hoping to captain a commercial freighter," Wade replied seriously. "If he were, he might have worried about it as much as Mark has. I had to swear to him I'd never tell, and only because he'd been briefed on my reputation did he tell me even then. That and his realizing that Ginger might be in some sort of trouble."

"You lied to him? Said the police were looking at Ginger?"

He shook his head. "Didn't have to. Just told him Hector was dead. Then he was eager to talk. Clear his name and hers, because he knows how she felt about Hector. Hated him to death, he said."

Interesting phrase. "How?" A seal popped its

sleek head up, eyed us briefly and dove again. "How could he clear himself and Ginger?"

Wade's gaze went unerringly to the distant place where the seal would come up again. It did.

"The thing is," he replied, "in the merchant marine you climb the promotion ladder by good work reviews and taking tests. Do well in both, you rise through the able-bodied seaman levels, then to second and first mate. But there aren't as many ships as there are people in those ranks."

"So you wait to get your own ship."

"Right. You have to be chosen. So you tell me, why would the owners pick a guy, if there's ever an accident the other side's lawyers can stand up in court and say, So Mr. Ship Owner, did you know your captain can't tell his right from his left?"

"But that's not true, and it's not fair! Sam can—"

"But it doesn't matter, because it might create doubt anyway. Whether or not they took all possible precautions to prevent an accident. It could be construed as a liability even if it never created a handicap."

Wade looked out over the waves. "And there are lots of good people waiting for their own ship, who *aren't* dyslexic. So Mark Timberlake could end up waiting for his command forever, without anyone ever admitting to him the real reason why."

"You know that's not the way dyslexia works,"

I protested stubbornly. "Sam has no problem driving a car, for instance."

"I know." He tightened his arm around me. "But not everyone does. That's the problem. And Mark's realistic about it, he knows it could hold him back. He didn't know how Hector found out, but he says he did take a lot of special classes in school, participated in some medical center studies."

"And Hector probably just kept digging till he found dirt," I said bitterly, thinking of the computer search Will Bonnet had done on Jan Jesperson. Probably if he'd paid enough he could have gotten her medical records, too.

"But how does that clear Mark and Ginger?" I asked. "Sounds like the opposite, that he told you what their motive would've been."

"Right. It doesn't clear them for sure, I agree. But he was at sea. That's easy to check. And from what you've said about Ginger, I doubt there's a third person she would trust enough to bring in on that kind of thing. To carry Hector, help her get rid of his body, after she'd poisoned him?"

I thought again about her loner lifestyle, way out in the woods with lots of things to occupy her in solitude.

"Probably not," I agreed. "On top of which I keep feeling that somebody picked George to be the fall guy on purpose. And Ginger wouldn't have any reason to do that, much less know enough about him."

"Right. And what Mark said confirmed that. He

said to ask around. You'll find Ginger plays it all very close to the vest. No tight buddies she would have told if she whacked Hector and needed a helper. Hell, the way Mark tells it, she doesn't even trust *him*."

"But then why would she lie about being in touch with him?"

The air changed suddenly as we reached the place where land was equally far away in all directions. I felt my shoulders relax as they always did out here, my troubles falling away.

Or lessening, anyway. For the moment. "Maybe she didn't lie, exactly," Wade replied. "Because Mark says he e-mailed her. He's got one of those wireless gadgets, bounces e-mails off satellites so you don't need a land line. But she hasn't replied. He thinks she's probably not even reading his letters."

"Oh," I said, comprehending. "So maybe she didn't tell us the facts. But in her mind, she could've been telling the truth?"

"That's how I'd read it," Wade agreed. One last thing didn't make sense, though.

"So Mark was at sea. But he still told you his secret, even though he couldn't have been the one who . . ."

"I wondered about that, too," Wade said. "Why tell me if he didn't need to? So I asked a little more. Turns out he thought if he helped me out by being straight with me, I might keep an eye out for Ginger, give her a hand if she needed it.

234

Just in case this whole thing did somehow end up getting stuck to her shoe."

Stranger things had happened. After all, it was happening to George. "To protect her from afar? That's pretty gallant of him."

"Yeah. Sounded to me like he's really in love with her. Not that she's giving him an easy time of it."

"Wade, he dumped her," I pointed out.

"Only because she wouldn't marry him right away, and she wouldn't take any money from him. Hector was threatening to fire her, too, not just rat on Mark. So what was the guy going to do, leave her here alone without a dime and without even a job?"

"Oh," I said slowly. "And she wouldn't let him explain. She told Ellie and me she hung up on him."

"Tell you the truth, I can see why he loves this woman. She sounds a lot like you. Bullheaded." He squeezed my shoulder.

"Oh, thanks." I grinned at him. But what he'd said earlier still bothered me a lot and I turned once more to stare out over the waves.

"Wade, do you suppose that'll happen to Sam, too? That he'll be passed over for things because . . ."

"If someone does it's their loss," he said. But he was too straightforward to deny the idea just to make me feel better. And there was something else as well; I could tell by his expression.

"What?" I prodded.

His shoulders moved unhappily inside his jacket. "Well, I don't know what this means. But it seems George's boat was out on Friday night. Some fellows saw it, I heard about it earlier this morning. They saw it heading out. Almost to the line."

The imaginary line between the U.S. and Canada, he meant. The line went down the middle of the bay; we were crossing it about now.

"They're sure it was the *Witchcraft*?"

The only flight of fancy in George's whole life had been the christening of the little vessel; that and his seemingly impossible dream that Ellie would someday marry him.

"Yup. Saw the strips of reflective tape on his life rings, knew who it must be."

The strips had been Ellie's idea. She had insisted that in an emergency all bets were off and any little extra precaution you took might end up being the thing that saved you.

"Huh," I said. "Not much chance of George's getting a stop-and-board, is there?"

Because the Coast Guard had Eastport pretty well buttoned up nowadays, every freighter and other unfamiliar large boat made to check in well ahead of the time they were expected to make port, all others investigated appropriately on arrival. The local work boats went in and out without excess hassle, though.

George's, for instance. "George was on the boat?" I asked Wade.

"Nobody saw him. But I'm starting to think maybe we'd better assume that he was," Wade replied. I'd told him what Clarissa had warned: that George was desperate for money.

Which Wade knew anyway. He frowned down at his hands. "If, for instance, he was moving something on the *Witchcraft* . . ."

"Wade, we know George wouldn't . . ."

"No." Wade cut me off. "We don't. I hate suspecting the guy, too. But if he needed cash, it's not like he had many other ways of getting it. He's already working right out straight."

I thought about it: a load of something, maybe even drugs. Because Coast Guard or not, the coastline around here had just as many places to conceal things as it had during Prohibition, and it was surely a whole lot easier to get into than New York or Miami.

The ferry reversed direction around the forested point of Deer Island, angled to port and made for the wooden pilings that marked the landing channel. A few small trucks idled on shore for the return trip to Eastport.

"I'd have lent them money," I said sorrowfully.

Wade made a "not-in-your-wildest-dreams" face. "He wouldn't take it. You know that. Ellie, either. It's hard enough for her letting you advance the money to Clarissa. And I don't think he knew his aunt was leaving money to him, no matter what they say."

Nor did I. "I'd hate to get him out of the murders

237

by implicating him in something he *did* do."

"Yeah. It's why I haven't told anyone else about the boat. The other guys aren't going to either, not without my say-so. They're rooting for George and they know this isn't necessarily good."

The ferry slid up, the ramp creaked down, and the trucks rumbled aboard. We didn't go ashore, so we didn't have to clear Customs; a few minutes later we were back on the water.

"It's a darned good bet there was something illegal on the boat, or why wouldn't George already be copping to the trip?" I wondered aloud.

We passed the return voyage in silence, Wade waving a thanks to the captain of the *Island Hopper* as we strode ashore. On reentry in Eastport, we had to account for ourselves to a Customs officer stationed at the landing, and show ID with pictures.

Speaking of which, what was wrong with this one? Then I had it, or thought I did.

"Wade, you can't count on slipping anything past Customs even if they know your boat. The border security is too tight. It would be too risky, because no matter who you are you could get a spot-check."

"So?" He headed the truck toward home. "You'd just pull in somewhere else, some little cove no one is watching. Offload your cargo, hide it, pick it up later."

He made the turn onto Key Street. "George does know every secret spot on this coastline, has since he was a kid. So he just goes ashore in the dinghy, hides his cargo, next day he takes his truck out there, grabs it up."

My shoulders slumped. "Yeah." For a minute there I'd been certain I had a reason why George couldn't be running contraband.

And now I didn't again. "Hey, thanks for the boat ride. I guess beauty parlor magazines have some good ideas, after all."

He made a wry face. "Next time I'll show you how to fix all the movie stars' favorite desserts."

I laughed aloud for the first time that morning. But I stopped when we pulled into the driveway and my father's truck was there, reminding me that George wasn't the only problem on my plate.

"You decided what you're going to do yet?" Wade asked. He turned the ignition off but didn't get out.

I shook my head. "I thought I did. Every time I go over it, I know what I should do. But I can't seem to face telling him he has got to go on the run again, that he's not safe around me." It was what it boiled down to. "I keep thinking it's a bad dream, or something. Jemmy must've given them my name, but why? Aside from the awful trouble it causes me, why arrange for me to testify *against* him?"

"No one else could have told them about you?"

"No one else would have," I corrected. "Plenty of big shots got introduced to me through Jemmy. People in government or high up in business who needed money help. But believe me, Wade, none of them will ever admit to knowing *him*."

I laughed once more, sadly, just thinking of it all again. "A mob banker? Even a whisper of a connection would ruin them."

"And Jemmy knows. About your dad, I mean. That he's here."

"Uh-huh," I confirmed miserably.

"So why'd he do it?"

I opened the truck door. "I don't know. Somehow I feel like he must've *had* a reason, and if I could just figure *that* out . . ."

But the mystery of why Jemmy Wechsler had betrayed me seemed about as solvable as the puzzle of George's behavior.

That is, *not*.

"You know what else would make George mad?" Ellie said as we drove up to Calais later that morning.

"No, what?" The bright morning had developed into a cool, brilliant late fall day. I was driving her to her regular checkup appointment at the hospital.

"That we don't trust him." Beside me in the passenger seat of George's old, unbelievably ramshackle pickup truck—

Wade had needed his truck and Sam was in his car on the way to a school thing in Machias, while Tommy's wasn't fixed yet and mine was still only a gleam in my eye—

—she gazed sadly out at the pristine landscape

240

whizzing by. A log truck thundered past us, heading south.

"Ellie, it's not a matter of trust. It's a matter of knowing the facts."

I hadn't told her what Wade had reported to me about the *Witchcraft*. She was worried enough already. Now a pang of guilt struck me as I decided to go on keeping it to myself.

"We don't know what George's been doing," I told her instead. "You know he's been taking on extra work. Lots of different jobs. And he'd probably rather we didn't go off half-cocked until we do know, is all I'm saying."

It was the nicest way I could think of to imply that George might have been up to something he didn't want publicized, and that bringing it to light might just possibly not be our wisest course of action.

Even so, with anyone but me she would've flown swiftly to George's defense. But it was just us chickens, now, and Ellie knew as well as I did that he was a proud man.

"It's a crunch just to pay the doctor bills," she conceded sorrowfully. "When it was only us two, we got along. But . . ."

We slowed through the S-curves along the water's edge in the little town of Robbinston. Across the bay to our right, the hotel in St. Andrews resembled a European castle: cream brickwork, red tiled roof.

"I even went looking for a job myself," she confessed.

I glanced at her. "You never told me."

She shrugged. "I figured I'd tell you if I found one. It was before I got so pregnant. But it turned out there wasn't anything, anyway."

We pulled out of the sharp turn at Redclyffe and onto the long wide straightaway, the truck accelerating without too much protest past the Robbinston Post Office.

"Well, telemarketing jobs in Calais," she amended, "but I'd need a car, which would put us up against it again. And don't mention borrowing any more than I already have," she added. "From you or anyone; we'd never be able to pay it back."

Which brought us around to George and his pride once more. As we entered Calais, passing the elaborate gingerbreaded cottages lining the mouth of the St. Croix River, I came to a decision.

"When George is better," I said, "I need him to paint the house." I took the left turn uphill toward the hospital. "To make sure he's available when I need him, I'll want to put something on deposit. Half up front."

It was about five grand that I hadn't planned on, because until that moment I hadn't planned on having the house painted at all. But it wasn't a loan and a deposit was standard practice, just not this early in the process. Ellie thought it over, then nodded slowly.

"All right. As soon as he's well enough I'll be

sure to let him know so he can start planning the job. Thank you."

"See if you still thank me after you see how I . . ."

Work him to death, I'd been about to say, but decided not to. We pulled up in front of the hospital entrance.

"I've got errands," I told her. "So I'm not coming in."

Just one errand, actually; Therese Chamberlain had said to call her but I thought a face-to-face meeting might be more productive.

"How about I meet you back here in an hour or so? You'll be okay?"

She managed a smile, still rigid with the burden of having agreed to accept money from me; standard practice or not, George would've pitched a fit.

"Yes, all right," she said. She'd talked to the nurses that morning by phone: no change in his condition.

"Give him a hug from me," I called, and she promised to. The lump in my throat felt as big as a bowling ball as I watched her go in through the glass doors, the sun putting yellow glints in her red-gold hair.

But the lump went down, as they always do.

Sooner or later.

I'd gotten Therese's address by simply looking her up in the phone book. It turned out to be at the

243

outer end of Bunn Street, a down-at-the-heels part of Calais a few blocks off the main drag where the business district dribbled away to small dwellings and vacant lots.

The street dead-ended at a cliff overlooking the river and the Bangor & Aroostook train tracks. The house looked vacant too, lowered blinds and a yard all gone to tall weeds. But a car sat in the drive and an animal had been at the garbage bin recently, strewing trash.

I left George's truck running in case I couldn't get it to start again and made my way up to the front steps. There was no answer to my knock. An old car rumbled by in the street, rap music blaring out of it. I knocked again, then went around to the side of the house.

It was nowhere near the time past which Therese had warned me she would be asleep. So I raised my knuckles to the old wood-framed door someone had inexpertly fitted.

And stopped. The door was open an inch and music was playing inside, a radio tuned to the local station. "Hello?"

The radio announcer said it was 9:43 Eastern time, 10:23 Atlantic, and that the next high tide would occur at 5:17 this evening. "Therese?"

I stepped into the kitchen: dirty dishes, gritty floor. A can of Campbell's chicken and stars soup had been poured into a saucepan, the burner left on low. The liquid had sizzled away and the empty can stood unrinsed on the grimy drainboard.

"Anyone here?" I turned the stove off. The air smelled of burned soup. A philodendron in a plastic cup was eking out a slow death atop the refrigerator. A calendar with pictures of big-eyed kittens was marked with her work schedule: N for dates she was scheduled to work the night shift, I guessed, and check marks for shifts already worked.

The S's, maybe, were for ones she'd called in sick. There were quite a few of those. For the weekend Hector Gosling had died, the calendar was marked with B's.

What that meant I didn't know. But . . .

"I have," I said aloud into the shimmering silence, "a bad feeling about this."

The sunny day and the lowered venetian blinds combined to suffuse the place in dim ochre light. As I entered the living room a black cat leapt off the sofa, which was draped with an afghan inexpertly crocheted in too many bright colors.

Yowrl, the cat said, and streaked for the door. But I paid it no attention because Therese Chamberlain was under the afghan.

Her head lolled back, her eyes gazing mildly at the cracked plaster ceiling over her head. On the coffee table beside her lay a small plastic bag and a cigarette lighter.

No more chicken and stars for Therese. I'd have known she was dead even without the tourniquet tied around her left arm, the stained, filthy-looking glass syringe screwed onto the needle still hanging from the vein tied off in her left forearm. Her forehead was blue, and a thin, dull film was beginning to form on her wide-open eyes.

Out in the kitchen the cat tipped over the Campbell's soup can. It hit the floor with a tinny clatter, startling me.

"Scat," I told the cat, chasing it out into the barren yard where it began immediately perusing the strewn garbage. As it did so I peered around.

The nearest house was a hundred yards away, its view of my truck blocked by its combination garage-and-toolshed. In the other directions were the burnt-out shell of an abandoned mobile home and the blank brick back wall of an auto-supply store.

So I thought it over for about a millisecond and then I went back inside Therese Chamberlain's sad little dwelling, locking the door behind me. It was clear there was nothing an ambulance or rescue crew could do for her. Not even Victor could bring her back from an hours-old accidental overdose of whatever Therese's narcotic of choice had been.

Heroin, I guessed. The plastic bag had a stick-on label with a little unicorn rubber-stamped on it. The unkempt, harrowingly exhausted look she'd had while alive made more sense now that I knew she was hooked. When you're high or jonesing all the time, hair washing and teeth cleaning drop low on your to-do list.

Way down there with eating and sleeping. I wondered how she had managed to keep together a regular work schedule. Thinking this I opened a cabinet under her kitchen sink, found an old pair of rubber gloves, and pulled them on.

Then, keenly aware that what I should've been doing was calling the police, I went through the house. Part of my mind automatically listed the many repairs the house needed. A stair tread was loose and would break someone's neck someday if it didn't get replaced. The tap in the ghastly bathroom was dripping, running up the water bill. And when I snapped on the light switch at the top of the stairs it made a *zzzt!* noise under my hand: yikes.

And that wasn't all. The place was a home-repair dream. Or nightmare. But none of it was my problem or Therese's anymore, so I walked past loose doorknobs and squeaky floorboards, the broken window and the stain shaped like Africa on the wallpaper below it, searching for anything that hinted of what Therese had intended to tell me.

That is, if she hadn't been just jerking me around. Angrily I opened drawers and pawed through her coat closet, then peered under her furniture.

You sad little lonesome loser, I berated her as I shuffled through scads of unpaid bills and catalogued her medicine chest. Visine, Tylenol, No-Doz, and NyQuil; all the standards. I perused her liquor stash, which contained everything from an almond liqueur to something greenly poisonous-looking called Zowie Malted Mint.

You silly twit, I scolded Therese. I dug through

her dresser drawers and cringed at her laundry hamper but explored it anyway, finding nothing.

But buried under some magazines on a table by a bed so unmade it looked as if my dogs had been sleeping in it, I uncovered some papers. They were copies of attendance forms for a nursing convention in Boston, including hotel registration, credit card receipt, and parking validation.

These I stuffed into my bag; B for Boston on that kitchen calendar, I figured, because the dates matched. More to the point, though, the last evening of the convention was also the time George wouldn't account for to the police.

Not that I knew what that meant. Back downstairs, I took a final look at the grey, lost face of Therese Chamberlain, still staring with filmy eyes at the nothingness that had been her life, there at the end of it. Finally I returned the gloves to where I'd found them, glanced around once more for anything I might've missed, and then called the police.

An hour and a half later by some miracle the truck was still running and I was driving Ellie home.

"What did you tell them?" she wanted to know. "About why you were there in the first place?"

"I said I'd stopped by to see her and found her that way, which was close enough to the truth to be convincing. I didn't say anything else."

"I don't understand," Ellie said, shaking her

head. "If Therese was a drug addict why was she attending a nursing meeting? And spending lots of money to do it if she stayed at a hotel and so on."

"Denial. Protesting too much. I doubt she saw herself as some kind of degenerate dope fiend. No one ever does."

Not until after we'd moved to Eastport did Sam stop viewing himself as a kid who just liked to have fun, even though by then he'd resembled Dracula's midnight snack.

Once Ellie's appointment was finished—all fine, pregnancy on track, the baby coming any minute according to the doctor but not for a couple of weeks yet, according to her—she'd gone in to be with George. I'd visited briefly too. And as the nurses had said, there was no change.

"Attending a convention might've been a way to tell herself that she was doing okay professionally," I told Ellie. "Her job would've been all that stood between her and becoming a dealer."

It was an activity I'd seen no evidence of in my search of her neglected home; no other proscribed drugs at all.

"Anyway," I added as we took the turn toward Eastport, "we can stop at the bank, I'll write a check for the painting work, and you'll deposit it."

Turning east onto Route 190 made me feel better despite the morning I'd had. That big pale-blue sky spread wide open over the choppy expanse of Passamaquoddy Bay on the left, the bright flat water of Carryingplace Cove on the right. Even the truck, which had developed a nervous-making carburetor stutter as I'd pulled away at last from Therese's house, now settled into a low grumble that promised to get us home.

"Ellie?" She hadn't replied. "We stop at the bank, right?"

But she didn't answer. She just gazed thoughtfully out the window as we sailed around the long curve past Quoddy Airfield. Then finally she turned to me, her green eyes speculative.

"Therese was a nurse. She worked in a hospital. Had access to the equipment there, the pharmacy, supplies, and everything."

"Yes, but I'm still pretty sure what I saw was heroin. And anyway, it's not easy to steal hospital drugs."

"Not the drugs," she said as we reached the Mobil station. Tommy Pockets raised a listless wave of greeting as we went by. "Tell me again about the syringe," she demanded.

We'd been over it before. The truck coughed hard, bucking a little as we slowed. But then it recovered. "Well, it was a glass syringe."

Which was somewhat unusual. Almost all hospital syringes had been plastic for a long time. Victor said they were cheaper, and disposable too, eliminating both the expense of sterilizing them and the risk that sterilization wouldn't work.

"And it was dirty," I said. "Grimy and used-looking. They glitter when they're new, you know.

But nothing else in her house was clean either."

We pulled into the bank parking lot. "So here's a nurse with access to clean syringes," Ellie said. "They don't count them, do they?"

In the hospital, she meant. I confirmed that they didn't.

"So you could," she theorized, "just drop a few into your pocket."

"Yes." When Sam was a baby, Victor had brought clean plastic syringes home for him to play with, in hopes it would get his son thinking about a medical career.

"So," Ellie went on, "Therese could've done that. Stolen all the clean syringes she might have needed. And even though she was an addict, she was functioning well enough to take proper cleanliness precautions with her hospital patients, or she would have been reprimanded for that. Yet for some reason she used a dirty syringe."

"Oh," I said slowly, realizing now what she was getting at. "Aren't you the clever one?"

"No," she said. "I'm not clever at all. I'm just someone who saw three different glass syringes on three different stainless-steel trays in the hospital today. Clean ones, used ones. I could have picked up any one of them and just taken it home."

I used to spend a lot of time on the wards when I was first married. So I knew glass syringes were used for arterial-blood drawing, among other things, because the barrels were slipperier inside than plastic. That meant the patient's blood would pump up into the syringe by itself, with less risk of artery damage than if it had to be sucked up by pulling on a plastic syringe's plunger. I even knew where those glass syringes were kept: on a cart in the clean equipment room. Soiled ones often lay out on a tray destined for the sterilization department.

"So someone could have taken one and used it," Ellie said. "To fake Therese's accidental overdose."

She rolled the window down; it went halfway, then jammed. "To try," she added into the rush of crisp October air, "covering up a murder."

Neither of us spoke as we took the shortcut down Clark Street to her house, passing between small houses and neatly kept mobile homes with garden plots on one side, the grassy bluffs overlooking the bay on the other.

"Even if you're right—and I'll admit her dying is one hell of a coincidence if you're not—you know it's not enough to go to the police with," I said as I pulled over in front of George and Ellie's cottage.

"Yes," she answered in a subdued voice. The burst of energy that had fueled her theorizing had vanished. "Because it could've been the way I said. Or not."

"They'll say she just didn't care enough anymore to bother with clean equipment. No one knew she meant to tell me anything. The convention dates are curious but they could be a coincidence, too. In fact, they argue the other way."

"Because if she was at the convention, then how could she know for sure *what* George was doing," Ellie agreed dispiritedly. "Yes, I guess you're right."

She managed a smile as she got out. "Thanks, Jake. Tommy can bring the truck back later."

I waited until she'd gone inside. Then, depressing the gas pedal carefully to avoid stalling the engine, I drove the truck home. There to my surprise I found my father in the cellar peering into the hole he'd dug.

With all that was going on I'd nearly forgotten about this repair work. "Dad, I'd have done that. You didn't have to . . ."

He smiled easily. "I know. But my fingers just got kind of itchy for it. Man can't swing a pickaxe for his daughter once in a while, what can he do? That old dirt," he added of the floor he'd just opened, "was soft as butter."

He leaned his spade against one of the old hand-hewn posts holding the ceiling up. Knowing the posts stood on butter didn't comfort me.

But knowing my dad was around to take care of them did, all of a sudden. I'd had him around for such a short time, and yet I already didn't know what I was going to do without him.

"You called the D.A. back yet?" he asked.

For his workday he'd tied a red bandanna around his thinning white hair. The sleeves on his flannel shirt were rolled over his ropy forearms and a battered leather belt held up pants so old, they consisted more of patches than of the original fabric.

"No." My head still wasn't clear of the sight of Therese, dead on her sofa. Then what he'd asked hit me. "How'd you know about it?" I hadn't told him about Attorney Farrell's call.

He shrugged. "Only logical. They get Jemmy, they come to you. His little running buddy."

"I was not his . . ."

But I had been. "I found another body," I said.

He nodded thoughtfully. It was another thing I liked about him; his I'm-so-shocked circuits had gotten burnt out long ago. Then he seemed to change the subject.

"You may be wondering," he intoned professorially, "why I've dug the new sump-pump hole so far from the old one."

A good six feet away. And I hadn't, but he was going to tell me. After his long fall in the 60s, my dad had landed hard on the facts of the physical world: how things worked, time and gravity and the unchanging properties of substances.

"Pressure," he said. I looked down at the metal barrel in the hole, its top removed and holes punched into its sides. The holes were about the size of the pointed tip of a can opener.

"Water flows into the holes, fills the barrels, lifts the floats, flips the switches on the sump pumps," he recited.

"I know that. I built one myself, remember? But I don't see why . . ."

"Why it matters how close the barrels are," he agreed. "But think about it. If they were always equally full . . ."

"I get it. But they're not and if the holes share a wall . . ."

His pale blue eyes gleamed. "I couldn't have said it better. Sometimes water in one hole will push toward the other hole, and sometimes the opposite. Stress, one way and then the other, until the wall between 'em starts deteriorating. Starts to collapse and then it *does* collapse. Not good."

"No. No, that wouldn't be good." Because the whole point of two holes was to have two pumps going independently.

To make even more sure the collapse didn't happen he'd begun excavating a slot about a foot wide, several feet deep, and three feet long, between the old hole and the new one.

"You going to fill that with concrete?"

He shook his head, applying the pickaxe again. "Stone and mortar. Stronger together than either one alone."

Of course. "I want to finish it today," he added. "Get the mortar in and give it plenty of time to dry before it's so cold outside that it might even freeze down there."

"Not much chance of that, though. It stays pretty warm." So far the furnace was the one thing that hadn't gone kablooie in my old house.

He looked wise. "No, I don't suppose so. But if the mortar does freeze it'll blow it all apart. Ice expands, pressure gets in there from a direction you didn't expect."

"Oh." Then, "Dad, I'm going to have to go down and see that district attorney. It's the only way."

"You lawyering up first?"

"Yep. Make them mad." I figured I'd ask Clarissa Arnold; she didn't have experience in this area of the law as far as I knew. But her lips were able to form the syllable, "No."

Which was all I wanted. If I drew fire by hiring a lawyer and then keeping my mouth shut, I figured the Feds would get so angry at me that they might be diverted from paying attention to anyone around me.

Such as my dad. "But you'll still have to go."

He plucked a cigarette from the rumpled pack in his shirt pocket and lit it, still leaning on that pickaxe. Only he could smoke in the house, and only in the cellar.

"What, you've got a better idea?" I demanded. "If they come snooping around me, Dad, they're going to find you." Because even I couldn't divert them forever.

He dragged on the cigarette, changed the subject again. "The dead person you found, who was he?"

"She," I corrected. "I think she was about to give me an alibi for George, only she decided to get high when she got home from work last night and miscalculated her cruising altitude."

I took a deep breath. "That or someone killed her."

"I see. Bad?"

He meant the experience of finding her. "Bad enough."

I told him about the squalor, the atmosphere of defeat that had seemed to hang in the little house like poison gas. "But we don't really know she was killed and if we say that to the cops, they'll think we're just drumming up a wild theory."

"Sure." He stubbed his smoke out carefully, took up his pickaxe again. "Don't want to cry wolf at this stage. And a dirty needle or syringe, that wouldn't ring any bells. Junkies are the other category of people cops think are always stupid."

They weren't; back in the city, one of Sam's little friends had figured out a way to get tax refunds by filing phony returns for nonexistent businesses. Another cut out the middle man and went right to the source. He'd hacked the city's computer so that it issued checks directly to him, without phony filings.

"What other items of interest have you come up with, any?" my dad asked.

Something in his tone said I should summarize it for him; that and the way his eyes glittered. In daily life it was easy to forget, but he was smarter than the average bear.

Way smarter. "Well, basically nothing." I went on to tell him about Ginger Tolliver, too solitary to have gotten help and not physically able to have moved Hector's corpse alone, and about the Condons, desperately strapped financially and their only chance to get out of it thwarted by Hector.

"But the thing about Therese is, even if she did have any information that would help George, I don't see how anyone would have known she meant to talk with me. And people do overdose, you know. It really could have been just a coincidence."

"Uh-huh. You believe in coincidence?"

"No." I took a deep breath. "Not usually. But like I said, there's nothing to convince the police of anything else. Meanwhile, Ginger's not much of a candidate anymore and the Condons have got a good story too, one they can prove. Besides . . ."

Seeing them together had crystallized the other thing I'd felt about them as well. "They've got this little boy. I think that's why they're hanging in on their marriage. And if you could have seen the looks on their faces at the hospital, when he was sick . . ."

"You don't think they'd do something to put their child at that kind of risk, of what would happen if they got caught? Or if *one* of them did?" he asked, very quietly.

"Right," I said, seeing too late how thin the ice had gotten beneath our feet all of a sudden. He blamed himself for what had happened to my mother.

"People do, sometimes," he said, evenly. "They do things that hurt their kids." His gaze rested steadily on me.

I looked straight back at him. "Not on purpose. Not them."

And not you, I added silently. But I hadn't always known that and some baggage is nearly impossible to get rid of; you get so used to the weight on your shoulder, you feel it even after you think you've finally put it down.

My father resumed digging. It was a big job. But he always said that every stone you moved was one to the good, and sooner or later in any project there were no more stones.

I hoped he was right. When he spoke, it was on the subject of Jemmy again.

"Think it over once more before you decide what to do, Jake. From what you've told me about him your pal wasn't born yesterday. He might have a plan. And remember what I told you about pressure, that it can come at you from a direction you weren't expecting."

In other words, I was missing an angle.

"What?" I asked. "What else haven't I thought of?"

He just shook his head. "Don't know. If I did I'd say. Seems like what you've got is all stones, though, no mortar to hold it together. Don't you feel that way about it?"

He was insightful, all right, but he could be infuriatingly cryptic too. Mostly it happened when he didn't quite know himself what he was talking about, just that there was something.

"Yeah," I conceded, "I do." *No mortar, all stones.* Mortar of course being the stuff that holds stones together.

Like the *why* of what was happening to George, and the *why* of Jemmy's having given my name to the Federal authorities who were holding him.

If I had the reasons behind those two things, I thought the rest would form a pattern as simple and stable as one of my father's stone walls.

But I didn't. "Anyway, be careful," he said.

"Yeah, you too," I replied, and was about to say more.

Maybe a lot more. Only just then over my head I heard three successive floor thumps as one after another the household pets abandoned the furniture they'd been lounging on.

For which in my experience there could only be one reason.

Someone had come into my house.

CHAPTER 9

"Tommy, what's wrong?"

The two dogs shoved their bodies up against him, sensing his distress but not understanding what it meant or how to fix it. He'd been crying and in the hand he'd bruised by slamming it against the wall the other night he clutched two grubby bits of paper.

"I should've given you these right away instead of hiding them, but I didn't. And I'm so sorry. Maybe they'd have changed things somehow, but . . . oh, jeez, I'm just so freaking sorry."

He thrust the papers at me. I peered at them, astonished. "Why didn't you tell us?" I demanded. "As soon as you found them why didn't you . . ."

"I couldn't," he replied wretchedly. "When I heard that the police were at George's house I knew they would search his truck. They always do that, the police, when anyone gets in big trouble. On TV, they always search their house and their car."

"Didn't they ask *you* about the truck? They must've known you'd been working on it and might've seen something in it."

He nodded, gulped in a breath. "Yeah. I said no. And I guess they all believed me. They never asked again."

"Tommy." I felt even more stunned at what he'd done. "You *lied* to the police? But why?"

It was as if Little Bo Peep had owned up to slaughtering all the sheep. Tommy's examples in life had consisted of a long line of sleazy guys, ones who lied, cheated, stole, and beat up women. Perhaps in reaction he'd rejected all forms of bad behavior, becoming an honest, hardworking—if underachieving—solid citizen.

Until now, when it seemed he'd begun thinking big: obstructing an investigation, concealing evidence, and I didn't know what all else. He had a swift answer, though.

"Because George didn't tell. Where he'd been, whatever he was doing, he *didn't want anyone to know.*"

As soon as he said it, it made perfect sense to me. Whatever George wanted was good enough for Tommy, even if he didn't have a clue to the reasoning behind it. Why wouldn't it be? Of the few adult males who had ever taken anything but a malicious interest in Tommy, George had gone the extra mile.

Standing up to Perry Daigle wouldn't have been a snap for George. Daigle outweighed him and was in addition the kind of guy who resorted to violence at the drop of a hat. But George had done it anyway to help Tommy and Tommy's mother.

And Tommy had felt that when push came to shove, he could do no less. But he couldn't stand keeping the secret any longer.

"I went over to the station right after Ellie called you, when they were searching the house," he said. "I figured maybe I could get into the truck before anyone else did. And I remembered seeing some papers in the cab."

"Where?" I demanded. "Were they hidden, or . . . ?"

"Stuck under the floor mat," he replied. "Like they'd just slid there. You know, like the kind of things that fall on the floor of a truck."

Sure I did. Grocery receipts, out-of-date coupons, and the tickets for church raffles I hadn't won tended to litter up the floor of my own car, when I'd had one.

"So I didn't think much of it when I first saw them. I just thought I'd give it all a cleaning after the repairs got done," Tommy went on. "He's always got stuff in the cab, like soda cups, junk mail . . ."

It was where the cup I'd used to pour gas into the truck's carburetor had come from. Probably that was still there, because Tommy's face said he'd lost interest in cleaning the truck or in anything else except for the papers he'd handed hopelessly to me.

They consisted of a parking-garage slip and a receipt from a store called A Taste of Honey Foods. The garage ticket said "parking" on it and was stamped with a time and date, but nothing more. The store whose name was on the receipt was one of a chain with outlets in every large city in the country.

Tommy didn't understand what that implied. But I did. The receipts told me that George had been away when Hector Gosling died. And perhaps more important, they told me he hadn't been alone.

And they hinted at how Therese could've known it. "If whatever he was doing was so secret he wouldn't even get himself out of a murder charge with it," Tommy said, "I wasn't going to tell. Or let the cops find out about it, either. I figured probably he *was* protecting someone, like you guys said. It made sense to me, it was what he would do. But then . . ." His face clouded again.

"But then," I filled it in for him, "George got attacked. Badly injured. And after that you felt you *couldn't* tell. Because we might think it was all your fault," I suggested gently, "that he got hurt."

A sob escaped him. The blow it must have been to him when he found out who'd attacked George hit me secondhand.

"Perry's nuts," he said. "He'll do anything. And George was on my side, so . . ."

"You think Perry attacked George because of you?" It would have made Tommy doubly guilty, not just that he'd possibly lengthened George's jail stay by failing to come to me right away, but also

264

that even the motive for the attack was on his shoulders.

"Tommy, I don't think so. You know how Perry hates being in jail." And what he'd done to George put him at risk for a prison stretch. "I was surprised he even bothered your mother again." Violating an order of protection had been certain to put Perry inside, where he least wanted to be.

On the other hand, maybe Perry had even fewer beans in his bag than any of us thought. "At least he can't get at George anymore," I said. "As long as George is in the hospital . . ."

"But what about when George wakes up? They'll send him back. And Perry will just try for him again."

"They will keep them apart," I assured Tommy. "If Perry's still even at the jail then, and not in the state prison system already."

And if, I added mentally, *George does wake up.* But there was no sense saying that.

"Hey," Sam said, coming in. The dogs danced to greet him. "What's going on?"

I explained briefly. "Tommy hung onto this stuff because he thought the police might be able to figure out where George was by looking at them, and he knew George didn't want that."

"Jeez," Sam said, and went over to punch Tommy gently in the shoulder. "You idiot," he said, but sympathetically.

"Now, though, I'm trying to figure out the same thing," I went on, "and I think Tommy might have given the cops a little too much credit. There's nothing here to say *where* these places are."

Then I saw the bitter dejection still on Tommy's face. "Tommy, it's all right," I told him. "You trusted George, is all. You did what you thought was the right thing. You couldn't know how it would turn out."

His look of misery eased a little. He'd been guilty and scared; convinced, I supposed, that none of us would ever forgive him.

"It's a hard thing to learn," I told him. "That your hero, someone you trusted so much, can make a mistake. That sometimes the guy you needed can end up needing *you*."

I watched him comprehend the bitter truth of this. "But I'm starting to think that might be what happened," I said. "George should've said where he was right from the start, but for some reason he didn't."

Sam had taken the parking ticket and receipt and was scrutinizing them.

"Anyway, it's a good thing you finally decided to bring the stuff to me," I told Tommy. "Now, is there anything you're still not saying? Anything left to tell?"

He shook his head morosely. "No," he uttered bleakly.

But Sam was still examining the two items. At last he spoke to Tommy. "The truck was at the garage last weekend too, wasn't it? I mean before all this started?"

266

Heavy sigh from Tommy. "Yeah. Checkup. Not that there was a lot to do. He's always tinkering on it, changes the oil about every other week. He buys it wholesale from a guy, by the case. Because . . ."

We recited George's auto-care mantra together: " 'If you want to keep a car on the road forever, keep the oil clean.' "

But in the midst of our laughter we turned instantly somber again. All three of us remembered where George was now.

"It needed a spark plug, fix a tire that was leaking. That's all," Tommy said. "Why?"

He looked impatiently at Sam, annoyed at being questioned about such trivia. But Sam wouldn't quit.

"A three-thousand-mile checkup. And for those, you write the mileage on the door sticker, don't you?"

"Sure." Tommy looked even more vexed. "But I don't see what that's got to do with . . . Oh."

He brightened cautiously. "Hey, maybe you've got something there."

Sam's face smoothed the way it always did when a problem suddenly straightened itself out in his mind. His trouble with mathematics was the opposite of most people's, purely numerical calculations being more difficult for him and "word problems"—"if Bob has two apples and he gives Jane one," for example—much easier.

Because Sam was good at *things,* the nuts-and-bolts physical real-world objects of any situation. Without them he required all the tutoring Tommy could give. But with them . . .

With them he was the prodigy his father had been, and more. "Can someone get me a map?" he asked, looking around impatiently. "And Tom, is that protractor of yours still around somewhere?"

When Sam's strangely literal brain got revved up, you could almost smell the ozone. "Okay," he said when we'd brought him the map, Tommy's protractor, and the receipts.

"Maybe I'm wrong," he said. "But with this stuff I think I might be able to get an idea of where George was when Hector got murdered."

Sam once fixed a turtle's shell while it was attached to the living turtle.

Rather, at that point it was a dying turtle; the animal had been hit by a car while trying to cross a remote road. Sam used a big darning needle, antibiotic powder, and some suture wire he'd gotten from his dad to bring along on his camping trip, plus a pair of needle-nosed pliers to draw the broken edges of the shell back together.

Later when he took the animal in for professional treatment, the vet said all that could be done was already accomplished, and the turtle recovered. Where to put the sutures, how tight to pull them, and how much antibiotic powder to use all came from Sam's remarkable ability with *things*.

Now Tommy and I stood in the driveway by George's old truck, hoping for similar magic. The door groaned, its grease sludgy in the chilly air, as Sam pulled it open.

"Tommy," he instructed. "Write this down."

Tommy brandished the legal pad Sam had equipped him with as Sam read the mileage from the sticker pasted on the inside of the truck's door.

"You wrote this here the weekend before last? When you did the check on the truck?" Sam asked.

Tommy nodded as Sam got behind the wheel to recite aloud the mileage on the truck's odometer. "Now . . ."

"Good old subtraction," Tommy said. He looked radiant. "Good old math. You can't beat it with a stick."

"You betcha." Sam slid from the truck cab and we trooped back into the house, where he spread the map on the dining room table.

"Okay, miles per inch," Sam said. "Where's that ruler?"

Tommy supplied it from the heap of study materials they'd been using to try getting geometry from a book into Sam's head.

"You, my man, are some kind of genius," Tommy breathed as Sam laid one end of the ruler on the map dot labeled "Eastport."

"Yeah, right," Sam said sarcastically, and kept working.

"I don't get it," I said. "What are you doing?"

He looked up. "The difference between the number of miles on the odometer now and the number Tommy wrote down when he did the three-thousand-mile check. That's how many miles it was driven in about ten days, right?"

I nodded.

"And we know that mostly it's been in George's yard or at the service station, because it wouldn't start," he said.

"Also true, but . . ."

"So," Sam asked, holding up the legal pad, "where'd a few over eight hundred miles on the odometer come from?"

"Wow," I said. Which was putting it mildly. "That's amazing. I don't know." It seemed to me just getting the thing to run that far at all was amazing. But then my jaw dropped even more as I understood what else my son was doing.

"Let's say a hundred miles around here," Sam said. Including my trip to Calais that sounded about right. "That means a round-trip of . . . okay, 700 miles. One way that's three-fifty."

He pulled the map in front of him. "On here, a hundred miles is half an inch. We measure out to the right spot on the map, and put the point of the protractor on Eastport, and—"

Neatly, Sam drew the proper-diameter circle with Eastport as its center. "Viola," he said.

Tommy and I looked over Sam's shoulder. Most of the circle he'd drawn was in interior Maine;

lakes and forests and mountains, few roads or none. But the southern part crossed neatly over Boston, Massachusetts.

"Maybe he lent the truck to someone else?" I wondered aloud.

"No way," Tommy said. "He would never let anybody else drive that truck anywhere near that far."

He looked around at us. "I asked him, once, could I take it to Bangor. George wouldn't let me. He said he could make it but the truck would strand me and I'd end up hitchhiking."

"You're right, George wouldn't have lent it for such a long trip," I agreed. "To an enemy maybe, but not to anyone he liked."

And until lately I'd have said he didn't have any enemies. "Tommy," I added, "do you feel like redeeming yourself?"

I wrote down the name of the hotel Therese Chamberlain had stayed in when she'd attended the nursing convention in Boston. "Get on the phone and find out whether there is one of these food stores anywhere nearby."

The literature for the nursing convention Therese had gone to named the parking garage for which paid convention registrants received vouchers. If I could put George in the same garage, it might account for her being so certain about his whereabouts that night, maybe because she'd been there that same night and seen him.

Not that I knew how I was going to place either

271

one of them there for sure, or even what good it would do if I could, now that Therese was dead. But it seemed worth a shot; for one thing, at this point it was the only shot I had.

"You got it," Tommy said earnestly. It was dawning on him that if George could make mistakes, maybe he could too, and be forgiven. "I won't let you down," he promised me. "Come on, Sam."

"No." I stopped them. "Sorry, Tommy. But you're on your own for this. I've got another job I want Sam to take care of for me. And another one for you as well."

I wrote down my long-distance PIN number so he wouldn't have to spend money doing the phone research I'd asked for.

"Take the truck to the garage," I told Tommy, "I think the cops probably have George's big key ring but the truck's spare key is still under the visor like always." I knew because it was the one I'd been using. "Do whatever you think the truck needs so it's absolutely one-hundred-percent ready for when George comes home."

That wouldn't be much, considering the recent tune-up. But as I'd suspected, the boy badly needed to feel he was doing something useful for George. My belief was confirmed when I observed that if he'd brightened before, he was positively glowing now.

"Pile all his lobster traps in the bed of the truck too," I said as an afterthought. "That way he won't have to do it himself when the season comes."

That George hadn't even woken up yet was a fact I figured didn't need discussing, just at the moment. "Okay," Tommy agreed happily. "Yeah, you bet."

"Mom, the hardshell lobster season doesn't start till winter," Sam said when Tommy had gone. "Stacking George's traps now is just busy work."

"Yes, but it'll make him feel better and after all he's been through over this, he deserves to. Meanwhile I would appreciate it if you would go over to Will Bonnet's and ask him for another jar of that wonderful caviar he fed us the other night."

"Fish eggs? What are you going to find out from fish eggs?"

"Just get it, please," I requested sweetly. "Tell him that I want to pay him for it. Say that Ellie's developed a late-term craving for the stuff and I want to give it to her as a gift."

Because among the many things I didn't know there was one I thought I did. George hadn't been visiting a fancy food store. To him, a french-cut green bean was as fancy as food needed to get.

Will was our resident food enthusiast, a likely customer for a gourmet specialty store like A Taste of Honey. And if what Sam brought back was a brand of caviar you could purchase there, I was going to start getting darned suspicious that maybe Will had.

That in fact he'd been in Boston, driven there

273

by George, when George was supposedly here in Eastport committing murders.

And that now, Will wasn't saying so.

Once Sam and Tommy had gone off on their errands, I sat back down at the kitchen table. The dogs nuzzled me, trying to cheer me up, then went away dejected, and even Cat Dancing glared ominously from atop the refrigerator for a while, trying to get a rise out of me.

But none of it was effective because for all the energy I'd fired up in the boys I was out of it myself. I needed to talk this all over with someone, to juice myself with theories, strategies, and hare-brained notions.

But Wade was at work, my father had quietly left while Tommy was making his confession, and having just commanded Ellie to lie down, I couldn't very well rouse her up again.

So instead I got up from my chair and looked around the big old kitchen. The channels of the tall bare windows were equipped with brass insulation strips; I'd learned to install them by the simple method of getting some and trying. The radiators worked too, on account of the air having been bled from their valves.

By me, with a wrench in one hand and a book of home fix-it instructions in the other. Even the little bathroom off the hall was in good order due to my stubborn efforts. In short, what I'd learned from my old house was that when something gets broken, usually there's a way to fix it. Maybe not one the old-house experts would endorse, but a way; all I had to do was find it.

I was still standing there thinking when Sam came back in. "Here you go, Mom," he said, tossing the little jar at me.

I caught it. The label was lettered in what I guessed was Russian, beautiful but unintelligible. "He says he's not going to take your money, though."

I'd figured he wouldn't. "And Mom—he says he's never heard of a pregnant lady craving fish eggs."

That too. And I hadn't heard of many with cravings this late in their pregnancies at all, other than the craving for it to be over with as soon as possible. But it was the best I'd been able to come up with on such short notice.

"I'm heading over to the boat school now," Sam said. "Unless you need me."

"Fine," I replied distractedly. The Taste of Honey receipt hadn't come from a bar-code reader, so there were no shorthand clues to what had been purchased. But I had a Boston phone book and as Sam went out I began paging through it. Moments later I was talking to a store clerk whose cah was pahked in the yahd.

After that it didn't take long to learn that the caviar I held in my hand was not available at that store, or at any of the chain's other branches.

"Sorry," the clerk said. He didn't know where the stuff I described to him could be had, either; so much for that.

As I hung up the phone, it rang again and Tommy informed me excitedly that the garage for the Boston hotel Therese had stayed at did have A Taste of Honey store very nearby.

Probably the one whose clerk I'd talked to. The store was open, Tommy went on helpfully, until eleven on Friday and Saturday nights. But the caviar hadn't been bought there. In fact, the receipt I had didn't even total enough. On it, someone had bought three of something that cost $12.95 each—not enough for all the purchases Will had suggested he'd made in Boston, either, now that I thought of it.

So the question was . . . well, I didn't know what the question was, and after a little while the whole confusing situation sent me fleeing up two flights of stairs to the third floor, to puzzle over it. Paint stripper had been simmering on the old door I was rehabilitating for many hours, now, and I needed to get my hands on it, because I needed to think and I wanted my hands busy while I was thinking, or I might start tearing my hair out.

What I found up there made me glad I'd decided to check that door for any reason, since its grungy old paint had transformed itself into a bubbly mess. Sticking a scraper into it I brought up a thick, satisfying amount of sludgy material. This I wiped onto a paper towel, noticing with pleasure the tight, rock-hard grain of the old wood I was exposing.

No hollow-core doors for those old craftsmen; this item was solid. Meanwhile, one thing was obvious, I thought as I scraped paint-and-stripper mixture off the door's surface. George couldn't have been out on his boat *and* in Boston, no matter what anyone said about the *Witchcraft* being on the water late that night. By the time I'd cleaned the paint from the screws holding the doorknob's faceplate to the door, I'd come to another conclusion, too.

Tommy was right. George might've lent the boat to someone but there was no way he'd allow anyone else to drive his rattletrap of a truck all the way to Boston. And it was too much of a stretch to think someone else with gourmet tastes had gone with George.

It had to be Will. Maybe he'd stopped at two stores, and the receipt Tommy had found was only for his minor purchases. But what else had they been doing?

I didn't want to march up to Will and demand that he tell me, though, because as Tommy had said if it was so bad George wouldn't even get himself out of a murder charge with it, maybe I ought to handle it with the equivalent of tongs, too.

And that was as far as I'd gotten when I confronted the knob on that old door. It should have been taken off before the paint stripper went on but I couldn't get a screwdriver into the screw slots until afterwards, a typical old-house Catch-22. Now I took the screws out of the faceplate, removed the spanner screws from the collar around the doorknob stem, and set them all aside.

Then, after loosening the knob and removing it—the knob on the door's other side had been missing for many moons—I slid the latch mechanism out. It was a block almost an inch thick and about four inches tall with a square hole in it for the doorknob stem to go through. Under a plate lay a spring mechanism that snapped the latch tongue out and also let it be pushed back in again; because of it, the door could be shut without turning the knob.

Doorknobs today still work basically on that same principle, which just goes to show how brilliant an idea it was in the first place. But my admiration of it was diluted by thoughts of Therese Chamberlain.

She might have told someone she meant to confide in me. If so, it would be great to find out *whom* she had told. But other than at a séance I didn't see how I could find out. A pang struck me as I recalled her at the CPR class, determined to resuscitate that idiotic rubber doll.

Scraping glumly at the old door, I imagined her before her addiction: young and vibrant if not actually pretty, possessing the hands-on practical kind of bravery a person had to have to be a member of her profession in the first place.

And then it hit me who might be able to tell me more about her; maybe a lot more. Because not that long ago she had indeed been reasonably attractive.

And she'd been a nurse.

"Yes, I knew her," my ex-husband admitted. "Not," he added hastily, "in the biblical sense."

The biblical sense being the only way he ever knew them, in my experience. But never mind.

"Drink?" he offered.

I'd had to wait until he got home from the hospital so it was six in the evening when I knocked on the door of his wonderful old Greek Revival house, waiting while the strains of a Schubert Liebeslieder waltz wafted out among the enormous white porch pillars.

"Sure," I said. He'd come to the door at last with a martini in one hand and a copy of *The New England Journal of Medicine* in the other.

The glass he handed me was cold, and one sip told me that a vermouth bottle had been waved delicately over the gin.

"Thanks," I said, and followed him past the antler-rack coat tree and the elephant-foot umbrella stand in the hall. The inside of his house hadn't had a thing done to it since the 40s, and Victor had kept all the safari memorabilia of the previous owner.

"I was about to phone Ellie," he told me. "George

is showing a bit of improvement. Nothing too dramatic," he added cautioningly. "But I think we can be pleased with his progress."

"I'll let you tell her." The pleasure of reporting decent progress was rare in his world; I thought he ought to have it. "But there's something else I need to ask you." I told him about my day, with emphasis on the finding-yet-another-dead-body part of the program.

"So what I want to know is who Therese might have talked to about her plan to confide in me," I said.

Victor frowned in disapproval. "Jacobia, I've mentioned to you how unwise it is, you getting involved in all sorts of . . ."

I noted that he was blathering, which in the old days always meant he was hiding something. "Victor," I said when he stopped, "are you sure you weren't sleeping with her?"

I hadn't really thought he was up to his old tricks, chasing after women as if they were gold-fish and he was a shark. I'd just thought he would *know* about her: a shark on a diet.

"No, I wasn't," he snapped, applying a gulp of his drink to whatever was paining him. "It wasn't that at all."

"What, then?"

Another swallow. "I tried to help her. You saw how well that worked out. Some doctor I am." His tone was self-lacerating.

"I knew something was going on with her," he

went on. "Everyone did. She was calling in sick more, appearance deteriorating. They put her on nights when she couldn't get along with anyone. And one more unauthorized absence, she'd be fired."

"Would a nursing convention count as unauthorized absence?"

"You bet. In fact she'd asked about attending one. I heard her with the nursing supervisor, they were arguing about it. Therese knew her performance reviews were going downhill. I guess she thought attending a convention would help."

Sure, and the CPR class too. "Wouldn't it?"

He made a face. "Yes, but showing up for work would help a lot more. And being on nights, the shift is short-staffed already so they couldn't spare her. But," he finished unhappily, "maybe her head was too screwed up by then to realize that."

So she'd gone anyway, which gave her a reason not to speak up for George right off the bat. She'd have to say she'd called in sick to take the Boston trip, and she might get fired for it. But after George was attacked she'd tried telling me, maybe hoping I could give information for her, keep her out of trouble.

"And you knew it was drugs causing her deterioration?" I probed.

"Not for sure. I really didn't know much about her, who her friends were, what kind of support she had. I asked, but she was too suspicious of me to say. She wouldn't open up at all."

He swallowed more of his drink. "No one else could get close to her, either. And pretty soon they didn't want to. She'd make really inept, off-putting remarks and then wonder out loud, sort of sullenly, why people avoided her."

I recalled the baffled way she'd tried to socialize with the other nurses at the CPR class.

"But a few days ago the nursing supervisor asked me to talk to her again," he went on, "so I tried one last time. I took her aside and gave her a lecture. Handed her a bunch of literature from a rehab clinic in Bangor, told her to shape up or ship out."

He laughed bitterly. "Well, she's shipped out now, hasn't she? Just the way I told her to. Very therapeutic, my advice."

"Oh, Victor." As usual, he was turning it around so *he* was the important one; what *he'd* done. But at the same time he really did feel bad.

"So you don't know of anyone she might confide in? A family member, even?"

He shook his head. "The way I heard it, she came from a bad situation. One of those kids who really did pull herself up by her bootstraps, school on a scholarship, all that."

And look how she'd ended. Victor frowned at his hands. "She reminded me of Sam. I was about as helpful to her, too."

I studied him, surprised. Victor hadn't wanted to admit there was anything wrong with Sam, back in the bad old days. He'd simply said Sam's troubles were all my fault and that I should deal with them.

Now he made a sad, helpless gesture with his glass. "She deserved better," he said, and his eyes said more. It was one of those rare shining moments of Victor as he could've been, honest and kind.

But the moments never lasted and they didn't now, either. "Anyway, that's all I know about her." His tone turned pettish as if I'd interrupted him during major surgery. "She didn't confide in anyone that I know of. It was a big part of her trouble. So was there something else? Because . . ."

He waved at the stack of medical journals on a table by his chair. "Because I have some catching up to do."

I suspected the martini glass would get more of a workout than his reading glasses tonight. But that wasn't my business anymore. "Don't give yourself a headache," I said.

He eyed me defensively but softened when he saw I meant it. "Anyway, Ellie can go up tonight and visit," he told me. "I believe George might even recognize her."

My heart lifted again. "Oh, that's great. You'll call her?"

He hesitated. "Do me a favor? I was going to, but . . . you tell her. She can call me if she has questions, but . . ." He glanced over at the martini shaker. "But to tell you the truth, I don't feel much like having a conversation right now."

Poor Victor, he was such a strange ranger. I

watched as he poured the rest of the liquid from the martini shaker. No one to talk to, indeed; I wondered if he ever looked in a mirror.

"Sure, Victor. I'll do it," I said, and let myself out.

By the time Wade drove us up to the hospital an hour later, Ellie's eyes were so bright Wade's truck hardly needed its headlights.

"I told you," she kept saying. "I told you he'd get better. And he is. He'll tell us where he was, now. He'll tell, and all of this will be over."

She sat beside Wade; I hunched on the half seat behind them in the extended cab. "Victor said that George was improving," I reminded her. "Not that he was all better. Don't expect a whole lot from him right off the bat."

But she didn't want to hear it, and I didn't even bother to say the other thing I was thinking: that if George got too much better they'd send him back to jail. Because Tommy had been right about that, too; the county paid for every day an inmate spent in the hospital. They'd have him back in a prisoner-orange jumpsuit the instant he was up to it.

"Thanks, Jake," Ellie said. "For all you've done. From both of us. I mean, all three of us."

Wade's eyes met mine in the rearview; she's going to be disappointed, his look said, and I feared so too.

But at first everything was fine. As we crossed the parking lot to the hospital's glass doors, I could see into the warmly lit lobby with groupings of tables and chairs, the information desk, and the nursing desk beyond. Inside, we found George sitting up, looking a little dazed but in possession of all his faculties.

He hugged Ellie, patted her belly fondly, and tried to make light of the injury he'd suffered. "Hard head." He grinned.

His tubes and wires were gone and they'd transferred him to a room in a less critical area of the nursing ward. "How'd it happen, anyway?" he asked. "Did I have an accident working?"

Ellie glanced at me, alarmed. "George, you were in jail and another inmate . . . Do you mean to say you don't remember?"

"Nope." He shrugged happily. "And I can't say I mind much. What you don't know won't hurt you, right?"

He appeared much better than I had expected, freshly shaven and with nothing left of his hospital dinner but the tray on his bedside table. Out by the nursing desk, the guard the county had posted stood listening, no doubt noting also how healthy-looking the prisoner was.

I felt like telling George to fake a seizure or something. At this rate the county would wise up so fast he'd be behind bars again by tomorrow morning.

"But I'd like to know," he went on. "What'd I

do, fall off a ladder or something? And what's all this about jail?"

"George." Ellie sat down on his bed, took his hands in hers. "George, I want you to try very hard to remember. What's the last thing you recall before you woke up here? Think hard, now."

He squinted, thinking. "Um, painting the baby's room. Yellow paint."

The baby's room had been painted weeks earlier. I gestured at Wade, who was in the corridor by the nursing desk talking to the guard on duty. Maybe Wade could jog George's memory more effectively.

But my hand stopped in midair as, looking past Wade, I saw something odd happening out by the main entrance. The glass doors were opening by themselves.

Or they seemed to. The dark glittering panes swung inward to reveal a woman and two children materializing out of nowhere as they stepped into the lighted lobby. They stopped at the desk, then went off in another direction, as the glass doors swung open yet again to admit another group of visitors.

"Excuse me," I told George and Ellie. In the lobby I passed between the waiting area and the information desk. Noting that I still wasn't able to see out through them, I approached the double doors. Then, as they swung open at my touch, I exited to the front-entrance drop-off area marked with No Parking signs.

A pair of wheelchairs stood empty on the sidewalk. Near them were an honor box for the *Bangor Daily News,* a large concrete urn filled with sand and cigarette butts, and a mailbox.

A dark blue mailbox. Ellie and Will had been standing near it a few evenings earlier. I'd seen them there very briefly while I was speaking with Therese Chamberlain.

And they could have seen us, I realized. From her furtive look and anxious behavior it must have been obvious that Therese was imparting something confidential, something she didn't want anyone else to know she was saying.

But someone had, without either of us realizing it, because at night you couldn't see into the parking lot from the interior of the hospital. From there, those doors were glittering black. From out here, though, the nursing desk was clearly visible.

Which was how I discovered that no one had overheard Therese talking to me. She hadn't told anyone about her plan to confide further in me, either. Someone had *seen* her, first in Boston and then here at the hospital as she was telling me something she didn't want anyone else to know.

Not to mention a final time, of course, on the morning when she was murdered.

"He doesn't remember *anything,*" Ellie agonized as we drove home. "Not since weeks ago. He won't be *able* to tell us where he was when—"

287

"He won't have to." Crammed into the truck's tiny backseat, I felt so full of knowledge that I feared I might explode. One bright burst of understanding had illuminated everything.

Someone had seen Therese talking to me and known the threat she represented, known that she could ruin everything by giving George an alibi for the night Hector Gosling was murdered. For she'd been in the garage in Boston when George was there, and had seen *him*.

"He won't have to remember anything," I said again. "We're going to clear him." I put my hand on Ellie's shoulder.

I could feel the tension in her neck muscles as she fought for composure. "But Jake, if they send him back to that jail . . ."

Wade interrupted. "The guard told me Perry Daigle's been sent to Thomaston. George won't have trouble with him again."

Thomaston, the state prison. "I think old Perry's going to have his world view adjusted real sharply," Wade continued. "He's tough when everyone else is smaller or more civilized." Small chuckle from Wade. "But down there, he's going to find out what it's like to be at the low end of the food chain."

Ellie laid her cheek on my hand. "Thanks, you guys. That does make me feel a little better, knowing that at least he won't be at Perry's mercy. But Jake, *how* will we clear George?"

I didn't want to burden her with more uncertainty

by telling her I wasn't sure. I couldn't even say what I suspected, not to Ellie or to anyone else, in case someone's body language or face communicated something sooner than I wanted.

Botox, where are you when I need you? All I could give her was a heartfelt promise.

"Trust me, Ellie. We're going to do it."

Or I am, I added silently. Because whether she liked it or not, in the snooping department she was out of action. No matter what she said, I knew the baby could show up any time. I couldn't risk her going into labor at an inconvenient, possibly even a dangerous moment.

Such as for instance during the unmasking of a killer.

CHAPTER 10

Just as I'd expected, George was sent back to the county jail in Machias first thing the next morning.

"Neanderthals," Victor fumed as Sam and I arrived for the CPR class at the firehouse. "You'd think they all had traumatic brain injury."

Fright stabbed me. "Does George?" It hadn't occurred to me that he might have long-term problems.

"No," Victor conceded grumpily. "He will likely regain his memory a little at a time. Eventually." But not immediately; not in time to do him any good.

"Listen," Victor said, "before we start can you help me out a little?" He walked me over to a window. "This won't stay open by itself and with all these people in here, it gets so hot," he complained.

He waved dismissively at the project. "It shouldn't take too long, should it?"

This was standard for Victor; if even his ex-wife can do it, he believes, any fool can. I considered just breaking the glass. That would keep the freaking window open, wouldn't it?

But that might be perceived as petty. And anyway, after I'd fiddled with the window a minute I saw that I couldn't fix it.

"Victor, it's the kind with a sash cord and counterweights inside. It'll need a new cord, we don't have one, and besides, I don't know how."

He looked at once incredulous and vindicated. "What do you mean? It's a window, isn't it? I thought you were the *expert* on household repairs."

Whereupon, having neatly disposed of *that* little notion, he accepted my verdict and we propped the window open with a Bangor phone book.

By now Sam was across the room kneeling by his Resusci-Annie doll and the other students were doing the same. That included my new partner, a big cop from the Machias police department standing by our own exercise mat. He sent a beckoning look my way. We were going to go through the whole resuscitation procedure today and he'd already made clear that he wanted to get it done with and vamoose.

"About Therese," I began to Victor. "You know it wasn't your fault that . . ."

But he shut me down. "Forget it," he said brusquely. "I can't save the world."

Which in a way was reassuring; if he ever turned into a fully functioning human being for more than a few minutes at a time, I'd have to start watching for other apocalyptic events, too.

"Got it," I muttered, and went to join my new CPR buddy.

"Hey," the cop said, positioning himself at the doll's head. Not friendly; like most of the students he was only here because he had to be, to re-up his professional certification.

"Let's do it," I replied, not chummily either. If anything, I wanted to be here even less than he did. But I had no choice; everything had to look perfectly normal if what I planned was to work out.

The cop responded to the briskness in my tone better than if I'd made some bogus try at being a pal. "Yeah," he replied. "Not that I got any big treat to look forward to."

Like Therese, he already knew CPR techniques, and he inflated the doll's lungs expertly while I pressed its breastbone down.

"What's that?" I asked as we switched positions. "I mean, what are you not looking forward to?" Remembering what Therese had showed me about extending the doll's jaw, I yanked firmly on it and pressed my lips firmly to its rubbing-alcohol-tasting mouth.

"Gotta transport a guy when I get done here." The cop pushed the doll's breastbone down energetically. The breath I'd blown in rushed back out of its lungs: *whoosh*.

"Guy named Ronny Ronaldson," he went on. "Local guy, I'll be getting him out of your hair for a while."

"Yeah, actually I know him. Friend of a friend."

Ronny, the not-too-brilliant helper that Will had

taken out fishing two days earlier along with the blond-ponytailed fellow, Weasel Bodine, whom Tommy had disliked so much.

The cop's verbal assessment of Ronny was less charitable than my mental one. "Guy's dumber'n a box of rocks," he commented.

Across the room, Sam and his partner were being singled out for praise; once again Sam had shown his handiness with the real world, absorbing the nuts and bolts of resuscitation in a gulp.

"How come? What'd he do that makes him so dumb, I mean?"

"Guy walks down Water Street," the cop told me, "puts a rock through a store window and runs. Broad daylight, what's he think, nobody's gonna see him?"

"Who picked him up?" Eastport was still being policed by the state cops, who last time I looked weren't doing foot patrols.

"Store owner ID'd him, I went to his house and grabbed him, he's locked in my squad outside right now."

The cop sat back on his heels. "Good news for Eastport," he went on, "bad news for me, I gotta do the paperwork before I can go home. I was supposed to be off this afternoon," he added injuredly.

"Who was the store owner?" I asked, suspecting the answer and trying to adjust mentally to this new, unexpected development. I'd thought I would have more time.

The cop shrugged. "Well, not a store, actually. Going to be a new restaurant downtown. Guy renting the space was there when it happened, made the complaint."

He shook his head. "That's what's so dopy, guy was standing right there watching him when he did it. Name of Will Bonnet?"

Victor strolled by. He'd been observing our performance from afar, which was the distance I preferred him to keep.

Especially now since he'd gone back to his usual, non-warm-and-fuzzy *persona*. "All right, you two. That'll be fine," Victor pronounced.

He handed us each a sheet of take-home exam questions and a date when we would all return, do the hands-on portion of the CPR test, and receive our certifications. Whereupon the Machias cop left before I could even try to talk him into hanging onto Ronny for a while.

So it was clear I had to do something. Ronny's arrest was not only bad news for the officer who had to transport him to the county lockup. It was also bad news for me, because Ronny was going to be in jail very soon. And unless I missed my guess, once he got there he would try finishing the job that Perry Daigle had started.

Back home I got on the phone at once. But the officer on clerk duty at the jail had little patience with me. The whole thing was nearly impossible to explain, the panic in my voice wasn't making me more believable-sounding, and

I wasn't halfway through it when he interrupted.

He wanted to know if I thought prank calls were funny, and did I realize my phone number and address were on a screen right there in front of him? He could send a cop out if he wanted to, bring me in for making a false report.

He did tell me that George was alone in the sickroom, that the beds were bolted down, and that there were no heavy objects or other items in there that could be turned into weapons. But he wouldn't promise George would *remain* alone. And when I asked him if Maine State Police Trooper Hollis Colgate was by any chance at the jail and if I could possibly talk to him, the officer hung up on me.

Trying to stay calm, I took deep breaths of the kind that are supposed to help your thinking by oxygenating your brain. But they only made me dizzy. What I needed were facts and with time suddenly so short I had nowhere to get them.

Nowhere but straight from the horse's mouth. I'd meant to get an unsuspecting Will over to the house tonight and somehow get the truth out of him. Tricks, lies . . . if worse came to worst I was ready to ask Wade to smack him around, if necessary.

And Wade would've done it. But now I would have to confront Will much sooner than I had wanted to, and manage to convince him that I knew for sure a lot more than I really did.

Jail officials might believe Will if he told them *he'd* sent Ronny to kill George. No one would say such a thing unless it was true, they would probably figure. So I had to make Will think he was caught, get him believing that if the plan to kill George went through, it would only make things worse for him.

And I had to do it in front of witnesses, or killing me could just put Will Bonnet right back in the driver's seat again. I just hoped it wasn't too late to stop him.

Grabbing up my keys and tossing them into the nifty little bag Ellie had given me, I rushed out to Harlequin House, where I thought Will might be this morning. It would've been perfect; the fix-up was back on track and there'd been a work session scheduled.

But no one was there and the door was locked. Taped to it I found a poster announcing a historical society meeting at Will's aunt's house, starting in a few minutes. Grimly I set off, intent on adding another item to the meeting's agenda.

A few blocks away just across from the Presbyterian church, Agnes Bonnet's lovely old Federal house was a near-twin to my own: white clapboard, multiple chimneys. I knocked, noting that cars were already lined up in the street.

Footsteps came to the door. "Coming," Will's voice called.

Steady, girl. A door latch clicked and the door swung open.

"Hey, come on in. The others will be here shortly," he said.

Step into my parlor, said the spider to the . . .

Anxiety seized me. But I couldn't very well run. That would surely tip him to my suspicions and perhaps seal George's fate.

Besides, I had plenty of company here with the meeting going on. "Hi, Will," I said brightly. "Got a minute?"

"Absolutely," he replied. "Coffee's on, we'll have some."

And sure enough, I did smell fresh coffee, yet another sign of the gathering about to begin.

So like a good little fly, I stepped inside.

"What's the meeting about?" I asked as I followed him into Agnes Bonnet's charmingly old-fash-ioned kitchen. A fire flickered pleasantly in the small isinglass-windowed woodstove. An elderly cooking stove, its rounded knobs and raised gas-grate burners reminiscent of the 1930s, stood nearby. The south-facing windows admitted bright sunshine through ball-fringed curtains.

From the other room came mingled voices. "Oh, you know. The usual. Who does what, all that," Will replied.

Into the serene setting he had introduced numerous large, shiny kitchen gadgets including an espresso machine and a fancy breadmaker whose contents seemed to have exploded out of its top, creating a crusted-on, neglected Vesuvius effect.

"The hot water pipe in the Harlequin House kitchen needs soldering before we can turn the boiler on," he said. "Ditto for the gas. I think we should get somebody over to look at it."

He got a cup down from a cabinet. "And they took the front hall banister down to the boatyard to refinish it there, in the spray booth," he went on. "So it'll have to be brought back and re-installed."

"Big job," I observed, looking around a little more. "But a spray finish will be faster than using a brush, I guess."

It was the result that might be horrid, too thick in some places and not enough coverage in others. Hardly anyone seems to rub down enough between coats of spray finish; thus the armies of garishly gleaming old tables and chests of drawers you see in so many "antique" shops.

"Anyway," I said, "anything's better than nothing." Again not my true opinion, but far be it from me to discourage anyone who was actually doing something, whether I approved of it or not, on a project as big as Harlequin House.

"Yeah," Will said. Back turned to me, he poured coffee from a badly-needing-a-scrub carafe. "Here you go," he added, handing me the cup.

Apparently his food enthusiasms only included cooking, not cleaning up dirty dishes afterwards. If it even included that; the coffee was bitter. I gulped at it nervously, keeping an eye on the back

298

door in case I needed to dash for it and wishing hard that some of the historical society members would join me out here.

Then as a burst of music interrupted the chattering voices, I realized that they were coming not from live people, but from a television set. No one was here.

"Will, I thought everyone . . . What are all those cars doing parked outside?"

"Church service. Memorial for Hector. Not that anyone much cared, but I guess they thought they had to do something."

"Yeah. Yeah, I guess." That back door started looking very good to me. On the other hand I was here now, and . . .

"Our group ought to be showing up soon, though," he said, glancing at the clock over the stove. "Stay here a second and let them in when they come, would you? Drink your coffee. I promised I'd bring Agnes a cup, too. Back in a jiffy."

He left with a tray. Upstairs I heard a door open, and then a low, incoherent mumble cut off as the door closed firmly again.

Sad as I was at this fresh evidence that Agnes was failing, I couldn't very well ignore the opportunity he'd given me to look around. I just needed to be careful: as he'd said, people would be coming in any minute.

So I got up and opened the nearest kitchen drawer. It held only a jumble of kitchen utensils including a spatula with egg dried on it and a cheese grater with a greying scrim clinging to it. But the next one contained papers.

Lots of papers. Hastily I rummaged through them. They included a report from the Board of Prisons of the Commonwealth of Massachusetts, numerous copies of probation reports, and a little card like the one the dentist gives to schedule your next appointment.

The card, dated nearly a year earlier, set a time for Will to see a probation officer. I didn't see any more recent cards. The paperwork said he was out on parole after serving a sentence in Walpole, in Massachusetts, for extortion and assault.

There were newspaper clippings too. I scanned fast: an arson fire at a Boston seafood place. Owner found inside with his legs broken, swore he'd fallen trying to get out.

Yeah, right. I opened a cabinet. Inside were a dozen jars of the imported caviar he'd fed us, but no other fancy foods unless you counted Fluffernutter, Froot Loops, and Ring-Dings, plus a variety of salty things in barbecue flavors.

In the freezer were stacks of frozen dinners and packages of prepared frozen codfish cakes, their label bearing an address in downtown Boston. The codfish cakes we'd had at the Harlequin House luncheon were, I recalled now, the only dish of Will's I'd ever eaten that didn't have serious preparation problems.

Because he hadn't made it. That was a lie, too.

He came back as I opened the refrigerator. "Looking for something?"

"No." Suddenly I realized I'd taken one of the little jars of caviar out of the cabinet and it was still in my hand, a dead giveaway to what I'd really been doing.

"I mean . . . yes." Nervousness made my mouth feel rubbery. "I was wondering if you had any milk."

Luckily my bag was still on my shoulder; when Will turned away I dropped the little jar into it, then stuffed the bag inside my jacket and zipped it halfway up so the bag wouldn't show, or so I fervently hoped.

He got powdered creamer out of another cabinet and handed it to me with a plastic spoon. "Here," he said flatly.

Which was when it struck me that he hadn't done much prep work for the imminent meeting. Where were the silver tea urn, the dessert plates and small sandwiches customary at such gatherings?

"I guess the club is bringing the refreshments?" I asked stupidly as I took a sip of creamer-adulterated coffee. In view of recent events, white powder wouldn't have been on my list of things I wanted to consume.

But the glass jar was brand new with the safety seal still on it. And dumping the stuff into the coffee hadn't made it taste better, but at least it tasted different.

"No," he replied finally. "I fibbed about that,

actually. I canceled the meeting. Aunt Agnes just isn't up to having people over today."

Then I did head for the door. But as I approached it the door began moving also: taller and shorter, fatter and thinner. Too late it occurred to me that a medicinal taste often indicates an actual presence of medicine in the tasted substance. Coffee, for instance.

Also, that medicine plus no meeting meant I might be in very deep do-do, indeed.

Or dee-dee indood. Oh, I was in trouble. Not the creamer; he had put something in the coffee much earlier, when he poured the cup. And I'd been drinking it all along, whatever it was.

The room tilted interestingly.

"Aunt Agnes," Will said, "isn't long for this world. Poor old dear. But she's had a good life and now it's time for her to move on. Let the younger generation take over."

I looked down at my cup. It was empty except for a tiny bit of undissolved something, a yellow muck-blob at the bottom of it. Not strychnine powder; if it had been I'd be past wondering about it by now. But powdered creamer didn't leave a residue like that.

Powdered creamer didn't even . . .

"Sink," I murmured aloud. It came out *think*. Which meant I'd better do the latter or I'd be doing the former real soon, now.

"May I use your bathroom? I'm not feeling very well."

A smile. "Of course. Top of the stairs, to your right."

Oh God. I made it upstairs, mixed my right up with my left, and flung myself through the wrong door. A grab at the doorknob saved me from falling right onto Agnes's bed with her in it; *tied* into it with adhesive tape. Agnes stared up at me, pale old eyes confused, mouth sagged into an O of beseeching semicoherence.

"Agnes, I'll come back," I gabbled. "I swear to you I will." I closed the door on this horror, confronted a fresh one: my own face in the bathroom mirror. Whatever he'd given me had already begun working its lousy magic. My pupils were dilated and sweat was beading on my upper lip.

I tried to make the stuff come up again but it wouldn't; whatever Will had given me, it had turned my digestion into the calm spot at the center of a roiling maelstrom. In desperation I yanked open the medicine cabinet.

Inside were the items of Will's much-vaunted first-aid kit, the one he'd been assembling so he could take care of his poor frail old aunt. But now I realized he was using the things to treat the scars of her imprisonment.

The "first-aid kit" consisted mostly of gauze, bandages, and some heavy-duty stuff whose label said it was for bedsores. There were several bottles of prescription tranquilizers, too.

But then I saw what I needed: the bottle of ipecac I'd given Will to complete his supply of remedies. Only just as I was about to twist the top off and guzzle the stuff—somehow I *had* to get rid of what he'd given me—he was pounding on the door.

"Jacobia? Are you all right?" His voice was saccharine.

"Yes!" I shoved the bottle into the pocket of my jeans, yanked my shirt down over it and got the cabinet closed.

The door opened a crack. His suspicious eyes met mine in the mirror, peered around. Then the door opened wide.

"Jacobia, I think you'd better come with me, now."

The window, I could hurl myself out through the . . .

His hand clamped around my arm, turned me, held me up as my knees dissolved without warning.

"Hey, hey. Can't have our star snoop passing out and maybe cracking her head open on the tub, can we?"

He guided me out into the hall. "No, we can't have that at all." His choice of words was smart-assed but his voice sounded frightened, unnaturally high.

"You're not George's friend," I blubbered. Gad, what had he *given* me?

I kept talking, hoping it would keep me from passing out. Not that my own choice of words was well considered, but I was doped up. And besides, he'd been onto me already for a while, now.

"You're a con man. The kind of bad guy who charms your socks off . . ." *Thocks.* I felt a goofy grin smear itself across my face.

". . . right up until the minute his fingers start tightening around your throat."

Froat. Oh yeah, I was doing real well. The hall looked miles long and I knew he was going to herd me into one of the other bedrooms, tie me up with adhesive tape like Agnes.

If he did I'd have a chance. It meant he was going to leave me alone, maybe long enough so I could squirm out of the bonds somehow and get help. But no such luck; he wasn't only a worried con man.

He was a careful one. "Ronny," I muttered as he half-carried me down the stairs. My feet kept tangling and my brain felt like a pinball machine. "What'd you tell him to make him do it?"

He cleared his throat uncertainly, his grip on my arm moist with nervous perspiration. And he didn't quite answer me.

Instead he seemed to be encouraging himself. "If at first you don't succeed," he recited. Then, more forcefully, "Too bad about Perry Daigle. I had hopes, but Perry always was a screwup."

"You paid him." We reached the downstairs hall. "You gave Perry money, made promises, so he would hit George on the head."

"Yup," he replied. "Decent down payment, a few years in jail, big payday at the end. More'n he could earn on the outside. And everyone knows

Daigle hates jail, so no one would suspect the truth. Not," Will said, "that he was going to reach that payday. But Daigle's not a long-term planning type of guy like I am."

If he tried taking me outside someone would see . . . but that hope sank too as instead he muscled me through a breezeway to the garage without ever going outdoors at all. "That's how I knew I had to have a backup," he went on, "in case Daigle missed."

He slammed the door behind him. "Which he did. George lived. But you're right, now Ronny can finish what Daigle didn't."

My knees buckled as he guided me toward the car in the garage. "Ronny doesn't bribe 'cause he doesn't understand about money," Will confided, "but he scares real easy. Pretty soon no more George, just the way I planned in the first place."

"So Perry Daigle killed Hector and Jan Jesperson while you and George were in Boston? And somehow you got George not to tell anyone where the two of you had gone. That way he'd have no . . ."

Alibi, I wanted to finish. But I couldn't remember the word. And anyway, that wasn't it. A triumphant look spread on Will's face as he opened the car's trunk.

"Wrong," he pronounced. "It's better than that. I had plenty of time to plan, back in Walpole. Get in."

I tried stalling him. Once he had me in there he

could take me anywhere. No one would know.

"You knew Jan was dead because you'd killed her. Saying your aunt wanted to see her, that was just to make it look as if you thought Jan was still alive?"

"There you go. Now you're back on the right track."

He shoved me hard. "I knew as soon as I laid eyes on her the Jesperson woman was bent. It takes one to know one," he added a little sorrowfully.

"Will, you don't have to do this," I implored.

"Really? You're going to let me get away, I suppose?"

Well, no. Not if I could help it. "Anyway I can't stop now," he added, turning sullen. "It's got to go the way I planned."

One last try. "No. No, it doesn't, and if you do stop now I'll help you."

I meant it, too. Partly because it could save my life, but for another reason also.

"Damn it, Will, there's no such thing as too late. Not while you're breathing."

I was looking at Will but I was thinking of my father, Sam, and myself.

All the second chances we fortunate people had been given to live down our mistakes. "You can turn this around and if you do I'll stick by you," I said. "I'll get lawyers, expert witnesses."

A forensic hospital and treatment was better than a jail cell. I was still looking straight at him, my own gaze managing to focus for a few moments. Something moved in his eyes.

Hope, I realized. But not for long. He was just too far gone. "I'll bet you would," he said quietly at last. Regretfully. "I'll just bet you would, and if you did go to bat for me, do you know what would happen?"

Yeah. I knew. That was, as Sam would've put it, the fly in the oinkment.

"I'd get out and do it again. Not the same thing, but something. Because that's who I am. That's what I do. I'm a bad guy. Truth is I wish I hadn't ever come back here."

He had, though. Back here to us. And now we were caught in his scheme like so many flies in a Venus flytrap. He had, I figured, about as much choice in the matter as one of those, too.

His expression hardened again. Oops, time to talk fast.

"How'd you know Jan was a crook?" I asked, hoping to keep the conversation going. When it ended I was sunk. And at first, my ploy actually worked.

"Hey," he replied, brightening. "You think she bought all that stuff in her house with sales commissions? No way." He chuckled.

Not a good sign. Now that he'd dropped his good-guy facade, he wasn't bothering to hide his mood swings, either. "So I found out more about her, figured out she must have assembled a stash. Which," he finished smugly, "she had."

"How'd you get them to come here? To this house?"

Howth. My little few moments of clarity were dissolving as the second phase of whatever he'd given me kicked in hard.

But he understood. "Jan and Hector? It was easy. Told 'em I could prove what they'd been up to. First her and then him. That Jan, she hotfooted it over here so fast . . ."

Yeah, so fast she hadn't turned off her coffeepot or locked her house, or even put away her laptop. Hector would've been extremely eager to know what Will had on him, too.

And each of them must have accepted a drink, right there in his aunt's kitchen where I'd done the same. It was a poison-laced concoction for Hector; for Jan probably a sedative like the one he'd given me, so she'd be easier to strangle.

After that, the back side of Harlequin House was so thickly overgrown that all he had to do was get the car in unseen, get the trunk unloaded, and open the coal chute. And presto, delivery accomplished.

The car trunk looked suddenly even more unattractive. He could drive to the wilderness on the mainland and leave me, walk or hitchhike home. Then he could come back later, bury me in the woods.

Or whatever. I leaned on the fender. "Will, is it about that boat trip? Is it drugs, are you smuggling them? Maybe with help from someone else?"

His laugh this time was genuinely amused. "Oh, please. Show some imagination. Try seeing the whole picture. The big show."

My head lolled back. I tried to fix it, but failed. My eyelids were lowering dangerously. "Tell me."

He inspected me. "Okay. Maybe I will. The boat was a ruse," he said cruelly. "You fell for it like a ton of bricks."

He checked my bonds—and where had *they* come from?—grunting with satisfaction as he yanked them. "You really believed I didn't know how nosy you are? I had Perry take the boat out just to give you something to chew on."

"I don't see . . ." God, I was out of it. He'd tied me up without my even realizing it was happening. But then I did understand. "The boat was to make it look as if George was involved in something illegal."

"Yeah. Slow you down a little. You dig too deep, you might come up with something nasty on Mister Goody-Two-Shoes. You sure wouldn't want to do that," he added sarcastically.

He was right. He'd been even farther ahead of me than I had realized. And now as if to reassure himself that he really was the villain he fancied himself to be, his manner roughened more, too.

"Tell you something else. You want to bring in a big score, you don't put it on a boat." He shoved me first one way and then the other, positioning me in front of the car's trunk.

I wobbled woozily, barely staying on my feet.

"Way too much security for that nowadays," he went on. "Those Customs guys see everything. So what you do is, you attach it."

He prodded me experimentally. I nearly toppled over but caught myself. "Underneath," he went on. "Then you move the boat. Out to Deep Cove, say. Haul your stuff up when no one's around."

"What stuff?" My feet felt as if they were dissolving and my head as if it were filling with concrete. *Thtuff.* "What did you bring in that . . ."

"You'll see. Real soon, you'll figure it out. For now let's just say it was the other reason I went to Boston, to finish the arrangements on a deal I've had going for a while."

His tone chilled to subzero. I didn't buy it. It was still as if he was trying to live up to some tough model in his head. But his efforts were working well enough to put a hitch in my git-along, as George would've expressed it.

"A *good* deal," Will added. "But right now I want you out for the count. Absolute silence, no ruckus while I'm driving, maybe somebody hears you. So we're going to just sit here till the junk you've got on board finishes working."

He grinned engagingly. Falsely. It was all bluff. Maybe it was always all bluff with guys like him, I didn't know.

And at the moment, it made no earthly difference to me. "The eyes are the window to the soul, Jake, did you know that?"

Yeah, I thought sourly, I've heard it somewhere.

311

Meanwhile his own eyes showed flickers of panic again. They'd begun darting around like little creatures hunting for an escape route.

It hit me again that he wasn't as sure of himself as he wanted to seem. But the cracks in his psychological underpinnings were not helping me. "You have," I mumbled, "an unoriginal mind."

He ignored the insult. "That's how I knew the jig was up. I could see it in *your* eyes, see it coming. And the minute Sam came for the caviar, I was sure. You wanted a better look at it, and that meant you suspected something. You want to put me behind bars again."

A slow head-shake. "Not gonna happen, though."

We'll see, you creep, I thought. I'd had enough of his deep traumas and I was way past the I'll-help-you-out stage, too. Hey, I'd offered him a hand and he'd turned it down.

So it was time for plan B, whatever that was; by now I was getting pretty unoriginal, myself. There's not much snappy patter to be found in la-la land, I was discovering.

Or a lot of clever planning ability. "What'd you tell George to get him to drive you to Boston?" I asked.

Didn't I? Maybe I didn't. I wasn't sure anymore how much I was saying and how much I was only thinking.

Perhaps dreaming. "And Ellie," I persisted, filled with drug-addled inspiration. "It's something to do with Ellie, too, isn't it? The whole thing, she's part of it?" I speculated aloud.

Or possibly not. By now, the gongs in my ears were ringing so furiously I could barely hear myself think.

"You want to know so much," he said. "Okay, I'll tell you a bedtime story. And I'll stop when I'm sure that you are fast asleep."

He reached out and gave me a little shove, just one-handed. I fell halfway into the trunk, flopped there. He loaded my legs in, bent them, and as an afterthought folded my hands together.

Like the hands of a child who is getting ready to float into slumber. Or praying hard. He lowered the trunk lid.

Darkness; the smell of old dust, the rubbery reek of a spare tire. I tried to push the lid back up and realized again with a bolt of fright that he'd bound my wrists.

Terror filled me. I was losing it. If I fell asleep now I wouldn't wake up in the morning, fresh and ready for a new day.

And not later, groggy but mad as hell. Not ever, unless I kept my eyes open. But from his manner I knew he didn't believe I had much choice in the off-to-dreamland department.

Sounds: the scrape of a metal lawn chair on the concrete garage floor. Faint creak as he settled into it. And then his voice, a bit muffled but still audible, and rich with the unexpected pleasure of pouring out his sad story to someone. Because for all I would ever be able to do about it, he could be talking to himself.

Among my final coherent thoughts was the too-late-now-dammit awareness of the mistake I had been making all along. To me the trouble had been that George's absence fell within the time frame of Hector's death.

But I'd never seen it the other way around: that appearances to the contrary maybe Hector's death *didn't* fall into the time frame of George's absence.

"Once upon a time," Will began in the age-old way.

The last story, probably, that I would ever hear. And though I didn't enjoy it, I will say this much.

It was a doozy.

"Once upon a time . . ."

I woke in near-darkness with my hands still bound and fresh tape over my mouth, propped up against a wall. A candle flickered on a nearby table. From somewhere nearby came a scraping sound, a very *familiar* sound, but I couldn't quite place it.

Then I did and a thud of fright hit me as I recognized my surroundings. Meanwhile Will had apparently started over: a story so nice he told it twice.

". . . there was a bad boy and a good boy. Best friends, right here in little old Eastport, Maine."

I was in the hidden room in Harlequin House

where Ellie and I had discovered the bodies of Hector Gosling and Eva Thane.

I battled my fear by tallying up all the physical things around me. There was the old red rug. The board floor, splinters sticking up from it, with a bent nail protruding from one of the boards where someone had tried inexpertly to fasten it back down. A candle like the one that had burned on the table by Eva Thane's body all those years ago was stuck in a mess of melted wax.

Its flame comforted me. But eventually it would burn down.

"All the bad boy did was get in trouble," Will went on. "And all the good boy did was get him out of it."

Beneath me I could feel the edges of the trap-door. My legs were getting numb, though; I'd been lying here for some time.

And while I was unconscious Will Bonnet had begun walling me up alive. That was the scraping sound I heard: a plaster trowel.

"It got pretty old," Will said. "The routine. Because it was not like the good boy didn't get into his share of trouble. Only no one ever held it against him. They were too busy shaking their heads over the bad boy."

A thoughtful pause. "All talking about him and wishing he'd go away," Will added bleakly.

Ellie and I had even speculated about it: quick-dry plaster, fresh wallpaper in the new pattern we'd picked. It would work.

"He did, too," Will went on. "The bad boy went away and once he was gone the good boy got everything. Even the girl."

Ellie, he meant. "It wasn't fair, you know. I tried. I did. But somehow I just always ended up in trouble again."

He sounded truly puzzled. "So what the hell," he finished. "I figured, try to make something of it. Being in trouble, in a weird way it seemed to be my strong point. So in the end I guess I just decided to go with that."

His voice turned vicious suddenly. "I mean, think about it, for God's sake. 'Take responsibility. Step up to the plate. Here, you're getting another chance, take advantage,'" he mimicked.

"Have you," he demanded, "got any idea how friggin' tiresome that crap gets after a while? I mean when you just *can't do it*?"

Another chance . . . Of course, I realized.

It was why George had remained silent. Sitting in jail, George had been giving Will one more chance to step up to the plate, take responsibility, and tell the truth.

Or what George believed was the truth. But Will had taken advantage in another way; his own way.

"He never was too bright, George. He always believed things turn out all right in the end," Will went on meanly.

More scraping. "Anyway, I've put up some thin lath. Not much so it won't show through, especially once the wallpaper's up. But good enough."

316

It was just what Ellie and I had planned to do. And once that plaster on the new lath dried, you'd need a battering ram to break out of it. I looked around frantically; no battering rams.

"You've probably figured out that Aunt Agnes wasn't being victimized by Hector Gosling or Jan Jesperson," Will said.

I hadn't, actually. I'd been too busy trying to avoid being victimized myself. And a fabulous job I'd done of it, too.

"But what a great story it was," he went on. "That the poor old dear needed me to take care of her. Perfect wedge for me to get into her house, set up a base of operations."

Thwack. He was generous with the plaster, I had to give him that. And it was dry in here; the stuff might not cure fully for a couple of days but it would be solid enough to imprison me nearly at once.

And the other walls of the room were made of thick boards. So I pinned my last hopes on the trapdoor. Spiked them to it in fact, because if it didn't save me I was going to end up like Eva, a shriveled corpse for future old-house fixers to find.

Would they ever know what happened? I thought of Wade and Sam looking for me. Not finding me until too late. Tears pricked my eyes; furiously I blinked them away.

"And Jan Jesperson *had* been squirreling away drug samples," he continued. "Using them on people, get hold of their property."

317

Another wallop of fear blindsided me, disorienting as a kick to the head. A desperate, gagging protest gargled past the tape pressed thickly to my mouth.

A scraping sound came from the plaster bucket. "Once I figured that out," Will went on, "I knew just what to do. Take her stash and use her for window dressing, like George got so mad he killed her, also."

Thwack. "George set his part up for me so well. Him and his righteous anger. What a motive he gave himself. Worked great."

A *thunk* as he dropped his trowel into the plaster bucket. "Anyway, it won't be long now," he finished.

Because Ronny would take up where Perry Daigle left off, if he hadn't already. Stay calm, I ordered myself. But my breath came in short, sharp gasps and my heart slammed painfully against my chest.

"Too bad about you," Will added. "You weren't in the plan. I'm sorry, Jacobia. Honestly I am. It's just one of those things that happens, unfortunately."

But he didn't sound sorry. I heard no trace of the mingled self-doubt and reflection he'd been tiptoeing around, earlier. Whatever story he'd had to tell himself to get through this part of his plan, that's the one he'd told.

The sad part was, probably a lot of the story was true. But it wasn't the worst part. The worst was that he'd gone all the way over from planning to doing. And for the life of me—literally—I didn't know anymore how I was going to stop him.

There was the sound of newspapers crumpling, being stuffed into—I guessed—a plastic trash bag. Probably he'd set it up so there wouldn't be any evidence of a fresh plaster job.

Now he was disposing of the newspapers he'd used to cover the floor. "I think if I just apply the paste to the wet plaster, press the paper on, it'll dry pretty neatly, don't you?"

He was right, it would. And even if it didn't, people would just think Ellie and I had hung the paper that way, a quick and dirty solution.

Which meant that if the trapdoor didn't let me out of here—assuming I could first get the tape off my wrists and get the circulation going in my hands again, so I could lift it—no one was ever going to see the wall and realize I was in here.

But if I thought I at least knew the grimmest element of the situation, I was all wrong. He had been saving the real chiller, the part that set me yanking at the tape on my wrists again.

"The kid, though," Will Bonnet said. "That stumped me for quite a while, the idea of Ellie having a baby. I wasn't counting on any little rug rat to screw up the picture. Especially not any of George's."

A needle of horror pierced my heart at this new depth, what this piece of damaged goods was actually contemplating.

"But hey," he went on, "accidents do happen. Kids can die in their sleep. She'll forget George and his offspring. And then . . ."

His aunt's house, his friend's wife, a sizable inheritance; I was seeing it all, now.

Too late. A choked noise came from my throat: fear, rage, and disgust, all in one tape-muffled outburst. But Will was too busy congratulating himself to hear it.

Meanwhile part of me was still arguing with him, trying to find the reason for his behavior. If I'd had his life, his biology, his upbringing, I might have turned out just like him, I thought. An outsider looking in, conscience-free and in the end perhaps simply unable to figure out how to be human.

Most of me didn't think so, though. Not really. Because Will might not have *had* a choice about who he'd turned out to be.

But he'd *made* the choice to stop fighting it.

And now his voice was moving away. With a thud of anguish I realized I hadn't heard any sounds of plastering or cleaning up for quite some time.

The job was finished.

A door slammed as he left the house.

Back in the days when I was a surgeon's wife I used to pick up lots of little hospital tips and tricks, none of which I ever expected to be able to use.

For instance, you can only tear adhesive tape if you don't let it see you coming. Approach it tentatively, it will beat you every time. But with a fast right-angle snap to the edge, it will rip straight across as easily as if you had cut it with scissors.

Unfortunately I'd already struggled with my bonds so much, the tape was blood-moistened and rolled at the edges. No hope of tearing it, so I didn't waste time trying; instead I rubbed my chin over its surface, trying to peel it off.

That didn't work either. It was too mushed together for a loose end to exist. And the candle was burning down . . .

Think. Something sharp. I scanned the tiny room, noticed something that hadn't been there the last time I was in it. Over in the corner where Hector Gosling had lain a few days earlier stood a pair of wooden crates, one with its top slightly ajar.

I inched myself over to them on my butt, bumped the top off the crate. Inside, the crate was completely filled with jars.

Caviar jars, and where the hell had *those* come from? But I didn't have time to wonder about it and they were packed in so tightly that with my wrists bound, I couldn't prize one of them out.

Then I remembered that maybe I didn't need to. The lids on these jars were like the lid on the jar I'd taken from the kitchen cabinet at Will's, then dropped into my bag . . . I rolled and felt the bag's lumpy presence inside my jacket.

Even better, I could smell fish, which was wonderful because it meant the jar had broken. I spent the next ten minutes working the bag up inside my jacket with my arms, all the while telling myself that if I could only keep my head and work methodically I still had a chance. That "method-ically" had never been an adverb that applied to me was a thought I decided to avoid confronting, just at the moment.

And eventually the bag popped out. Then of course I had to get some broken jar pieces out of the bag; fortunately I hadn't had time to zip it back at Will's house. And it is astonishing what a person can do to avoid having her life flash termi-nally before her eyes; I finally got hold of a piece. But there was now only a quarter-inch of candle left and the flame fluttered dangerously.

An eternity passed before I managed to position a biggish shard of the broken jar between my sneakers, sharp edge up. Then, working with care so as not to add a severed artery to my list of diffi-culties, I sawed at the soggy tape till it fell off.

Which freed me to dig in the bag again. It didn't contain what I really needed: a rocket launcher, say, or one of those handy combination ratchet-tool-and-help!-flare gadgets they sell in the TV ads around Christmas.

Also while I was digging in it my keys fell out and vanished with a jingle and clank through the iron grate over the old heating duct. But . . . *there*. I dug the miniature flashlight out and turned it on just as the candle died.

All right, now, dammit, I thought furiously, encouraged by the flashlight's beam. Ripping tape from my mouth I tore the old carpet from over the trapdoor, pushed my fingers into the crack.

Let's see how our buddy Will likes having the nasty story he told thrown right back in his . . .

Damn. The trapdoor was nailed shut from below. He could get the nails out when he wanted to when he came back through the cellar to get his boxes of caviar.

I couldn't.

Don't panic, I instructed myself firmly again. There was still the door he'd covered with plaster. And since I was free sooner than he'd expected, there was a slim chance that the plaster had not yet hardened enough to keep me from bashing through it. The lath would be thin, little more than popsicle-stick width; he'd said as much. I need only get the door open and . . .

That was when I noticed that the door lacked a doorknob. Of course; you couldn't plaster *over* a doorknob stem. Now the square hole for it was a small, darkly staring evil eye. I stared back, thinking of Ronny arriving at the county jail.

Ronny, whom Will had threatened with something dreadful if he didn't kill George, and afterwards endured in silence the prison term that would result. Not that poor Ronny was going to survive long enough to do otherwise. I had no doubt that Will would find a way of shutting that particular mouth forever, too.

But I was still staring at the door, and it still wasn't open. Unless I could *get* it open, it wasn't going to be until someone opened it and found my body.

Someday. *Poor Sam,* I thought as self-pity washed over me. I wished he were here right now. Oh, did I ever.

Then it struck me that if Sam *were* here, he'd probably have this problem solved already. To do it he would use *things,* ones he found here, jury-rigged to suit his purpose. All I needed to do was identify them and use them, too.

This I thought shouldn't take long. But the way my day was going it should've come as no surprise that I was wrong again.

Once I started looking, I found several more items I hadn't known were there. The gun, for instance.

And the suicide note.

I don't know why I hadn't understood it all earlier. Maybe because once you start thinking of someone as a victim, it's hard to envision them as the villain.

The heating grate pulled up easily; its bolt-holes had been stripped long ago by repeated removal and resetting. Once upon a time the house had suffered heating trouble, it seemed. The grate itself was a lovely, heavy old cast-iron object, its open-work the shape of a fleur-de-lis, substantial enough that I figured I could use it to bash through the plaster. But when I'd lifted it I spotted something lying barely visible in the duct below.

Not my keys. They'd apparently slid on down. Instead I found the sweetest little antique derringer you ever saw, small enough to fit in a lady's purse, and a crumpled piece of deckle-edged notepaper.

The cops, I realized, hadn't opened the grate. I plucked the gun and the note up out of the duct. Covered with writing, the note was signed "Eva"; in it, the woman whose body Ellie and I had found here confessed to murdering three Eastport girls in the 1920s.

But she couldn't stand seeing Chester Harlequin blamed and didn't have the courage to tell the truth while she was alive, the note explained. An especially clever bit was how she'd removed the doorknobs and doorknob stem, then pulled the door of the tiny room shut till it latched. She'd known workmen were coming the next day to plaster over the door and hang wallpaper. They wouldn't realize she was inside, dead.

Or as Eva had put it, that she'd gone on to meet her Maker. What a little hysteric she must have been, I thought. She'd surely known the impression she would make when she was found; nothing like time to turn a tawdry soap opera into a tragedy.

And by doing things the way she had, she'd arranged a double triumph for herself. *Saying* she wanted Chester cleared. But since neither she nor the note would be found soon, making sure that in fact he remained a suspect. Let's see, now, how slowly can you spell m-a-l-i-c-e?

Sure, Eva, I thought bitterly. Now that it's too late you spill your guts. And naturally even after almost a hundred years it's still all about you. How about a few hints from the grave on how I'm going to get out of here?

But on this topic the murderous flapper was unhelpfully silent. Why she'd crumpled the note and dropped it down the grate instead of just leaving it on the table I supposed I would never know either; just another quirk of bad-girl mischief, probably.

I could guess how the gun got there, though. I could see it in my mind's eye. Eva's right hand, the one that almost certainly held the gun, would've jerked reflexively in the moment of her death. The little gun flew across the table, hit the old floor, and fell through one of the openings in the heating grate to the duct below, where it landed with the note.

Sheesh. Chester Harlequin had been framed, all right, just as Ellie insisted, by someone he trusted. Just like George.

But I didn't have time to dwell on the ironic parallels. Instead I took a page from Sam's book and pulled a thick splinter out of an antique floorboard. This I jammed as firmly as I could into the hole where the doorknob stem should have been.

There: not quite a doorknob. But wrapping Eva's note around it made it thick enough to grasp, to try turning . . .

Damn. The wood broke off in the hole. Now I was worse off than before, unless . . . Okay, I told myself, fighting panic once more. So maybe it was a two-step process.

But it had better be a fast one because now my flashlight was failing; just finding a bent nail in the gloom was a project and wiggling it back and forth until it came out of the floor was worse. Then I had to bang the nail's sharp end into the wood in the doorknob hole, using the heating grate's edge for a hammer.

Careful, careful . . . Mindful that this was my absolute last chance, I grasped the head end of the bent nail, its pointed end firmly lodged—or so I very much hoped—in the wood jamming the doorknob hole. Then gently, gently I pushed down on it, using the nail as a latch-handle.

If the nail turned in the wood I was doomed. But if the wood turned the latch mechanism inside the door, there was a chance—just the barest chance—that the door might open.

Holding my breath, I felt the latch-set's inner mechanisms turn gratingly. The door moved a fraction . . . *outward*. There hadn't been room enough in the little chamber for it to open *in*.

That was why Eva had had to *pull* it shut . . . and now Will's lath-and-plaster job was blocking it.

Which was when I went a little crazy. I grabbed up the grate and began demolishing the old door shred by shred. By the time I smelled fresh plaster, my throat was raw from screaming; every time I slammed the grate's pointed corner into the door, it cut another wound into my hands.

Finally came the moment of truth. With the door

327

apart at last I stood sweaty and exhausted, gasping and weeping. Staring at the fresh plaster seeping through the lath strips and already half-hardened, I knew there was barely a chance in hell I could ever break through.

But Wade was on the other side, and Sam was too. Fresh air, and Ellie and the baby. My dad was outside; likewise that damned district attorney who was trying to put Jemmy away.

All there. Even Victor.

And Will Bonnet.

Thinking about them all, I backed as far away in the little room as I could get. Physics, I thought. Time and gravity and the unchanging properties of substances.

Things. And . . . pressure. Never mind if I got hurt.

Soon I'd be hurting a lot worse, unless . . .

. . . *now,* I thought. *Now or never.*

Whereupon I *charged* the wall, slammed into it with my whole body, much harder than I'd ever hit anything before in my life. On impact the lath bit hard into my flesh, bowed out, and . . .

Splintering with a fast, sharp series of *cracks!* it suddenly gave way, slicing me in a dozen places as I burst through.

On the other side I staggered wildly to keep my balance and failed. When I fell, my head hit the floor so hard I saw stars for a minute, bright fluorescent explosions I tried blinking away. But I couldn't do that, either. They had to fade on their own.

Lying there gasping, I tried to think of where Will would be right now. Or rather, where he *wouldn't* be; it was crucial to know this since I was certain I wouldn't survive another encounter with him. I was bleeding, still half-drugged, and if there was a part of me that didn't hurt like the hounds of hell were using me for a chew toy, I couldn't find it.

But as Wade said once when he drove himself to the ER with a boat hook stuck through his arm, pain is for when you have time. And this wasn't only about saving George from a murder conviction anymore. It was about saving his life.

I staggered outside. The fresh air was sweet. But I couldn't pause to glory in it.

I needed something sweeter.

Somehow I needed to stop that son of a bitch.

CHAPTER 11

The new phone officer at the jail was no more helpful than the old one had been, but he had better manners.

"Your friend's arraignment has been postponed due to his injury," he told me. "He remains in the infirmary but his physician has requested that he be allowed no visitors."

Victor's doing: trying to make sure no one came in from the outside to clobber George again. *Good try,* I thought at Victor. *Way to be paranoid when it's actually appropriate, for once.*

But it wasn't going to help. "All right, now, please listen to me," I told the officer. "There's an inmate named Ronny, he'd have been brought in a little while ago. He was picked up in Eastport this morning and I know this sounds crazy, but—"

"Yes, ma'am," the officer said. "Ron Ronaldson."

When they start calling you *ma'am* in that humor-the-civilian tone, the conversation is over. But I tried a last time anyway.

"The thing is, Ronny's going to try to kill George. Believe me, I know he is going to, and—"

"And you know this because . . . ?"

"Because his accomplice told me, the guy whose orders Ronny is taking, he had me in a room all drugged up and he meant to—"

"When did you take the drugs, ma'am?"

"I didn't *take* them, he *gave* me—"

A radio sputtered in the background. "Ma'am, I can't stay on the phone with you unless you need assistance. If you do I can send an officer or an ambulance to your location."

My location was that I was roaring down Route 190 toward Route 1 in George's old truck, and the only assistance I needed at the moment was a pair of jet engines. Or maybe just a regular one that didn't threaten to conk out on me any minute.

"No. Sorry," I mumbled, "to have troubled you." I pressed the off button of the cell phone that George had installed at Ellie's insistence in the cab of the truck.

Like the reflector strips on his boat, the cell phone was a safety feature. Staggering home from Harlequin House, I had found the truck in my yard with George's lobster traps stacked in the bed. Probably Tommy had stopped off while bringing the truck over to George's, so Sam could come along and give him a ride back.

But now both boys had gone off somewhere else in Sam's car. Wade wasn't around, or my father. Nobody home, house locked up because Wade's gun shop was full of weapons, and me with no keys; they were down the heating duct at Harlequin House.

For a stupefied moment I'd just stood there wondering what to do. I couldn't call Ellie because I didn't want to risk Will being at her house, figuring out it was me on the phone, and knowing I'd escaped. And I couldn't stumble around town looking for help, for the same reason; he might *not* be at Ellie's and if he realized I was free, who knew what he might do?

Worst case, he could get a message to Ronny somehow, tell him to hurry up. And then good-bye George. What Will would do about me I wasn't so sure but I didn't think I'd like that, either.

Bottom line, I had to get to the jail in Machias. The truck key as always had been under the visor and for once the old heap had actually started on the first try; Tommy's doing, probably. Now, slamming the phone back into its holder, I turned the truck onto Route 1; pressing on the accelerator I got the old rattletrap up to sixty and then to sixty-five.

It wouldn't go faster, coughing when I tried to make it, but the engine noise didn't change from its low, amiable hum. It gave me confidence, that sound like the buzz of an aging bumblebee. Passing first one hitchhiker and then another—around here the thumb was a common method of transportation, but I couldn't risk stopping—I even began to think I might reach the jail without further disaster.

But my optimism was premature. Nearly thirty miles of forest and fields, divided occasionally by glittering saltwater inlets, went by without a cough, lurch, or shudder from the truck. As I approached the long hill on the outskirts of Machias, however, the engine gave a shuddery gasp. The battery light came on as I got the vehicle over to the side of the road. The starter motor ground valiantly but to no effect as I turned the key.

But as luck would have it, I'd pulled in right alongside another thumb-jockey. My luck, not his, as he saw immediately. He'd be better off walking than trying to promote a ride in this junk heap.

"Need any help?" he asked, approaching the truck. He was a good old boy from the backwoods, his boots muddy, beard scraggly, and blue eyes bright with the messianic light that comes to men who've been hunkered down in their cabins for too long, brewing up crackpot theories.

But he was all I had. "Yeah. Get behind the wheel?"

The look on his face as he scrutinized me told me how I must appear to him: bruised and bloody, lips raw from the tape I'd torn off them, eyes like a pair of peeled grapes.

In fact, in the possible crackpot contest I took the prize. "Please," I added humbly.

The guy nodded. That's one thing about hermits out of the backwoods. With them, your personal grooming isn't an issue.

He got in and popped the hood in a way that made me think he'd done this sort of thing before. I filled the same Big Gulp cup I'd used the last time from the gas can George kept in the truck bed, hoisted myself up onto the front fender, and peered into the engine compartment.

Now, which hole had I poured that gasoline into? Not the oil dipstick, not the radiator . . . Gingerly, I found and unscrewed the fuel line from the carburetor. Which luckily this truck had; no fuel injection, bless the old beast, just an old-fashioned carburetor, fuel pump, fuel line, and spark plugs.

Very carefully—if I messed this up, a big ball of flame was going to be the result—I began dribbling gas from the soda cup into the carburetor. "Okay, turn the key."

The hermit guy obeyed. The engine turned over a couple of times but then coughed irritably and stalled again.

More gas, just a teensy stream. "Turn it again. Please."

Cough, cough. But then—bingo. Gas began spurting out from the disconnected fuel line; with trembling hands, I screwed it back on. Truck exhaust spewed in a fragrant plume from the back of the vehicle, and the engine noise smoothed out.

I slid off the fender, slammed the hood, and swung into the cab again as he slid over. "Where you going?"

"Bangor."

In the side mirror, a line of cars approached from behind us. I let them pass, waiting for my chance. And then I saw it.

334

Not my chance. Something else. "You don't want to ride with me," I said.

The guy looked over, not sure he'd heard correctly.

"I mean it. You really don't want to ride with me, trust me on this. Get out."

His eyes met mine, his brow furrowed with the injustice of my pronouncement, and I saw him thinking about whether or not to protest vehemently. After all, he had helped me, so didn't I owe him a ride? But then, to my relief, he gave me the benefit of the doubt and hopped out. Meanwhile I kept waiting for my chance to get back into the traffic lane, at the same time watching a vehicle making its way up the hill behind me . . .

I hit the gas hard, spinning gravel as the truck shot out onto the pavement. Probably it wasn't a good way to treat an ailing engine. Or the backwoods guy either.

But coming up behind me, passing everything in its way, was a collection of mismatched fenders and out-of-square chassis with the big front grille of an old Buick Roadmaster and a windshield held on by a row of C-clamps on either side.

It was big, it was fast, and it was without a doubt the same car that had been following Ellie and me the day we'd visited the Condons and Ginger Tolliver.

Wildly the vehicle swung out and shot past two more cars, just missing a log-rig loaded with a pile of thirty-foot tree trunks, speeding uphill. We hadn't hit the steepest part of the grade yet and George's truck was already slowing, laboring in third gear.

Will was even more thorough a bad guy than I had thought. He must have gone back to Harlequin House to check on me, found me gone and George's truck nowhere around, and drawn the correct conclusion.

There was a blare of horn and a harsh squeal of tires as my pursuer narrowly missed hitting an oncoming vehicle head-on. I tromped the gas. The truck lurched and backfired, barely avoiding a stall.

And then with a sudden hard gleam of his ferocious-looking front grille in my rearview, there he was.

Right behind me, bumping me.

Hard. Behind the big car's wheel I glimpsed Weasel Bodine's unattractive face, his two big front teeth hanging out as he gripped the steering wheel one-handed and grimaced with the effort of rubbing his few brain cells together.

He hit me again. The lobster traps piled in the truck bed lurched alarmingly, and the steering wheel tried to jump right out of my hands. With the next impact—or maybe the one after, which was not to my mind a particularly better option—he would force me right off the road or into the path of another car.

Bang! The lobster traps jostled again, the entire pile of them sliding backwards a foot. Too bad, I thought grimly, that the truck bed wasn't filled with iron spikes. They'd be at about the level of Weasel's head, and . . .

Wham. The truck's tailgate flopped open, its spit-and-baling-wire repair job not quite up to a game of highway bumpercars.

And neither was I, as I desperately wrestled the truck back into its own lane. What Mister Overbite meant to do once he caught me I wasn't sure, but I had a feeling Will's instructions had been X-rated for violence. Will needed me silenced, and after all, the promise of a big payday had worked on Perry Daigle. Why wouldn't it also banish the fear of prison from Eastport's very own home-grown version of Bucky Beaver?

But then as a new thought hit me my mouth imitated Weasel's and fell open, too: I didn't need spikes. What I needed were the brakes, good timing, a bit of luck . . .

And a reason for Weasel to hit even harder, next time. So gazing into the rearview, I smiled my sweetest smile and let my middle finger send an unmistakable message.

Which infuriated him, as I'd expected. These guys, they take everything so personally.

Well, so did I. Gripping the wheel I watched Weasel roar up behind me again, waiting until the instant when I felt the first metal kiss of his big front grille on the rear of the truck.

Then I stomped on the brake. The impact whipped my head back, snap-ratcheted the seat-belt against my chest, and sent twin bolts of pain slamming through my knees as they slid forward and smacked the lower dashboard.

It also sent lobster traps sliding relentlessly downhill off the truck bed, right into the C-clamped windshield of Mister Future False Teeth of America's junkyard-dog chase vehicle.

The C-clamps let go and then the windshield did. He tried swerving to avoid the traps, which sent him into the guardrail lining the side of this steepest part of the hill. The last thing I saw as I pulled away was steam rising out of the hood, as he climbed out.

Gosh, I wished I had a camera. And time to use it.

Instead, five minutes later I pulled the truck into the lot outside the courthouse in Machias. The building also housed the jail, the registrars of deeds and probate, and numerous other offices where people were in the habit of behaving soberly and respectably.

But respectable behavior had gotten me nowhere. It was time for a new strategy.

New and different; my only reason for thinking I could pull it off was that I had to. George's life depended on it.

If he still had one.

The Washington County courthouse was a lovely old redbrick building on a narrow side street. Built when there were fewer inmates and far less litigation, its surrounding streets were jammed with traffic and parked cars.

The small lot near the front door was reserved for official vehicles. I pulled the truck in there. Leaning on the horn, I made sure that I would be noticed.

Then I got out. Fell out, actually. Yelling while I did it.

Clambering up, I spied two uniformed officers ambling from the sheriff's office. Their long-suffering looks said I wasn't the most disruptive drunk they'd met that day.

I'd soon fix that. Digging around in my bag, I pulled out the bottle of ipecac I'd taken from Will Bonnet's medicine chest and swigged thirstily from it, then threw it as hard as I could. It shattered on a squad-car windshield.

The cops' faces hardened; perfect. Now if I could just keep the ipecac down for a little while longer . . .

"Lady, you're intoxicated. You need to come with us."

As firmly as they could without actually lifting me off the ground, the two officers seized my arms and escorted me up the front steps, down the tiled corridor, and into the booking area of the jail.

Fussing and squalling, I let myself be propped in front of the officer in charge of accepting me into the county's custody.

"Name?" he asked tiredly.

"Who wan's tah know?" I gave him the old

bleary-eye. His glance in return was the one you might give to the bottom of your shoe, while you are scraping something off it.

Oh, this was going fine. Or it was until the strangest thing happened. State Trooper Hollis Colgate stepped out of a side room, still talking to whomever he'd been visiting. I tried turning away quickly but it was too late.

He'd seen me. And recognized me. Now Colgate was headed toward me and whatever he did or said, it would cause a delay.

I couldn't afford one. *Go away,* I thought at him. But he stopped right in front of me.

"Okay," the booking officer said to the two cops still holding me. "Is there any ID on her?"

"None that we saw," one of the officers replied.

And then in one of the most inexplicable events of my life, Hollis Colgate turned his back on me and walked away.

"Not on her, anyway," the other cop confirmed, as Colgate went out through the front door of the building without another glance at me.

Baffled, I turned my attention from Colgate back to the matter at hand. They'd gone through my bag, as I'd expected they would. It was why I'd stashed my license and other ID items in George's glove box, and why I'd had to swallow the ipecac syrup so dratted early. Any time now the syrup would produce the effect that made it such a useful, even lifesaving, first-aid remedy.

Which—abruptly—it did.

"Aw, Christ," yelled one of the officers. "Horace! Get a mop out here, will you?"

Horace was apparently the inmate on janitor duty that day but I never got to meet him. Instead I was hustled rather roughly through a door marked "Intake," and into a small holding area.

"Think you're gonna be sick again?" inquired the hard-eyed female officer in the holding area. She patted me down with brisk thoroughness; fortunately I hadn't made a mess of myself, only the floor.

The officer was immaculately groomed and her expression said clearly what she thought of me: not much.

"I'm not really like this . . ." I managed.

"Yeah, sure. Until now, and all of a sudden you are. Take my advice, when you get out of here, get with the program. Come on," she added, not unkindly. "You can sit in the sickroom while they finish your paperwork."

"Am I going to jail?" I put the proper fear in my voice.

"Probably." She escorted me toward another door. "If you were just intoxicated, maybe not. But now you got destruction of official property, disorderly conduct."

I held back. "Who's in there?"

She urged me along. "One guy says he's dizzy, I'm pretty sure he's faking but we've got a nurse coming. The other one's getting over a big headache. Don't worry, I'll be there with you. That's my job

341

today—baby-sitting," she added with a grimace.

Again just what I'd hoped for. The dizzy one, I figured, was Ronny. It's what I would have done, faked a symptom, if I wanted to get in there with George.

In fact, it *was* what I was doing. But George must be the one with the headache so it sounded as if I had gotten here in time, albeit with my mouth tasting like the bottom of a bird cage.

There was a drinking fountain by the door. "Can I get some water first?"

She stopped impatiently. "Yeah. Hurry up."

It was plain old city water and it tasted like champagne. "I mean it," the officer went on while I was savoring it, "I'll give you a card for some people who will help you."

I raised my head as she unlocked the sickroom door. "Because after today, I really hope you'll have learned a lesson. I don't want to see you again in this condition . . . oh, son of a bitch."

She crossed the room fast, removing her baton from the loop on her utility belt as she did so. She hit Ronny Ronaldson across the back with the weapon, and she must've had some serious upper-body strength because despite his impressive size Ronny went flying.

Then she yanked away the pillow that Ronny had been holding to George's face. Placing two fingers on the side of his neck, she cursed again, then slammed her fist to the intercom button in the wall above the head of the bed.

342

"I need the crash cart and an ambulance. We have an inmate in cardiac arrest."

Finally she turned to me, and I must not've looked quite as skanky as I had a few minutes earlier, because the four words she said to me then were the ones I'd hoped never to hear again.

"Do you know CPR?"

She was already beginning to perform it, and as I'd learned at Victor's class it works better with two people doing it.

Even if one of them is me.

"George! George, are you all right?"

The two of us moved him to the floor. I knelt beside him with the heel of my hand three fingers' width from the end of his breastbone: compressing, not gently at all, between the breaths she blew into his lungs.

"One-one-thousand, two-one-thousand . . ."

I timed the breaths and chest compressions aloud as all the things Victor's class had taught me whirled in my head.

"Leave her alone," the woman cop snapped when someone tried replacing me. "I'm getting a pulse on her compressions. Let's not fix what ain't broke."

Which meant my efforts were circulating his blood, while her rescue breathing—when the crash cart arrived she'd switched to a mask with an oxygen tank attached to it—put precious air in his lungs.

So he wasn't blue anymore. But he wasn't responding, either; every time we stopped compressions to see if he had any pulse of his own, he didn't.

Someone led Ronny out. He'd been weeping, mumbling over and over again that he wanted to know if his mother was all right.

That, I realized with the tiny part of my mind that could still think, must've been what Will threatened him with: harm to his family.

"Ambulance is on the way," reported one of the officers who'd brought me in. "But he says he's got a ten-minute ETA."

Estimated time of arrival, in other words. The room was full of people; even Horace the janitor had wheeled his cleaning cart in to observe. But they were a blur to me; all I could see in my mind's eye was Ellie's face, sweetly radiant with soon-to-be motherhood.

And all I could hear was Victor's voice, dithering on about all the numerous ways that resuscitation could fail.

Somebody jostled Horace's cleaning cart and swore as the contents of its top shelf fell. "Damn it, Horace, get out of here and take this crap with . . ."

"Wait." Among the fallen items was a box of baking soda, used here I supposed just the way I used it at home: to deodorize garbage cans, drains, and the inside of the refrigerator.

But when I spotted it something pinged in my

memory. Baking soda. *Bicarbonate* of soda. The stuff, Victor had said, that your blood uses to keep from being too acid.

Because if the blood is too acid, resuscitation won't work. The fact printed itself in boldface on the front of my brain, superimposed somehow atop a mental picture of Sam, pouring that antibiotic powder into an injured turtle years ago.

"Pour some under his tongue," I heard myself saying. "The soda bicarb."

I waved at the box, went back to doing chest compressions as all the faces around me creased in skeptical looks. All but the female cop doing the rescue breathing, that is. She gave me an odd glance, then spoke up.

"If the ambulance people were on scene now, they'd be giving IV bicarb, wouldn't they?"

"Yeah," I gasped in reply. Chest compressions are strenuous, and my hands were killing me. "But they're not. Here. Giving it."

She eyed me again. "You weren't drunk, were you?"

"Give the little lady a round of applause," I grated out. "You can hear all about it later. Now are you going to, or not?"

"Do it," she snapped at one of the hovering cops. "Open his mouth, pour some in. Do it fast so I don't miss any breaths."

The officer obeyed, dumping a bunch under George's tongue where it began dissolving. Then we went back to the same rhythm we'd been in before.

Push, push, push, breath. And again.

"You need relief?"

I shook my head. My arms were aching, my back was on fire, my knees felt as if iron spikes had been driven into them, and my torn hands were bleeding onto George's shirt. But I would stop what I was doing when he responded positively or when hell froze over, whichever came first.

"So what makes you think under the tongue will work?" she asked.

"My son used to do cocaine. When his nose bled and he didn't have anywhere left on his arms to skin-pop, he'd put it under his tongue."

She nodded thoughtfully. "Pause," she said as an ambulance screamed up outside. She checked George's pulse. "Nothing."

Black misery hit me. I put my hands on his chest again. But then . . .

"No, wait," I heard her say. "It . . . I think I got something."

She repositioned her fingers on his neck. "Pulse." The hard look faded from her eyes, replaced by something like wonder.

"Hey, he's got a . . ."

George's chest shuddered wheezily up. He took a hitching breath and then another. And then he coughed hard and moaned.

The female cop who'd been ready to send me to AA jumped up and flung her arms around me as the EMTs raced in and took over.

"Jeez," George complained thickly as they lifted

him to a gurney. "What's a guy gotta do, get some rest in here . . . hold his breath till he turns blue?"

Then his eyes found me and focused. "Will," he said, and struggled, trying to get up. Apparently Ronny had felt the need to talk during his try on George's life.

"Now, George," one of the EMTs soothed him, "I'm going to need you to cooperate a little bit with me, here."

Whatever Ronny had said, it had been enough to clue George in. Not to the why, probably. But to the *who*.

"Where is Will?" George added, not sounding cooperative in the slightest. Then he got a look at me, all cut up, bloody and disheveled, and a wry little gleam came into his eye.

"I told you to be careful with power tools, Jacobia," he said. *Powah:* the Maine way of pronouncing it.

I began weeping.

"Wade," I said urgently into the phone. I was in a squad car, speeding toward home. "Don't let on that it's me."

He performed beautifully. "I'm afraid she's not here now. Is there a message?"

Not a quaver, bless Wade's devious little heart. Trees and road signs went by in a blur. At the tops of the hills the tires didn't quite fly up off the road, but they almost did. "Bonnet's our bad guy," I said. "Is he there? And Ellie, too?"

When they couldn't find me they'd congregate at my house to decide what to do next. Or I'd hoped they would, anyway.

And they had. "Yes," Wade replied. "He's here."

We roared into a curve, careened through it, hurtled across a bridge; any faster and we'd have needed a flight plan. "Good. I'm two minutes away," I said. "Don't let him leave."

At last, Trooper Colgate took the long curve into town with the casual flair of a man who is accustomed to hundred-mile-an-hour highway pursuits.

Swiftly I explained to Wade. "Bonnet's going to be charged with three murders and a whole raft of other stuff as soon as we get there. So . . ."

"He is, huh? Well, then, hang on a minute." He put the phone down; then his voice came from a distance.

". . . Will? C'mere a minute. Yeah, just stand right there."

Next came the flat, meaty *swock!* of a fist connecting hard, the crash of a chair overturning, and the *thud* of someone hitting the hardwood floor.

Finally Wade came back on. "I don't think our pal Will is going anywhere for the foreseeable future."

"Oh, good. See you soon," I said.

We drove some more. Fast, but not quite as fast as before since Hollis Colgate apparently had just as much confidence in Wade's right hook as I did.

"What I don't understand is why Eva Thane killed those three girls," I said. Partly it was to take my mind off the rate at which we were still rocketing along, light-speed being only a bit less terrifying than warp-speed.

Colgate chuckled. "You know, I've been hoping for a chance to talk to you about that. Because her name sounded familiar to me and I couldn't figure out why. But eventually it hit me, so I called my mom in Lewiston and she reminded me."

"Your mom knew Eva Thane? But . . ."

"Nope. My mom's not old enough. But her mom did. Eva Thane was a Lewiston girl."

"Ohh," I breathed, beginning to understand.

"And Eva was not a poster girl for mental health," Colgate went on. "Not," he added, "that she had any reason to be. She had a family right out of a Tennessee Williams play. Booze, incest, the whole nine yards."

I turned curiously, thinking of Colgate reading Tennessee Williams. It is absolutely astonishing what people find to do in the winters around here.

"And she'd done it before," I guessed. "Killed someone. And that's why she ran."

"Yup." He slowed at last for the speed zone across from Bay City Mobil. "She'd wangled herself a boyfriend from the rich side of town. Figured he was her ticket out, I suppose."

"But then another girl butted in?"

Colgate nodded. "That's the story my grand-mother told. Eva took care of that problem with the blunt end of a fire axe. Then she got scared, I guess, and took off."

We crested the Washington Street hill and headed downtown past the white-clapboard Methodist Church and the granite-block Post Office. Out on the water some little sailboats were having the season's last regatta, bucking a stiff, cold breeze.

"Eva must've latched onto Chet Harlequin somehow," Colgate continued, "charmed his socks off. She was good at that. But from what I under-stand, police were about to move in on her here in Eastport when she vanished again."

A spindrift of grit and the last of the summer's cheerful litter whirled lonesomely in the middle of Water Street. Colgate turned right, up Key Street toward my house.

"And that," he finished, "was the last anyone ever heard of her until now."

"Huh. Poor Eva," I said.

He glanced at me. "Sure," he replied, his voice hardening in a trooperish way. "I guess you could think of it like that."

Moments later Colgate swung into my driveway. By the time I got my seat belt off he was striding toward the house and the handcuffs were already unclipped from his utility belt. He passed Wade as Wade half ran to the squad car but didn't stop to talk.

"Okay, take it slow," Wade warned me, opening

the passenger door and catching me as I fell out. "You," he added as he wrapped his arms around me, "have had quite a day for yourself."

"Is Ellie okay?"

He nodded. "She's going to the hospital in a minute, so she can be there when George arrives. Victor called the ambulance guys, they're transferring George up to Calais from Machias Hospital so Victor can check him out. But they say he seems fine, so in a little while we can all go up there, too."

In the kitchen, Trooper Colgate hauled a groggy Will Bonnet up off the floor and snapped the cuffs onto him, and recited the warning. "Anything you say can and will be used . . ."

But the warning wasn't needed. The shock of being found out must have paralyzed Will's vocal cords because for once he didn't have anything to say. He just cast a surly glare at us as the cop muscled him roughly out.

We all watched him go; all but Ellie, who seemed preoccupied with something else, her brow knit into a frown of concentration.

She got up, walked in a circle, and sat down again. "I'm not going in the car," she announced. "To the hospital."

"But why not?" The dogs had romped joyously up to greet me, their nails clicking on the hardwood floor, and even Cat Dancing uttered a grudging meow from her usual perch.

Ellie took a breath, let it out slowly. "You're sure

George is okay? And you are, too? Your poor hands."

They were raw meat. "Never mind that. I'm sure. But Ellie, what's wrong with you?"

As I peered at her it occurred to me that in the space of a few hours I'd been drugged, tied, and walled up in a room, not to mention my experience with a stomach-emptying concoction that for prompt, effective action, I'd rank right up there with dynamite.

But compared to the way she looked I was fresh as a daisy.

"I'm not going in the car because there isn't time. Just now while Wade was outside getting you, I called the ambulance. It's on its way," she said.

"You mean . . ."

She nodded, wincing. From outside came the distant but fast-approaching *whoop-whoop* of yet another siren.

"But you know," she said, an odd, insistent look coming onto her face, "I might not be going in the ambulance, either."

It screamed up outside. Moments later two EMTs hustled in, pushing a gurney.

But Ellie wouldn't get on it. "Never mind the gurney," she told them. "And never mind the ambulance, either."

Her eyes met mine: wide, frightened, and exultant. Her hair was wild, her face sheet-white and pasty-looking. A bolt of pain snapped her head back, blue veins pulsing visibly at her temples.

"You *said* . . ." she began accusingly to me.

Then she seemed to relax. But not for long; gripping my hand so hard I could practically hear the bones crunching, Ellie spoke clearly, distinctly, and as it turned out, absolutely correctly:

"Jake, this baby is coming *now*."

CHAPTER 12

"Wow," said Tommy, his eyes huge with wonder, as Ellie put the baby into his arms. "It sure is *new*."

"She," Ellie corrected proudly. She touched a tissue to a bubble on the infant's rosebud mouth. "Her name is Leonora and she's two weeks old today."

Two eventful weeks: Will Bonnet had been arrested, George had been released, and Will's astonishingly resilient Aunt Agnes was out of the hospital. Now we were gathered at the gala celebration of the reopening of Harlequin House.

All around us rose the delightful spectacle of sparkling windows, fresh new paint, and the mellow patina of old woodwork rubbed to a honeyed glow. The house positively shone with the love that had been denied it for decades and poured so unstintingly into it over the past fourteen days. I turned back to what Trooper Hollis Colgate was saying.

". . . What you have to realize is that when the medical examiner said twenty-four to forty-eight hours, that's just what he meant," Colgate went on. "You *assumed* a time because it fit your problem. Cops, too. But Hector didn't die while George and Bonnet were away in Boston."

"Will killed Hector Thursday night," I said. "Not Friday night. But we all got so focused on the time when George was gone . . ."

"Right. You figured it must be the time of death, just the way Will planned. The last thing he did before leaving town on Friday was hustle over to Gosling's place, slip inside, and call Ellie from there so the number would show up on her caller ID. Saying he saw Gosling *alive* on Friday afternoon put the cherry on the cake."

Little Lee gazed up at Tommy and gurgled pleasantly. "Wow," Tommy breathed again, his expression melting.

"Later," Colgate went on, "he killed Therese Chamberlain. He'd seen her in the parking garage in Boston and he recognized her, of course, at the hospital. But until he spotted Therese talking to you, he hadn't realized *she'd* seen *George*."

"So she really *did* know George couldn't have killed Hector that night. And if she said so, it would've spoiled Will's whole plan."

Ellie came up beside us. "Will knew George wouldn't rat on him by revealing that he was on probation," she said. "Will had set things up that way, by asking George not to. Meanwhile George was waiting for *Will* to step up to the plate and tell the truth. It never even occurred to him that Will wouldn't."

George would have tumbled eventually, of course, and spoken up. But Will never planned for George to live long enough to tell anyone. And George nearly hadn't.

"He still thought Will was his friend," Ellie said, her tone indignant. "When all along . . ."

George had already recited to us the litany of Will's lies. First he'd begged George to take him to Boston for the probation visit, saying his aunt's car had conked out again. That the car was in fine shape the next morning he'd explained away by saying it'd turned out to have a bad spark plug wire, and that he'd fixed it.

Then there was the probation visit itself; fictional, too. Will hadn't kept a date with a probation officer in more than a year. But that hadn't stopped him from pretending to go to one and swearing George to secrecy, Will's story being that he didn't want his fresh start in Eastport destroyed by news of his old bad deeds.

In short, Will Bonnet had spun a tangled web and eventually gotten ensnared in it. "But why didn't he just kill George himself if the whole idea was to get rid of him?" I asked.

Colgate shook his head. "He's been questioned about that. And at different times he's given quite a few different reasons. Sometimes he says it would've been too easy. He's got a pretty high opinion of himself, you know."

"You think?" Fresh fury at Will made me clench my fists for what he'd done.

And for the way he'd fooled me. If he hadn't, Therese might still be alive.

"Other times," Colgate said, "he gets a little closer to what I suspect is the real story. He says it wouldn't have been enough for George just to die, that George had to be ruined first, his reputation demolished." Colgate finished his drink. "Will knew you two would be working in that parlor but if you hadn't found Hector he meant to 'discover' the body himself."

"Sure," I said. "Makes sense. Bad enough for a jerk like him being compared with George alive. It would've been even worse if George ended up being turned into a saint."

"Right," Colgate agreed. "Myself, though, I think it's more complicated even than that."

His brow knit. "I'm not sure he knows it, but I think it was the one thing he couldn't quite bring himself to do. In a screwy way he still looked up to George almost as much as Tommy does."

"Killing his old friend with his own hands would've been like murdering the last, vestigial little bit of good in himself," I agreed. "Not that there was a lot of that."

Another question occurred to me. "Therese was already high when he got to her house?" I asked, theorizing aloud. "So he'd have talked his way in easily and slipped her the same mixture he gave me?"

Colgate nodded. "After which it was also easy to smother her and set things up to look as if she'd simply OD'd. If your ex-husband hadn't gotten on the horn and expedited her autopsy, though, I'd never have known it wasn't a simple heroin overdose."

"He did that? Expedited the autopsy?" Victor hadn't said anything about it. What he had said, emphatically and at length, concerned using baking soda during a resuscitation attempt.

In short, don't. It hadn't helped George; that it had seemed to was the only coincidence in the whole sorry affair. But it had messed up George's body chemistry enough so that if things had gone differently—if he'd needed further resuscitation once he'd reached the hospital, for instance—it might have killed him.

"Will set the Harlequin House fire, too, I suppose?" Ellie asked. It was a part of Will's scheme that had gotten overshadowed by other events. But it could have been a disaster in its own right.

"Oh, yeah." Colgate nodded at her. "Back in Boston he was an arsonist among other things, so he knew how. Cute little device, no wonder no one found it the first time they looked." He grimaced. "You two triggered it," he added, "when you forced that door open. Once the body was found, the fire was meant to take care of any self-incriminating details Will might have missed. Didn't spread quite as fast as he expected, that's all."

Just then another well-wisher came up to Ellie and guided her away. "Why did you ignore me at the jail?" I asked Colgate. "I thought I was finished for sure when you came out of that office and saw me."

He looked wry. "Well, for one thing I'd just heard from your ex about Therese's autopsy result. And I'd also just found out Bonnet had a warrant in Massachusetts for probation violation. I'd asked him if there was anything I should know and he'd said no. He probably figured with George already on the hook, I wouldn't check anyone else's background."

"But you did." If my opinion of him got any higher it would shoot right through Harlequin House's mansard roof.

"Talked to Massachusetts and they wanted him," he agreed. "I had the order to drive up and grab him when I ran into you."

I drank some champagne. "That still doesn't explain why you didn't say anything. . . ."

"Yeah, I guess it doesn't," he conceded. He sipped lemonade, having explained that he only drank on airplanes. "But I already felt like I was missing something, things not zeroing out, when I got a load of the look on your face."

"And you got the message," I interrupted, pleased at having transmitted it to him so flawlessly via my expression.

"Well, not exactly," he demurred. "Unless you were trying to tell me you were getting ready to lose your lunch."

"Oh," I replied, crestfallen. "What, then?"

"Just a hunch. What I thought of, actually, was Sam. A kid like yours, his whole presentation of himself . . ."

He glanced across the room at his own two kids. It was, he'd explained, his weekend to have them, so he'd brought them along. The pair of young teenagers had latched onto Sam like a couple of bright barnacles, to Sam's bemusement.

"Sam's a genuinely good guy and he got it from somewhere," Colgate said. "From you, mostly, I figured. But that didn't jibe with you being drunk and disorderly. So I guessed you weren't. Which led me to wonder if maybe you were up to something else."

"And you just let me go on with it, whatever it was?"

He laughed. "Hey, snap judgment. I could've been wrong. But I didn't see a downside. You were already in custody, after all."

"Yeah." I repressed a shudder at the memory. "Luckily not for long. So anyway, Will confessed to all this? It doesn't seem like him."

Telling *me* about it was different. I'd been supposed to die. Colgate set his glass down. "He stonewalled hard for a week or so. But Massachusetts wants to talk to him about quite a few things, not just his probation beef. That caviar, for instance. They got his associates on it."

Two hundred pounds of the valuable stuff; besides framing George he'd been arranging delivery of it during the Boston trip.

"One way and another it turned out to be worth his while," Colgate added, "us not giving him up. So he spilled his guts."

The Maine State Prison at Thomaston, I gathered, being a less brutal destination than Walpole, Massachusetts. But Thomaston would do nicely as far as I was concerned.

Near the refreshment table I spied Siss Moore, Tommy's old teacher. Dressed appropriately in battleship grey, she fixed her sights on him and began steaming toward him.

Tommy stood his ground. In fact he looked glad to see Siss. She must've wondered about it.

I didn't. But Colgate was speaking again. "So how's that other matter you were worried about turning out?" he asked me. "Your friend and the Feds?"

Standing nearby, Clarissa Arnold overheard and shot me a look of warning. Bob's mother was better; their family was back in Eastport and beginning to settle themselves after the crisis.

"That's been cleared up," I replied carefully. "My friend is no longer a target of the investigation."

Because as Clarissa said after I'd told her the whole story, a picture is worth a thousand words; a picture, for instance, of a well-known and eminently recognizable political bigwig chummily entering a money expert's office in the company of a mob banker. No matter how long ago it had happened it would make said bigwig into a "known associate" overnight.

Bad news for the bigwig. "But good news for you, Jake," Clarissa had said. "If you're up for a game of hardball."

She was, it turned out, quite a bit more blood-thirsty than I'd ever given her credit for. Bottom line, I'd promised never to show the photographs to anyone in return for the bigwig's not using all the considerable powers at his disposal to try getting them away from me.

It was a major deal; between them, my father and Jemmy had a lot of charges pending. But I'd done major deals before. And I had a *lot* of pictures. So it ended up being to everybody's benefit that we trust one another.

Sort of. I still had the pictures and they still had the ability to bring new charges. But Jemmy was free and after three decades on the run my dad was no longer a wanted fugitive. It was the kind of resolution I now believed Jemmy had intended all along.

And one I could live with. My father came up to us and put out a gnarled hand, touching the pink, chubby one thrust out to him and laughing when the tiny fingers curled around his own.

"Dinner on me tomorrow night," he said. "Jody Jones paid."

The guy that he'd been building a chimney for, he meant; I blinked at him. "That's amazing. You must hold the record for getting Jody to . . . Dad, how'd you *do* that?"

"Oh, it wasn't much. A little chimney magic.

Thing wouldn't draw till he did pay up, is all. Smoke from the fireplace poured right back out into the room. Old mason's trick."

He spoke confidentially. "What I did was, I cemented a piece of plate glass in there. Blocked the chimney but when you looked up, you couldn't see it. He paid, I went up on the roof, dropped a brick down the chimney."

"Breaking the glass, so the smoke would . . ." I gazed at him in admiration. "But don't a lot of people know that old trick?"

He smiled innocently. "Yes, they do. But not the other old trick I know, to get around what *they* know. And I," he added with sly satisfaction, "am not telling that one."

Ellie returned to check on the baby as my dad strolled away. "Ellie, she's so beautiful," I said. "Thank you for . . ."

Leonora had been my mother's name. Ellie looked levelly at me. "There should be one. Another Leonora, don't you think?"

Ellie looked lovely too, her red hair tucked up into a topknot, soft tendrils of it curling around her face. George wrapped an arm around her shoulder as she spoke; his own hair was growing back in the place where Victor had shaved it.

"I told Agnes Bonnet we'd take her home early," he said to Ellie. "Ginger wants to finish moving in today."

Ginger herself had just come in with Mark Timberlake, the two of them shaking off the downpour outside in a flurry of shed raincoats and happy greetings. If Mark Timberlake ever washed out of the merchant marine, he could get a job modeling for Greek statues. Even Siss Moore's face softened when she saw the two of them together.

"Gosh, he's young," Ellie commented.

"And she's gorgeous." Her face glowing and her hair piled in a coronet, Ginger resembled the mythic heroine of some impossibly romantic German opera. And although pain still etched tiny lines around her eyes, at Mark's insistence she was about to begin new treatments; they'd married three days earlier, so she was now covered by his medical benefits.

"What persuaded them to reconcile?" Ellie wondered aloud as the newlyweds moved away toward the refreshments table.

"Well, as I understand it," I said, "Mark and George had a little confab in which George advised Mark to try, try again."

Which was precisely what George had done, fervently and unceasingly, to persuade Ellie into marrying *him*. Now the newlyweds had undertaken to care for Agnes Bonnet, with whom Ginger would live when Mark was away with the merchant marine.

"So all's well that ends well?" Ellie asked.

"Oh, yeah," Tommy breathed, with his arms wrapped around Leonora. He looked as if he might never want to give her up.

But just then Siss Moore reached him and planted herself before him. "Young man," she intoned into a chance silence, and everyone laughed; it was that kind of moment.

Except for me. Turning away, I guessed only I was imagining poor Eva Thane's sad ghost fluttering in the old house. For one thing, only I knew what had really killed her; Wade had gone over her little derringer rather carefully as he'd restored it, then placed it with a photo of her in a display case he'd made and given to the historical society.

Now as I glanced at it, hung in the hall by a portrait of Chester Harlequin whose name had at last been cleared, I wondered again how close I'd come to repeating Eva's mistake.

But suddenly a different question occurred to me. "George," I asked, "what *did* you buy at the Taste of Honey store, anyway?"

Will Bonnet had been obdurate on this point, Colgate said. He had done some shopping during the trip to Boston, but not at Taste of Honey. Then he'd left George alone for a few hours and they'd started back.

Which meant the receipt in the truck was from some purchase of George's after all.

"Oysters," Ellie replied embarrassedly. "Smoked oysters, not the usual kind. Those little French ones?"

She'd gotten some in a gift basket once. From me, actually, and months earlier she'd been heard saying she craved a few more. So when George got a chance he'd braved the fancy food store to grant her wish. Will hadn't known or he'd have destroyed the receipt. And they'd both forgotten the parking stub, apparently.

Outside, rain began crystallizing into snow; it was getting to be the season for more indoor projects, I realized. Plaster and new tile for the bath; over the winter, I might even finish that panel door. . . .

But now I watched with interest as Siss Moore stood before Tommy. He'd told me the night before what he intended to say to her; I wondered if he really would.

"Um, Mrs. Moore?" he managed faintly. "I was wondering . . ."

"Yes, Tommy," she replied, her tone authoritarian; she had the voice of an experienced teacher.

He quailed. Then, perhaps emboldened by the infant in his arms, he rallied. And in the glance he sent me, so youthful and yet so manfully determined, I knew he understood just exactly what he was doing and that he would follow through on it.

"Mrs. Moore, you used to say I was smart."

She tipped her head. "And?"

"You said I could go to college, make something of myself. You said," he continued as she fixed him acutely in her steel-blue gaze, "you'd help me if I decided to try."

No reply from Siss. "Mrs. Moore," he persisted,

"back then you said you believed in me. Trouble is, I guess I didn't believe in myself."

Siss glanced over at Ginger and Mark, then at me. "Anyone," she said, "can make a mistake. What is it you want, Tommy?"

He shifted from one foot to the other. "Well, that's the thing. I reckon . . . I mean I've *observed*"—he corrected himself as her lips tightened—"that lots of guys go to college. They can't *all* have that much more on the ball than I do. Can they?"

He took a deep breath. "So I wondered, would you still help me now?"

"*Why?*" she demanded. "Why, after all this time?"

But Tommy was up to it. "Well, because it's like you always said. Experience isn't the best teacher. But maybe sometimes it's the best *first* one, Mrs. Moore. It was for me. So now I'm ready for the other kind. I mean . . ."

He paused. "That is, if you still want to be one."

Her lips pursed consideringly. Then: "Tommy, is that foolish vehicle of yours outside?"

The jalopy, she meant, complete with raccoon tail and *oo-oo-gah!* horn. The fuel pump had arrived and for the moment the car was in running condition.

"Yes, ma'am," he said eagerly as Ellie took the baby back. "Just let me pull it up out front." He hustled away, returned an instant later with her coat.

"It's snowing out. I'll drive you home. We can,"

he added boldly as he helped her on with the garment, "talk on the way."

"Indeed." But it was clear that she was immensely pleased. Moments later we all heard the blast of that astonishing horn, as in a thunder of engine backfires Siss's chariot bore her off.

What can I say, it was too sweet for my taste. But then, I'm from New York. Wade appeared from somewhere, put an arm around my shoulder. "Hey. Nice party."

"It is, isn't it." Candles had been lit, bristling swathes of them on the tables and above us in chandeliers. There were fires in the fireplaces and music had begun playing; after supper, we were going upstairs to the ballroom, where there would be dancing.

Wade looked down at me. In the candlelight his eyes were the mysterious sea-grey of a fog-bound coast, alluring and a little dangerous. "I helped deliver that champagne," he said, nodding toward the ice buckets.

He held me tighter. "And," he whispered in my ear, "I stole a bottle. It's home now, waiting for us."

"Really. That's fascinating."

"Oh, good." Whereupon he kissed me, which always tends to blot out anything else that may be happening in my vicinity.

But not for long because next came a prime rib dinner, and angel food cake with ice cream and homemade chocolate sauce. More champagne too;

the whole evening was, as George put it later, a real wingding.

So it ended up being long past midnight with the temperature plummeting and our breaths hanging in frozen clouds when Wade and I finally started home, through the snow sifting through the cones of yellow light under the streetlamps.

"I still don't understand about the paperwork from George's aunt's lawyer," Wade said puzzledly. "I know Will must've gotten hold of it somehow and planted it at George's house, but . . ."

I laughed. "That was easy. He just faked it all. Got some good stationery somewhere and mocked it up on a computer at the public library." Clarissa had filled me in on this part.

"Some nerve," Wade said. "But wouldn't that be discovered?"

We stopped at the top of Key Street and looked back over the sleeping town, the big lights over the breakwater standing like sentinels against the black water. A foghorn sounded.

"Sure," I replied. "But not in time to do George any good." Wind blew the snow up into little spirals that whirled briefly in the street before collapsing again.

"Examination of the evidence wasn't in Will's plan. George wasn't supposed to live long enough to go to trial," I added.

Across the water the lights on Campobello were bright blurs behind a thickening gauze of white. Wade drew me nearer.

"So it was worth it to risk that the fake paperwork might be found out later, as long as it couldn't implicate Will."

"Yup," I agreed. "It sealed George's fate arrest-wise. Maybe it *would* have tripped Will up eventually, but I'm glad we didn't have to find out."

"He got the poison from George's shed?"

"Uh-huh."

But now a related thought struck Wade. "Darn, so George doesn't inherit after all?"

But actually, he'd hit on a bright spot. "In fact he still might. With Hector gone and George the next of kin—"

"And the suspicion growing about Hector and Jan Jesperson's undue influence?"

"Exactly. Because it turns out Jan *did* keep backup disks for those computer files. Clarissa warns it's no slam-dunk. But there's a decent chance George and Ellie will end up contesting his Aunt Paula's will successfully."

"Huh." Wade brushed snow out of his hair. "Here we are."

"Home at last," I agreed. With flakes twinkling around it and lights glowing from within, the big old house shimmered like the scene in an old-fashioned snow globe. Inside—

—once the dogs had been taken out and the furnace had been checked and the proper radiators had been turned on or off in the various rooms, so the oil wouldn't quite make an actual *glug-glug* sound while being sucked down by the oil burner—

—we sat at the kitchen table in thick robes and warm, fuzzy slippers, drinking hot cocoa instead of champagne.

"We're domestic," I observed, too exhausted to say more.

Wade smiled tiredly. "Yeah. Okay by me."

Domestic, I thought, and lucky; me especially.

I wondered what Wade would say if I told him it hadn't been ipecac in the bottle I'd guzzled from that day. Later Victor had sniffed at the licorice smell still lingering on the shards.

Tincture of opium, he'd said; a morphinelike drug. Will must've dumped the ipecac, using the bottle to disguise its new contents for some hideous reason of his own. Victor surmised it could've been used to keep Agnes Bonnet's stomach from rejecting the pills Will was dosing her with.

And atop the other narcotics Will had administered to me, Victor had informed me gravely, what I'd drunk had likely held enough sedative to kill me. That is, if my stomach hadn't been so nervous, it revolted, and if I hadn't been so primed to believe the stuff would do what it had.

Otherwise I might've ended up with Eva Thane in the special fool's purgatory reserved for accidental suicides. "Wade, do you really think Eva's gun went off by itself?"

"Yeah," he confirmed. "Shoddy piece of junk.

It could've fired if you just looked at it the wrong way. Could've happened easy."

He frowned, considering it all again. "What I think is, she changed her mind at the last minute, then put the gun to her head. Just experimenting, but feeling safe because she'd already decided not to. And—bang."

It would have been just like Eva, I thought, play-acting the ending of her life instead of doing it. Thinking she could still escape, that Chester would go on being blamed for murdering three girls.

"She'd have gotten an awful surprise if she'd tried getting back out of that room, though. No doorknob."

"Uh-huh," Wade agreed. "She hadn't expected to want one. And she got a surprise anyway."

Because the gun had gone off. And there you had it: in the end, you attracted your own sort of luck.

Or not. The murdered girls hadn't thought so, probably, and neither had poor Therese.

Even Jan and Hector, I imagined, didn't think so.

Anyway, I had asked Victor to keep quiet about the opium and he'd promised to. And I wasn't telling, either.

For now. Wade ruffled my hair. "Hey, it's getting late. How about if the both of us head on up to bed?"

Music came faintly from upstairs; it meant Sam was home. Not that he had to be when I turned in, but I preferred it. All three animals were settled too, Cat Dancing atop the refrigerator and the dogs in their dog bed, their soft paws twitching in dreams.

So as frost-fronds etched silver witchery on the windowpanes of our old house, the both of us did.

ABOUT THE AUTHOR

SARAH GRAVES lives with her husband in Eastport, Maine, where her mystery novels are set. She is currently working on her eighth *Home Repair Is Homicide* novel, *Tool & Die*.